Kyoko Nakajima was born in Tokyo in 1964. After working at a publishing firm and as a freelance writer, she made her debut as a novelist in 2003 with *Futon*. In 2010 her novel *Chīsai ouchi* (The Little House) won the Naoki Prize. This was followed by the Izumi Kyōka Prize for Literature for *Tsuma ga shiitake datta koro* (When My Wife Was a Shiitake – available in English on *Words Without Borders*) in 2014 and the Kawai Hayao Story Prize and Historical Fiction Writers Club Award for *Katazuno!* (One-Horn!) in 2015. Her other works include *Itō no koi* (Itō's Romance), *Chōbō zekka* (A Magnificent View) and Things Remembered and *Things Forgotten*, published in *Granta 127*, translated by Ian MacDonald.

Ginny Tapley Takemori has translated fiction by more than a dozen early modern and contemporary Japanese writers, ranging from such early literary giants as Izumi Kyoka and Okamoto Kido to contemporary bestsellers Ryu Murakami and Miyabe Miyuki. Her short fiction translations have appeared in *Granta, Freeman's, Words Without Borders,* and a number of anthologies. Of her book translations, Tomiko Inui's *The Secret of the Blue Glass was* shortlisted for the Marsh Award, and Sayaka Murata's Akutagawa prizewinning novel *Convenience Store Woman* was named on of the New Yor~~~~~~'s Book of the Year 2018.

D1440369

KYOKO NAKAJIMA

The Little House

Translated by
Ginny Tapley Takemori

DARF PUBLISHERS,
LONDON

Reprinted in 2021

First published by Darf Publishers, 2019

Darf Publishers Ltd
277 West End Lane
West Hampstead
London
NW6 1QS

The Little House
By Kyoko Nakajima

Originally published as *Chīsai ouchi* (Bungeishunjū Ltd., 2010)

The moral right of the author has been asserted

English translation rights arranged with Kyoko Nakajima / Bungeishunjū Ltd.,
through le Bureau des Copyrights Français

Copyright © 2010 Kyoko Nakajima

Cover by Luke Pajak

Printed and bound in Great Britain by Clays Ltd, Elcograf S.p.A.

ISBN-13: 978-1-85077-316-0

This translation was possible thanks to grants provided by:

JAPANFOUNDATION

The Great Britain
SASAKAWA
FOUNDATION

Chapter 1

The House with a Red Tile Roof

There's something I must make clear right off the bat: this is not a housekeeping guide. I am not giving any more housework tips. I want to make sure we have that straight from the start.

Having at long last retired from the Watanabe household, I now live alone in the Ibaraki countryside. I manage to get by, and feel quite blessed in my old age. My nephew and his family live nearby and we sometimes have dinner together. I have some savings from my many years of hard work, and I have my nephew invest in stocks on my behalf so that I might pay for an old people's home when my body gives out. I live frugally on my meagre pension, and making do is steeped in my bones, so I'm better off than most young people today.

So this isn't about making money, either.

I suppose you could say the turning point in my life came two years ago when Master Watanabe's daughter enthusiastically introduced me to her publisher employer, and they produced *Granny Taki's Super Housework Book*. Youngsters nowadays appear to know nothing about how to select and prepare vegetables, or how to clean the house. I suppose nobody ever taught them, and the fact they have to turn to someone like me for guidance shows just how much the times have changed.

I was stunned to learn at the time that an author doesn't actually need to write anything in order to complete a book these days. I find it deplorable how everything nowadays is mass-produced with no thought for quality, although admittedly, I have this to thank for my own book. And after all it was a pretty good book, even if I do say so myself. It sold well, and I was able to buy more shares with my earnings from it.

But everything I know about housework is in that book, and I don't feel like talking about it anymore. There's no need for more books saying the same thing: one is enough. That in itself is a lesson in economy.

Today, a young woman introducing herself as an editor from the publisher came to my house to discuss the next book. I've been talking about my idea for the next book for some time, and she was clearly aware of this.

'Naturally, we're not thinking housecleaning tips anymore,' she said. 'So instead, we'd like you to talk about Tokyo in the old days, things that only you know about—your sense of the four seasons, your favourite dishes, social niceties. That sort of thing.'

Well, it's not such a bad idea and I can see where she's coming from. It's just not quite what I've got in mind.

People probably think that all the likes of me can talk about are the best ways to clean limescale deposits from the sink. I used to be the same. Now I'm in my nineties though, and nearing the end of my life, I realize there are more important things I want to write about.

There's not a single person left who remembers what things were like when I was a housemaid. As for when the word 'housemaid' disappeared from use in Japan, no doubt there are scholars looking into it, but if my memory serves, I believe it was still around in the sixties.

I recall when my nephew was in high school, he told me about some character in a novel popular at the time—*Little Red Riding Hood*, I think it was, or maybe it was *Little Black Riding Hood*—who got upset at being called a 'home help' and demanded to be properly addressed as a 'maid'. He said it reminded him of me. I think that was the last time I heard it, though. These days, my nephew tells me, people use something called a 'housecleaning service'. It sounds so humdrum.

When I went into service in the early Showa period, there was a shortage of maids for company workers' households in the well-to-do Yamanote area of the city, so I was always properly addressed as 'Miss Taki' and apparently thought quite highly of. It must have been the same in any good family in Tokyo. At that time, the common wisdom was: 'A family that can't keep a good maid is not a good family.'

It so happened that I never married and remained a maid all my life, but the job was effectively domestic training for young women pre-marriage. An apprenticeship for brides, although not exactly on a par with women's colleges today, nor was it the mindless job akin to slave labour it's often made out to be.

I can't say it wasn't ever difficult, but it was after all a job, and whoever heard of a job that's all fun and no hardship? On the other hand, I can't say categorically that I was never looked down on during the course of my work.

As for whether or not I was ever ogled by the master of the first house I served in, well, between you and I, there was some of that. But with him being a famous author I can't possibly disclose what went on, so that side of things will go with me to my grave.

There were times when he'd furtively touch my leg or bottom as I went about the dusting, or give me pocket money behind his wife's back, then summon me to give him a massage. But, well, it was what it was. Indeed it was.

It was the spring of 1930 when I finished elementary school and went to Tokyo.

Of my five siblings, the eldest four had all already gone into service somewhere or other, so I thought it only natural that I would too. My next sister up, Tami, was sent to the house of a local big shot where she had a really hard time of it and was wretched. Listening to Tami talk tearfully when she came home on her days off, her skin chapped and chilblains on her hands and feet, I realized how tough it was for her, but what choice did a country girl have back then?

I was more fortunate than Tami in being able to go to Tokyo. In those days, though, a daughter sent from a rural community to the capital in order to reduce the number of mouths to feed was at the mercy of the recruiter and might find herself sold off to a whorehouse by an unscrupulous agent. Geisha houses would even come to the village to buy the fairest-skinned, most popular girls. By the age of seven, girls either went to primary school or were sold off.

But I was no beauty, so there was no chance of that happening to me, and thanks to my aunt's good connections my destination was decided in advance. Having been assured that I was being sent to a very good family, I could rest easy on that score. Yet a girl of twelve or thirteen can never really be ready. That's still true now, however much the times have changed.

One good thing was that my first experience of a train journey was surprisingly enjoyable. Once on the train, my aunt lectured me earnestly on the skills required of a maid: getting up earlier than everyone else in the household; going to bed later than everyone else; how important it was to use your head, not just do as you were told; not talking longer than necessary with tradesmen; not neglecting other jobs just because you liked cooking best; not confusing childcare with playing… the typical sort of sermon, but thanks to my cheerful nature I couldn't help thinking, 'Childcare sounds like a lot of fun!' and I didn't feel particularly dragged down by it.

'Look, in Tokyo, right, youse can't be at yer leisure. You gotta do everytin quick, lickety split. An' the first tin youse gotta do is lose that bumpkin way of talkin'. Youse gotta learn to speak Tokyo right off. Gottit?'

'Yeah, gottit.'

'Okay, so hows about startin' right aways? Stop speakin' local and talk proper. Gottit?'

'Gottit.'

'Gottit ain't proper.'

'But youse said it first. Howja 'spec me to speak proper if youse don't?'

'I did?' She looked at me in surprise. After a moment, she said without a trace of an accent, 'When I'm with people from home, I slip back into our way of talking without even realizing it. You've got to be on your guard, you know.'

I didn't know how to speak standard Japanese, so although I felt like chatting I kept quiet, while my aunt, as if realizing there was no point lecturing me in dialect, closed her eyes and fell asleep.

Unrefined country lass that I was, you can imagine my astonishment upon arriving in Tokyo. I'll never forget the scene that met my eyes as I alighted from the train at Ueno. The station was swarming with people, and endless tracks stretched out one after another. Of course, this was Tokyo, there was nowhere in Japan you couldn't go to from here, I thought with a sigh. Train whistles shrilled incessantly and sooty smoke belched from the freight trains coming and going. It was like being caught in a strange dream.

We took another train to Otsuka, where we alighted at a shop-lined street thronged with people on their way to work, a sea of bicycles, laden packhorses, gleaming black cars, and streetcars coming and going. It seemed impossible to walk in this teeming mass without bumping into something. I still remember how dizzy I felt.

As my aunt pulled me through Otsuka Sakashita-machi dodging the streetcars, on our right I caught sight of the magnificent Gokokuji Temple, then slap in the middle of the greenery in Kubomachi was the newly built University of Science and Humanities. It was all so imposing and dignified! On the corner was the brown, Western-style building of the Otsuka women's lodgings. As I gazed at it, a woman with her hair in a fashionable bob emerged carrying a small handbag under her arm, her heels clacking as she walked.

Everything in the imperial capital of Tokyo was so utterly different from the rural village where I was born and grew up. In those days, it really was a beautiful city.

It's quite laughable how young people these days, upon hearing that I'd been sent from the far north to serve as a maid in Tokyo, tend to narrow their eyes pityingly and say sagely, 'That must have been really tough for you.'

Master Konaka, the novelist, lived in an elegant, traditional-style residence right in the heart of the city. He already had two older maids, Miss Masa and Miss Ine. Miss Masa was in charge of the cooking and cleaning, while Miss Ine looked after Master Konaka and his wife, ran errands and did the laundry. I was given the task of childcare and assisting Misses Masa and Ine. And boy, they kept me so busy my head span.

The following year, Master Konaka told me his friend's daughter needed help with her child, and so I was sent to be her maid. The house was small compared with Master Konaka's large mansion, but my most cherished memories are all of the time I spent with the lady of the house and her son.

When I told the young woman editor that I wanted her to tape what I was saying, for a moment she looked as though she had no idea what I was talking about, but then said, 'Oh, right, yes of course. Once we've decided on the concept.'

Concept? Young people these days use so many English words that people my age have trouble understanding what they're saying. I was beginning to feel that this editor and I weren't going to get along too well. I wasn't sure what to write about, so I wanted to talk about things and record it all on tape first, but here she was insisting that she would only record it once I'd decided what to write. We weren't going to get anywhere like this.

'So, what you want to write is something along the lines of your personal history, is that it?' the young woman said. *Personal history?* What on earth did she mean by that? Literally speaking, I suppose you could call it my personal history, but that's not what I want to write. What does it even mean? History is a word that goes with Japan or England, or the Meiji or Edo period, that's the sort of thing that you can write a history of.

'If that's what you want, I'm afraid we won't be able to publish that,' she went on irritably. 'In which case, I could introduce you to someone from vanity publishing services, if you like.'

That was a rather disagreeable way of putting it. I was beginning to feel that if it was a matter of vanity, I didn't need to have them publish it after all.

For a maid, the most important thing is not only being good at cleaning and cooking and the like. You have to be really quite clever. Come to think of it, it was none other than Master Konaka who said that about me.

'You've got a good head on you, Taki. You're really quite clever. It isn't like being good at studying and able to become a scholar, but it is really important, you know. At least it is for those of you who work for other people.'

It's almost sixty years since Master Konaka passed away. My oldest, fondest memory of him is not from when I first went to meet him, but from my very first day there, when I went to clean his study.

'No need to clean in here.'

The study was a Japanese-style room with a low, imposing reading desk, and south-facing shoji that opened onto a garden with a goldfish pond. Around the desk were higgledy-piggledly piles of very difficult-looking books, some of them in English.

The desk was covered in sheets of spoiled manuscript paper, although they can't all have been mistakes, for Master Konaka then told me, 'If you inadvertently burn those thinking they're just wastepaper, I'll be in a right pickle. You know there was once one such maid in England, who tossed an extremely important manuscript the master had received from a friend into the fire and burned it,' he said, looking at me mischievously over the top of his glasses.

I must have felt really disconcerted at this. How thoughtless of a maid to burn an important manuscript without realizing it!

But maybe Master Konaka could see in my thirteen-year-old eyes how I felt, for he then said, 'The maid's master and his friend were both scholars, so you could say the two of them were rivals, so to speak. The friend had spent several decades completing his work. The maid's master, on the other hand, had not yet reached the stage of producing anything worth publishing. Maybe he was envious of his friend. What if his friend's essay was reduced to ashes in an instant? The friend would have to rewrite that massive tome. Or he might have to give up on publishing the work altogether. Meanwhile, the master himself could get a step ahead of his friend. Hadn't such a fancy crossed his mind, even just for a moment?'

At the time, I didn't have a clue what Master Konaka was getting at. However, it was a story he seemed quite taken with, and I had occasion to hear it again a great many times after that.

And every time he related how the maid of the scholar called Mill or Gill or whatever burned the manuscript of his friend, the scholar who had a name that sounded like curry rice—Carlyle or Carris or something—he would conclude his account by wondering, 'But is it really possible that he never, even for one moment, wished his friend's manuscript would just disappear?' At any rate, thanks to Master Car-thingy's manuscript being lost, Master Mill was apparently able to publish his own work ahead of his dear friend.

Some years later, when I'd learned the ropes of a maid's job, it finally hit me what Master Konaka had been trying to tell me. That's why even now, the story of the maid who for the sake of her master threw his friend's manuscript into the fire is still clear in my mind.

The English maid hadn't inadvertently thrown an important manuscript into the fire. Wanting her master to succeed, she'd taken it upon herself to burn his rival's manuscript, then took the rap for it. This story left a profound impression on me as a parable demonstrating the lengths a maid is expected to go to for the sake of her master.

What with this and that, I shall never forget my short term of service at Master Konaka's, but more profoundly memorable for me are my days of service in the pleasant household of company worker Mr. Hirai, whose modest house was quite unlike Master Konaka's luxurious mansion.

***

Properly speaking, I didn't go straight from Master Konaka's house into service with the Hirais, but first served in the Asano household.

The first time I met Mistress Tokiko was on a hot summer's afternoon in the coolness of a wet street sprinkled with water by local housewives.

I was just arriving for my interview, accompanied by her mother (the Mistress Suga, who was attired in a silk gauze kimono secured with a linen obi and carrying a parasol), when the young Mistress came dashing out of an alleyway between rental houses intended for company workers, wearing a dress with blue polka dots on a white background. She was carrying young Master Kyoichi, then around a year and a half old, but from the sprightly way in which she'd come dashing out, she looked less like his mother than a neighbourhood lass who had playfully swept the boy up in her arms. She was so youthful I almost addressed her as Miss.

Her mother looked amused. She had employed me on behalf of her daughter, and now told her, 'See, at last you'll be released from ironing your husband's shirts.'

Chuckling at this witticism, the young woman turned to look at me. The first words she uttered to me were, 'Taki and Tokiko… our names are quite similar, aren't they?'

I had the feeling I was seeing a true urban young lady for the first time. Master Konaka had a daughter too, but she looked so much like him that the impression she gave was more of a middle-aged man than the young lady of the house. Mistress Tokiko, by contrast, was a beautiful, bright-eyed young bride.

Having entered the ranks of those with a maid for the first time, she threw herself into teaching me in minute detail tasks like how to cook and speak properly. In that respect she had the humility of a young mistress, and since my former employers had trained me in everything from childcare to cooking, I even felt she was modest enough to depend on me. Compared to Master Konaka's portly wife with her middle-aged spread, I found her utterly charming and so I too threw myself into my work.

At the time, she had just turned twenty-two years of age, and I was eight years her junior at fourteen. It was the beginning of a really very rich time together.

Mistress Tokiko was the one who taught me how to suppress my regional dialect and speak in a Tokyo accent, who first took me to eat Western-style food in a restaurant in Ginza, and who generously gave me the meisen silk hand-me-downs she wore during her childhood, telling me I should alter them to fit me.

She was cheerful and always behaved as though she was happy, but her first marriage wasn't exactly a bed of roses.

Her first husband had apparently worked for a decent company, but by the time I was taken on he'd already been laid off as a result of the recession. He was then doing some kind of clerical work for a factory managed by a relative, a sort of temporary job on a daily wage, which must have been demoralizing, for he drank away all his wages and rarely came home, despite having a child.

When I think about it, though, perhaps the reason he didn't come home was precisely because he had a child. I've heard there are men who tend to steer clear of a woman once she has given birth. I can't for the life of me understand why anyone would neglect such a beautiful wife and angelic son, but being a man of small calibre with an attractive wife who had an idealized vision of married life, he probably felt guilty for not making her happy and couldn't bring himself to face her.

The Mistress was not one to nobly sigh over a tray of food gone cold, declaring that she couldn't be bothered to prepare food for someone who never came home, but in private there were times when she couldn't stop the tears. I was probably the only one who knew that.

Nevertheless, this first marriage turned out to be very short due to the husband's untimely death in an accident. One rainy night, the very same year I started working for them, he slipped and lost his footing on the outside staircase of the factory.

I swore to myself that I would keep my mouth shut as long as I live so that no one would ever know, but secretly I was glad he was dead.

The husband was only the third son and the head branch of the family already had sufficient male children, so the Mistress took Master Kyoichi and returned to her own family. I went with them.

And so, when the Mistress married for the second time, it was as though I too was marrying into the family. It was towards the end of 1932 when, with son and maid in tow, the Mistress joined the Hirai family.

I'm now living in a one bedroom flat my nephew rented for me. The municipal housing I'd spent many years in was pulled down the month before last. Most of the residents there had been single elderly people, and we were given priority on this low-rent place, for which I'm grateful.

On the other hand, it's one of these new-fangled, all-electric places and even when all you want is to run a bath, you have to press so many buttons it's like you're issuing orders to the electrical system, which is really quite exasperating.

My nephew's second son very kindly came over to set it up for me so I can get by, but it's a nuisance having to call them up whenever I can't work it out.

Homes these days are very different to the way they used to be, and I don't understand them anymore. I don't feel attached to things and don't mind where I live, but if I may be permitted to give my opinion, between you and me there was just one house where I was resolved to remain until the end. You may consider it strange and even impudent of me to wish to live out my days in the small servant's room I was allocated in the house Mr. Hirai built in 1935, but that's how I felt. Master Konaka's mansion was right in the middle of Tokyo, but the Hirais' small residence was in the suburbs. New houses were being built at a remarkable pace in the major developments that were happening along the private railways.

In any case, Mr. Hirai had apparently told Mistress Tokiko at the marriage negotiations that he intended to build a house right away, a Western-style house with a red tile roof, and she was fond of telling me that this had been the clincher for her in accepting his proposal.

Three years after she married for the second time, the two-storey house topped with red tiles was built. This photo from the day it was finished shows the Master and Mistress, young Master Kyoichi, and myself. The Master and Mistress are seated with the child on the Master's lap, and I am standing behind the Mistress to her right. Nobody today would think I was a maid, they would probably assume we were a family of four. There aren't any plants in the garden yet so the porch shows up dazzlingly white, even for a black and white photograph.

But for some reason, I can't remember much about the day we moved in, or about the day the photo was taken. My first clear memory of the house is a scene on a winter's day soon after we started living there. I had just come back from running errands, and as I entered through the tradesmen's door I heard a voice coming from the direction of the drawing room.

The Master was at work and young Master Kyoichi was supposed to be taking his afternoon nap, so I thought a visitor must have turned up unexpectedly and hurried through to see. However, I could only hear the Mistress's voice. I peeped around the half-open door and saw her seated comfortably before the lit stove.

I had never before seen the Mistress indulging herself, taking tea alone when nobody else was at home, but perhaps now she had that house she was finally able to relax and be herself. She had poured tea for one in a Koransha blue-and-white porcelain teacup with gold edging. It was apparently part of a gift set from her aunt on the occasion of her first marriage and had been stored away without being used for quite some time, but I had heard her say a number of times how much it suited this house.

'Oh my goodness, no! The house is ours, but the land it's built on is leased,' she said, looking down bashfully despite being alone.

It appeared she was practicing answers to hypothetical questions, such as what to say if someone commented, *My,*

I never imagined you would be able to build such a splendidly elegant new house! I'm really very envious, you know.

The imaginary conversation apparently continued, *Even if the land is leased, the house is your own, isn't it?* for she now answered, 'Well, that's true, but we scrimped and saved, economizing on everything. You'd never be able to build a house otherwise,' waving her hand before her face in modest denial.

'And we borrowed money from the bank, you know. A mortgage is a must, it really is. On top of that we've juggled this and that to make ends meet. It doesn't make all that much difference financially whether you rent or buy, and once you pay the mortgage off, the property's yours, so it's cheap at the price.'

Having said this, the Mistress frowned and made quite a scary face. Perhaps the conversation continued, *Oh yes, that's a good way to do it, it's cheaper than I thought*, for she didn't seem at all pleased.

'Well, that's true, but we scrimped and saved, economizing on everything. You'd never be able to build a house otherwise,' she said, repeating the same line as before, and this time added rather boastfully, 'It's just a regular suburban house but my husband insisted on having a porch, so it is on the large side.'

Then she went on, 'My husband said at the marriage negotiations that he was planning to build a house, you know. That was three years ago, and I didn't really believe him.'

Oh, it was a promise he made when you married? What a good husband he is! As if in response to such a comment, the Mistress smiled sweetly and brought her teacup up to her face. She looked delighted by the sweet scent of Lipton's tickling her nose.

Then she abruptly shifted in her chair and I was about to go in, but what she did next was so graceful that I continued to watch, unable to bring myself to disturb her.

Reflected in the glass of a display cabinet was a twenty-five-year-old woman in her prime, her hair in fashionable waves painstakingly created with a curling iron and gathered demurely at the back of her head. Checking her reflection, she patted her curls and smiled to herself. You could say it was a rather youthful hairstyle for the mother of a child who would soon be starting at elementary school, but the Master was apparently very taken with her youth and didn't want her clothes and hair to become too housewifely.

I don't think anyone could deny her former husband, the drunkard, was more handsome than Master Hirai. After all, the Master was over ten years her senior, middle-aged, short and bespectacled, with thinning hair. He was on his first marriage, and certainly seemed more interested in work than women.

But the Mistress knew very well that having a man as handsome as the heartthrob actor Kazuo Hasegawa at her side did not make a woman happy, and surely had no illusions about her second marriage.

Given her painful experience first time round, she clearly considered the most important aspect of the marriage to be that there was sufficient money and that she would be able to afford some amount of luxury. I myself never married but, well, I can understand this.

When I close my eyes, I can vividly recall that suburban house with its triangular red roof. Going through the gate, along the path and up three stone steps brought you to the porch that the Master was so proud of.

You slid open the east-facing front door to enter the cool and spacious entrance hall, from which a wood-floored corridor led straight ahead, dividing the house north and south in a layout that was fashionable at the time.

There were three rooms on the sunny south side of the house. Next to the entrance hall was the Western-style reception room-cum-study the Mistress was so fond of, with bookshelves, a display cabinet, a solidly built desk, and a fine dining table and chairs purchased in Yokohama. The ceiling was crossed with black beams, like the rafters in a mountain lodge, from which hung an electric light bulb encased in a pretty lampshade.

Next to that was the tatami-floored living room, and beyond that the couple's bedroom. Those two rooms were separated from the southside garden by an enclosed veranda generally referred to as the sunroom, which broadened out by the bedroom where a coffee table and two chairs with armrests had been placed so they could sit looking out over the garden.

On the northern side of the central corridor were the rooms that required a water supply: the kitchen, bathroom and lavatory. The maid's room where I lived was on this north side. It was beneath the stairs leading up to the first floor, located to the right of the entrance hall. Upstairs there were two rooms, one of which would one day be young Master Kyoichi's bedroom.

This layout encompassed everything they needed, but it really wasn't big for a house built at that time. But houses don't need to be large to be good. Something I learned from that house is that functionality is what matters. At the time, the usual size for a master bedroom was eight tatami mats, so theirs was on the small side at only six, and the upstairs rooms were just six and four respectively. Had they rented a house, they could certainly have found somewhere a little bigger.

Instead, pretty touches like the stained glass in the front door and round window in the reception room that Mistress Tokiko had coveted were all incorporated, and she seemed truly satisfied with the design.

She would often say that some of the girls she'd been at school with now lived in a much higher class of residential development and others were renting somewhat grander houses than hers, but if you look above yourself there's no end to it. She was just happy to own a house that suited her.

I was reluctant to interrupt her when she looked so content having tea on her own, but having just come back from running errands I could hardly stay silent.

'Well, I wonder. Things will be hard from now, I suppose,' she said.

I didn't know what was going to be hard, but perhaps she felt she should at least show some humility when people praised her. Continuing her imaginary conversation, she put her right hand to her mouth, then gently put her left hand alongside it, tilted her head to the right, narrowed her eyes to a bowstring, and laughed. Seizing my chance, I quickly returned to the tradesman's entrance and called out breezily, 'I'm back now.'

'What did my sister say?' the Mistress said, turning to me unperturbed as I went into the reception room. 'Oh my, another gift?'

That day I had taken some cakes to her elder sister in Azabu, to thank her for the gift she'd sent to congratulate them on moving into the new house.

'She instructed me to tell you they'd just happened to receive the same gift from different people, and it would be such a pity to waste it. She'll be sure to visit soon, but just now it's such an important time for young Master Masato, what with his exams coming up, so she'll come once they're over.'

Mistress Tokiko frowned with displeasure upon hearing this. The Mistress in Azabu, or Mistress Azabu as I called her, was obsessed with her son Masato's exams for entrance into middle school and had started sending him to cram school from year five of elementary with a view to getting him into a prestigious seven-year secondary school. Every Sunday, she would drag him by the scruff of his neck to the mock examinations held at the Aoyama Kaikan cultural centre.

Mistress Tokiko was sick to death of hearing about how this year it was the real thing, and he would at least be made to take exams for the most selective schools, be they city or prefectural schools. 'If she waits that long,' she said in vexation, 'Our newly-built house won't be new anymore, will it?'

She turned off the stove, picked up the pot and teacup, and took them through to the kitchen. I followed her, still holding the paper-wrapped package, and muttered half to myself, 'Yes, and what's more…'

The Mistress frowned. 'There's more?'

'No, no, it's nothing.'

'What? Tell me!'

'Um, but…'

'What is it? Did my sister say something bad?'

'Yes, well…'

I was fairly bursting with indignation and wanted to talk about it, but I was afraid the Mistress would fly into a rage and couldn't bring myself to say it. Mistress Azabu often said things that rubbed people up the wrong way.

'What did she say?'

'Are you sure you don't mind me telling you?'

'Yes, it's fine. I'm prepared.'

'She said she couldn't understand why you would want to build your own home even after Tokyo burned to the ground following the big earthquake. It should be clear that houses and property are not things to own, that's what she said.'

'Oh my.' The Mistress's nose flared with anger.

'Even after the Takarazuka Theatre in Kobe burned down last month, she said too.'

'Dear me!'

'All she can think of is Master Masato, you know. While she was at it, she even dragged Master Kyoichi into it.'

'Oh dear, what did she say?'

'She was going on about how if you're going to spend money, better to spend it on your child than on a house. Since there's also the matter of his father, if you don't get Master Kyoichi studying hard soon, it'll be nigh-on impossible to get him into a decent middle school. I swear I was getting quite vexed.'

'Oh, school, school! Really, these mothers fixated on their children's examinations are just too much,' she said, not bothering to hide her irritation. 'Well, I suppose there's a touch of jealousy there.'

'There's no doubt of that,' I concurred vigorously, noting her tone of defiance. 'Being siblings, there's surely some rivalry. It's best not to say anything, you know.'

I was furious at the snide comment about her first marriage. Her first husband had had his faults, it's true, but this was hardly the time to bring up the past. Since she had remarried, the national economy had been rapidly picking up, exports were brisk, and at last she seemed able to put those days of poverty behind her.

At any rate, the company Master Hirai worked for was prospering. The year he married Mistress Tokiko, he resigned from his previous employment and took a position as sales manager of a toy manufacturer. From what I heard, he had consequently received an astonishing increase in salary.

The toy business was booming, with military toys such as fighter planes that flew around and around, and figurines of the Three Human Bombs—the brave soldiers who sacrificed their lives in the siege of Shanghai—fairly flying off the shelves, and Japan-made Kewpie dolls were selling well abroad, too.

No doubt this had enabled him to build the house within three years, as promised. On the other hand, I did feel a little sorry for the Mistress Azabu, whose husband was a civil servant for whom pay rises were unheard of, so all she could do was pin her hopes on her son's success in life.

'Would you get Kyoichi up soon, Taki? It's best to have him play a while outside while it's still light. If we keep him shut up inside because of the cold, he'll end up being a frail slug of a child.'

I'm sure that in that moment she was picturing the frail figure of her sister's son, young Master Masato.

'Ah, before I do that…' I said, then hesitated.

'What's the matter?'

'Mistress Azabu gave me a handkerchief. May I please go and leave it in my room first?'

'Yes, okay.' She looked me closely in the face for a few moments, then gave me a knowing look. 'Do you like your new room?'

'Oh yes, I do!'

I'm sure my seventeen-year-old-girl cheeks flushed pink. I absolutely adored my room. It even had its own toilet, and everything was brand new.

'Ma'am,' I blurted out, then pulled myself together and said formally, 'Ma'am, I'll look after this house as long as I live.'

The Mistress laughed merrily. 'Oh no, that wouldn't do. You yourself will soon be of an age to marry, won't you?

'Why would I ever get married? Even if the likes of me got married, there's no way I could have a better life than I have right here in this fine house. And apart from anything, I can't bear the thought of anyone else being in my room.'

'Goodness, I'm not sure how I should take that,' she said laughing, although she did seem rather struck by my seriousness.

'I'll just put the handkerchief away and then I'll take the young Master outside.'

I was just turning to leave, when the Mistress quickly unwrapped the gift from her sister, took out a bean-jam bun, wrapped it in some tissue paper, and handed it to me.

'Have one of these. You must be tired after going all that way, so how about eating something sweet in your room first? When you take Kyoichi out, will you go and buy some vegetables at the same time? We're having chicken stew for dinner tonight, so get something like carrots and turnips to go with it.'

I nodded and looked up at her. What I saw was an intimate gaze full of meaning, that only kindred spirits who understood each other's feelings could exchange.

When Master Hirai came home from work, the family sat down at the low dinner table in the living room and I served them their meal. After they finished eating, they sprawled out on the tatami to enjoy some after-dinner fruit.

The Master liked to speak as though he was a mover and shaker in the world, often touching upon some headline or other in the evening newspaper he'd read on his way home from work.

'It's pretty much decided the next Olympics will be in Tokyo, then.'

'What's Olympics?' asked young Master Kyoichi, remnants of the cream stew still caked around his mouth.

'It's a sporting event where they decide who the world's fastest runners and world's fastest swimmers are,' the Mistress explained in simple terms.

'What's a sporting event?'

'It's a competition where you run races and play ball and things like that. You'll have a sports day too, Kyo, when you start going to school.'

'Italy apparently gave their unconditional backing for Tokyo. The Rome Games will be four years after Tokyo, I suppose. Finland's also a candidate, but Tokyo's a much bigger city than Helsinki.'

'Well that's for sure. I can't believe Tokyo would compare unfavourably to a town with a name like Hell Stinky.' The Mistress always concurred with the Master's opinion on everything. 'If we hold the Olympics, I suppose there'll be another parade or something like in the Reconstruction Festival, won't there?' she said, a faraway look in her eyes.

No doubt she was recalling the Imperial Capital Reconstruction Festival five years earlier. I didn't go to it myself, but the Mistress had told me about it any number of times, and had shown me photographs, so by now I almost felt as though I had seen it with my own eyes.

She had apparently gone with her school friend Miss Mutsuko. There had been lots of decorated tram cars in the centre of Tokyo, the streets were lined with crowds of people waving Japanese flags, and rows of bright paper lanterns lit up the night. She loved gaiety and would often say what a joyful festival it had been.

And she was probably right. It had been a huge event to show the world that seven years after being devastated by the major earthquake of 1923, the imperial capital had at last been reconstructed and was now the world's second city, after New York. If I closed my eyes, I could almost hear the sound of the brass band.

'It won't be anything like that,' the Master said self-importantly.

'Oh my, do you mean it will be even bigger?'

'Oh, I'm sure it will. After all, people from all around the world will be there. The Reconstruction Festival was big, but it was limited to Tokyo, or at most Japan, but the Olympics is a worldwide event. It's never been held in an Asian country before, so it's absolutely a historical undertaking. This means Japan's economy will be secure for a while.'

'Is that so?' the Mistress answered noncommittally, and instructed me to bathe young Master Kyoichi and put him to bed once I'd had my dinner. Upon hearing the word 'bath' the young Master would start throwing a tantrum, but he always cheered up when I promised to read him a bedtime story.

'If we do host the Olympics, they'll build sports stadiums and facilities to welcome the athletes, and they'll improve the roads, too, so the economy will really take off. It's a good opportunity to show the world Japan's good points, so more and more people from all over the world will want to come here, trade will boom, and we'll all be in the money. That's what it's all about, you know.'

'So it's win-win all round, then,' the Mistress said, offering him some of the apple I'd peeled and taken into them.

Nowadays everyone knows that the Tokyo Olympics were held in 1964, not 1940. In 1935, however, everyone believed that five years later Tokyo would be the stage for a major event—and if it wasn't, it would be because some European city with a funny name had beaten us to it.

Even now I feel happy whenever I remember how light-hearted Tokyo was at that time.

***

By the way, I've neglected to mention my nephew's second son, Takeshi, who's now in university. Recently I had him come over to fix my bath for me, but I was unfortunately out when he arrived, so he let himself in with the spare key and whiled away the time waiting for me reading my notes. Ever since then, he's started saying some quite odd things.

'You're wrong, Nan. No way could it have been so light-hearted in Tokyo in 1935. That's the year Tatsukichi Minobe was denounced for claiming the Emperor was merely an organ of the State, and it was just the following year that there was the attempted coup by the young officers in the 26th February Incident. Come on, you must be going senile,' he said.

'What an awful thing to say! Nobody's going senile.'

'But Nan, Japan was at war at the time!'

'No, there were various incidents, but—' I started, but Takeshi frowned and interrupted angrily, 'I'm not talking about incidents, it was war! Calling it anything else is just equivocation.'

I tried to tell him that although there had been some 'incidents', Japan wasn't yet at war—war was something that was happening in Italy or Ethiopia, or the Civil War in Spain, but then he really did blow his top.

He probably thought his great aunt was awfully ignorant, but actually I wasn't as uneducated as he seemed to think. At the time I was reading things like *Housewives Delight*, the magazine where Miss Tokiko's old schoolfriend, Miss Mutsuko, worked. The magazine called for a worldwide reduction in arms, and ran dignified articles such as how, if all the women in France and Germany were to join hands as mothers of their respective nations, they could probably bring about international peace.

They never featured sensationalist topics like Manchuria or Chiang Kai-shek.

The 26th February Incident was indeed horrifying. Tokyo was blanketed in deep snow that morning when several leading government officials were assassinated by a group of rebel army officers, sending shockwaves through the imperial capital.

Nevertheless, with the arrival of spring it felt increasingly like something that had happened far away. Apart from anything else, the Hirai household was out in the suburbs, so we felt somewhat detached from a major incident in the city centre.

Plus, I have a fond memory related to the 26th February Incident. After dinner, as they relaxed together as usual, the Master told us, 'Still, it's an unexpected stroke of luck that Prime Minister Okada is alive and well, when he was thought to be dead. It's a pity about his brother-in-law who died in his place, though. Apparently, he was so loyal that he had no qualms about routinely serving as his stand-in. That aside, something interesting emerged from today's newspaper extra, you know.'

'Really? What was that?'

'It was under the headline, "Daring Servants: Maids Save the Day". Prime Minister Okada survived because his two maids hid him in the servants' quarters. Look, here it is. *Since their Master was reportedly dead, they seized the opportunity to take some provisions to him. However, they heard loud snoring coming from the quarters where he was resting. It would be terrible if he were overheard, so the pair took turns pretending to be asleep, doing their best to breathe in time with his snores to cover up for him,* it says. And look here: *Miss Fukawa is in her third year of service after graduating from*

Odawara Girls School, but Miss Akimoto has been in the employ of
the family for over twelve years. Taki, if anything ever happens in
this household, I hope I can rely on you to snore too.'

'Oh, come on! That sort of thing is hardly likely to ever
happen here, is it now?'

The Mistress seemed highly amused by the account, but I had
to fight back tears as I cleared away the dinner table. I was so
happy and proud that a pair of inconsequential household maids
had heroically saved the life of our nation's prime minister that I
could hardly contain myself.

And I recalled at that moment what Master Konaka had
said to me about being 'really quite clever'. There and then I
resolved that, for all that the Hirai household was small, as the
maid in their employ I would do everything in my power to
protect them.

If I tried telling that to Takeshi, though, he would just criticize
me for being stuck in the past. He apparently reads quite a lot on
the sly. I had better decide on a good hiding place for my notes.

The matter of the Tokyo Olympics was settled that summer. At
the opening ceremony for the Berlin Olympics, it was formally
announced to the world that Tokyo would host the next Games.

How impressed we all were by Japan's performance that
year! Tajima and Harada won medals for the Men's Triple Jump,
Nishida and Oe for the Men's Pole Vault, and Maehata for the
Women's 200m Breaststroke.

'Just wait until it's in Tokyo! We'll sell so many toys!'

This was probably the main reason why Tokyo hosting the
Olympics was such a major topic of conversation in the Hirai

household. Olympic playing cards, an Olympic version of the board game Sugoroku, and even a swimming doll that bobbed up and down doing the breaststroke when you put it in water would sell like hotcakes worldwide. No doubt the Master's firm was already busy gearing up for the occasion.

I thought about what I could say to Takeshi, but my only memories for 1936 and 1937 were peaceful and full of nostalgia.

The Hirai household was always congenial, the Master and Mistress's marriage was harmonious, and the young Master was really attached to his stepfather, too. The only slight cause for concern was the fact that they had not had a child between the two of them, and even then people gossiped that it was because they got along too well.

In the autumn of that year, I recall, a young man set up his easel outside the house to paint.

The Hirais' house had been constructed at the top of the narrow road that ran straight up the hill from one of the new stations on the private railroad that was rapidly expanding westwards as Tokyo grew. There were quite a few Western-style bungalows in the burgeoning residential area one stop along, but it was quite a rarity here and had instantly changed the atmosphere of the neighbourhood. Cosy yet also elegant with its striking red roof, the house had become a local landmark. I will never forget the scent of the seasonal daphne and osmanthus blossoms in the garden, or how the beautiful red roof was complemented by the dazzling fall colours of the maple tree and crimson-fruited rowanberry beside the front door.

That day I was sweeping up leaves outside the house when the Mistress opened an upstairs window and called out to me.

As the breeze caressed her soft hair, several strands escaped her neatly bundled chignon and she smoothed them back down with her hands. It was such a natural move, but she looked sublimely graceful in that moment.

I liked doing my errands inside the house, and I liked gazing at it from outside, too. And I liked my room. I don't think anyone would understand how much I loved that room, even if I did write about it.

Chapter 2

Tokyo Modern

Takeshi has apparently been sneaking a look at these notes when I'm not around. At the weekend, I was just about to go over to my nephew's for dinner when the boy grinned and said, 'Nan, you really shouldn't romanticize the past, you know.' When I didn't say anything, he went on, 'Nobody'll believe you when you say things like being a maid was equivalent to going to a women's college.'

I don't recall having written anything about serving as a maid being the same as women's college. Apart from anything, I have no idea what was taught at such institutions, or anything else about them. What I wrote was that a maid's job was an apprenticeship for brides.

I'm sure Takeshi, brat that he is, looks down on me for my lack of schooling. I only completed ordinary elementary school, but if young Master Kyoichi hadn't lost the use of his legs, I would probably have received my high school diploma. I've never told anyone about this, so Takeshi and the others think I'm just dumb, but at that time just getting a place in a girls' high school was really hard.

It must have been in 1936 when Mistress Tokiko came into the kitchen where I was going about my work to discuss the matter with me. She really did come out with the most astonishing things sometimes.

'Taki, would you like to attend the Evening Girls' School from next year? I've seen you sighing over the ads in magazines. I'm right, aren't I?'

I stuttered in surprise. Lately the women's magazines around the house had been full of advertisements for girls with only elementary level education to study by distance learning for middle school and high school qualifications, so as not to be left behind in the world. Moreover, they often ran articles about maids who had worked to pay their way through women's vocational college.

To tell the truth, every time I saw these, I would secretly worry that once young Master Kyoichi was old enough to start elementary school the family would have no more use for an uneducated nursemaid like myself.

'I asked a friend of mine about it. It just so happens there's a one-year course at the Evening Girls' School. It's aimed at girls from poor backgrounds, so there aren't any fees. It would be hard work, I'm sure, but if you want to do it, Taki, then I don't mind. Kyoichi will be going to elementary school from next year too, so it'd be good timing, don't you think?'

I was absolutely ecstatic. The very fact that the Mistress considered I should be better educated for the sake of young Master Kyoichi made me feel that it was my duty, and I was determined to take up her offer to go to the Evening Girls' School from the following year.

My grades at elementary school hadn't been bad, and I had always wanted to continue studying. Back home in the countryside, though, the assumption was that I would inevitably be sent into service then brought home to be married off, so I never really had any high hopes. Nevertheless, in the modern atmosphere of Tokyo I had been made acutely aware of the educational possibilities for girls.

Every time I read articles in the magazines about how this and that maid had graduated from high school, and maids that oversaw the studies of the children in their care, I wondered why I, too, couldn't do the same, and was seized with a youthful desire to improve myself.

But towards the end of that year, young Master Kyoichi broke out in a high fever, slept for a week, and by the time his fever abated, he wasn't able to move his legs.

At the time, polio was the most terrifying illness imaginable. Numbness and paralysis in the limbs after a high fever was enough to instil dread in any parent and the Hirai household was thrown into confusion. I had never, either before or since, seen the poor Mistress look so wretched.

I recalled from my time in Master Konaka's mansion having overheard talk of a doctor in Nihonbashi who was skilled in treating polio. I mentioned this to the Mistress, and she sent Master Konaka a letter through the offices of her mother. Having received a splendid letter of introduction from Master Konaka, we immediately set out for Nihonbashi with me carrying the young Master on my back. The doctor ran an electric current through his legs and said that since there was a response it should improve if treated quickly, so we should bring him in every day.

And so, every day, I carried the young Master piggyback to the doctor's surgery. However, it was almost the end of the year and the New Year holiday was not far off. I was shocked when the doctor told me that he would show me how to massage the young Master and that I should do it from now on, but the young Master's future depended on it, so I did my best to learn the method.

Starting with his toes, furthest from the heart, I rubbed each one in turn from tip to root and circled them, then applied pressure to the bones on the top of the foot, pinching them one by one before moving on to the anklebones, shins, calves and front of the thighs, turned him over and pressed the soles of his feet with my fists, then pummelled him, gradually moving up along the bones, and finished with a thorough massage of his lower back and buttocks. It generally took about an hour to get through it.

Maybe I got the amount of pressure just right, for the young Master said, 'It tickles when Mummy does it. You do it better, Taki,' and meekly let me get on with it. When I finished, he was so relaxed he fell asleep.

Gazing at the sleeping young Master with a troubled expression on her face, Mistress Tokiko said, 'I wonder how it's different?' and told me to massage her legs. She took off her socks, turned up the hem of her kimono, and told me to do the same on her. I placed her lovely, slim feet with the blue veins showing beneath her milky white skin on my knee, and demonstrated how to do it. Hers were completely different to the young Master's skinny stick-like legs, but I massaged them as best I could. As I did so, her skin took on a transparent kind of vitality.

She submitted to the massage for a while, then looked up suddenly. 'It feels warm,' she said, covering my hands with hers. 'Your hands are warmer than mine, Taki.'

It's funny how even now, after all these years, I can still recall how pleasantly cool they felt.

I spent the next year devotedly rubbing the young Master's legs. His entrance into elementary school was postponed. The doctor had said he would recover quite well if they waited a year, so the Mistress thought they might as well devote themselves to treating him at home.

I think I became enormously more important to the Hirai household because of this situation. The bond between the Mistress and myself deepened and she started taking me with her wherever she went, even on visits to her parents and to the home of the president of Mr. Hirai's firm. Of course, there was also the fact I had to carry the young Master on my back.

Nobody ever mentioned the matter of the Evening Girls' School again.

After a year, it was no longer necessary to massage the young Master every night, yet I couldn't bring myself to raise the matter of my education again. There was also the fact that the war with China had intensified and keeping a maid had come to be considered a luxury. The only reason I was able to continue in service at the Hirais' for such a relatively long time was because the young Master was still weak and I was trying my hardest to care for him. I do think these things were related.

The Mistress often used to give me women's magazines and her old schoolbooks. I believe she felt sorry for me not being able to go to school, and was somehow looking out for me.

Other than the matter of the young Master's legs, the Hirai household was bright and cheerful, and everyone was in high spirits. Preparations for the Tokyo Olympics were well underway, and the Master often talked animatedly about the 1940 Grand International Exposition of Japan due to be held at the same time.

It was apparently well known all over the world that Tokyo was unaffected by the recession. The Master gleefully related a true story about a rather silly-headed young lady in London, who had applied for work to the labour exchange in Iidabashi in advance of the Olympics. I recall how the young Master surprised everyone by repeating his father's mocking words, even though he didn't understand them: 'There-are-Olym-pics-so-is-there-any-work?'

Exports were brisk at the toy company where the Master was employed, and they were making so much profit they were laughing all the way to the bank, I heard. Their business record was so good that a year earlier they had built a large new factory and started mass production from the spring of 1937. As their operations expanded, the Master was promoted. He was extraordinarily successful, apparently. I'm not sure exactly what his standing in the company was, but as executive director I think he was pretty much second to the president.

I recall seeing the Mistress scribble down, 'Tokiko Hirai, Executive Wife'. She then burst out laughing and ripped it up, but the words 'Executive Wife' had a nice ring and she seemed quite taken by them.

When she met up with her mother to celebrate, her mother said, waving her hands modestly, 'Well, it's a small company, after all. It's not such a big thing,' although she was clearly delighted.

I also tried it out in my room, writing, 'Maid Taki, in the Employ of Executive Director Hirai', but it didn't sound all that grand, really. Still, now the Master had been promoted he would be getting to know a lot of important people and I had to brace myself, since it wouldn't do to be clumsy.

'I wonder if our home is a little too cosy for the wife of an important executive,' the Master joked proudly. 'Although if it were bigger, it would be a lot of work for you to clean it, Taki. Still, no matter. We can take on one or two more maids. And we could think about building an extension.'

'I like the size of this house, myself. Although it'll be another matter if we do have more children,' the Mistress said innocently.

Because of the young Master's legs, I was closer to the Mistress than before. You could even say we were inseparable.

I fondly remember being taken to dinner at Restaurant Alaska in Kyobashi to celebrate the Master's promotion. On that special day, the car ordered in advance came up the hill to pick us up. Restaurant Alaska was a favourite of the Master's, and he would often take the Mistress and the young Master there whenever he had a customer from the provinces or there was a celebration of some sort. I feel awful when I think that the only reason I was treated as a guest at the family table was because I was needed to carry the young Master on my back, but I will never forget those rare occasions I joined the family for an elegant meal in the city. I was terribly clumsy with a knife and fork and became known as 'Curry Taki' for ordering curry and rice wherever we went because it was eaten with a spoon.

Since the doctor treating the young Master's legs was in Nihonbashi, there were times when the Mistress decided to stop off at the restaurant in the Mitsukoshi department store on the way home and would take me with them too. The young Master would sometimes childishly demand that she treat him to the children's lunch special there if he behaved well at the doctor's, so it usually went well.

Taking the elevator up to the fifth floor, the sight of the huge restaurant took my breath away. It had a high ceiling with round, disk-like lights, and ceiling fans going around and around above numerous sturdy long tables. I loved seeing the Mistress with her pretty chignon chatting with the staff as we ate our meal.

Next to Mitsukoshi, there was a shop called Nagafuji Confectioner's that was managed by the bakers of the same name in Ueno, where the Mistress and her old schoolfriend Miss Mutsuko often met up. It was cosier than the department store restaurant, they served quality food, and it was to the liking of career-oriented Miss Mutsuko. The ground floor was a Western-style cake shop, so sometimes I was charged with buying whatever cake was in season on the way back from the young Master's doctor visit.

Miss Mutsuko was rather an eccentric, having gone onto the women's college in Mejiro after school, then found employment in a publishing house. I recall at that time she was working feverishly on bringing Helen Keller to Japan. She was particularly proud of an article that said, 'In these times of crisis, Japanese women have much to learn from the many great achievements of Madame Keller, whose extreme benevolence was gained from the extraordinary effort of overcoming her triple handicap of not being able to see, hear, or speak, to eventually become an accomplished public speaker.'

Young Master Kyoichi, now seven, hated Madame Keller and would pout and complain that she had a 'weird face', earning a reprimand from the Mistress. He had always been thoroughly spoiled, showered with pity for his illness and treated like a little king, but now with the appearance of Helen Keller everyone was suddenly telling him that he shouldn't be indulged just because of his illness, that there were people with worse disabilities than him whose extraordinary efforts gave hope to others. He must have felt suddenly besieged. He especially disliked Miss Mutsuko, who always lectured him to follow Helen Keller's example: 'You can get over polio if you try hard. Just think of all the difficulties that Madame Keller's faced.'

The editor who said she wanted me to write another book has not been back again to see me. I suppose it's inconvenient for her to come all the way out here to rural Ibaraki from Tokyo, but still, at my age it was rather awful of her to encourage me to do it only to neglect me afterwards.

'I don't know what you want to write, but you mustn't write lies, you know,' Takeshi said.

How conceited of him to force his opinion on someone who has lived four or five times as long as him, even though he knows nothing. He probably meant something stupid like we can't possibly have had so much fun in 1937, since that's the year the Marco Polo Bridge Incident happened.

Well, looking back, other than Helen Keller, I recalled that it must have been around that time that the stock phrase 'Think of the soldiers!' started going around. Whenever children became sulky and peevish and were being unreasonable, someone would always use that phrase. Not that the adults thought all that seriously about the soldiers either, though, it was just a convenient way to scold children.

It was around then, too, that I started to get letters from home telling me that this or that classmate from my old elementary school up north had been conscripted. I wasn't really all that close to them, so didn't think much beyond registering that their turn had come. Everyone was in the same boat, so you couldn't feel shaken up every time. What's more, the one I knew best of all, Masakichi from my neighbourhood, was a B-grade conscript and a reservist, meaning he wouldn't be sent abroad, so I was told.

I was by now accustomed to life in Tokyo and letters from home all seemed so colourless. I was so completely immersed in city life that even the crisis that started in July felt somehow festive, but if I'd told that to Takeshi, no doubt he would have been angry with me again.

'Everything will be fine if we leave it up to Mr. Konoe.' The Master was so taken with the handsome Prince Konoe, who had just become prime minister, that he actually said this at the time of the Marco Polo Bridge Incident.

'Yes, indeed. With his upbringing he's completely different to your regular politicians, isn't he?' the Mistress responded emphatically for the sake of conversation.

The Master frowned and said, 'What's different about him is that he's cultured. I have no doubt that he is fair and proper, and progressive in everything. The mess in China will probably be sorted out now. But it will be tough for a while. We're already in a time of crisis, but it's going to get worse. A crisis within a time of crisis. Given that modern warfare is all-out war, we mustn't let our guard down.'

The phrase 'Time of crisis' had been a kind of buzzword ever since the incident in Manchuria the year before the Mistress married into the Hirai family, but for those of us going about our daily lives, we didn't quite know what the crisis was, exactly. The Master parroted everything that was said in newspapers and magazines, but he had a big grin on his face and was evidently pleased with the boom in business.

After all, the toy planes, gliders and steel helmets for children that his company produced were flying off the shelves. Sales of tinplate toy aeroplanes shot up after the Asahi Shinbun's entirely domestically produced aeroplane, the Kamikaze, became a worldwide sensation following its successful flight from Tokyo to London. The Master often boasted that it wasn't just domestic demand, that exports were strong, too.

Every time the company released a new product, the Master would bring one home for young Master Kyoichi. The boy might have crippled legs, but he was a privileged child with enough warplanes to beat whoever he went into battle with.

And he didn't just have warplanes. Since he wasn't able to go to elementary school, the Mistress bought him a magazine called *The Elementary School First Grader*. The following year he would be learning alongside children one year younger than himself, so if he started this year, he would be better than anyone else, which she hoped would help him overcome his feelings of inferiority on account of his legs.

I was put in charge of reading *The Elementary School First Grader* and picture books to the young Master. Even I was good at Japanese language study and maths at this level. First I would read it to him and, once he got the hang of it, I would get him to read it aloud while I massaged him, helping him only when he got stuck. I loved having this role.

And then, in an effort to cheer him up, his Granny and Grandad Suga came over for a magnificent celebratory feast on the Boys' Festival on 5th May. All the young Master's favourites were served: ham rice with omelette, croquettes and lobster salad and a mousse pavlova made with canned peaches and whipped cream, and they sang songs at the tops of their voices.

I was rushed off my feet in the kitchen, but I pressed the ham rice sweetened with ketchup into a jelly mold before turning it out on to a plate and decorating it with green peas and corn. It went down really well with him, reminding him of some of the children's set lunches in restaurants, and I fondly remember it as a fun day.

That summer the Master was invited to the company president's summer villa in Kamakura.

The company president had kindly enquired about the young Master's legs, and said he could bring the whole family as medical treatment. I say 'kindly', but given that he was the boss, it was also an order.

The villa was located about a seven-minute walk from the beach. Much bigger than the Hirais' house, it was practically a mansion, with a mahogany spiral staircase from the entrance hall up to the first floor. A foreign car called a Buick was parked out front. American music was playing on a magnificent Victor Phonograph in the reception room.

Carrying Kyoichi in my arms, I followed the Master and Mistress into the reception room and made myself small in the corner. I would have felt more comfortable helping the servants, but there were already three maids and I would just get in their way. So, I obediently sat and listened to the conversation, mechanically chewing on the sweets we were offered. But the company president mostly just talked about America.

'And the women! There are so many beautiful women with long, straight noses, I'm telling you. I can't wait to see what a fantastic specimen Shirley Temple will blossom into. It's all down to good nutrition, you know. If we Japanese focus on nutrition to produce beautiful women, we can catch them up. It sounds like a line from the movie *Priest of Darkness*, but if you only eat whitebait and fried tofu, the bits that should curve out don't curve out, and the bits that should curve in don't curve in. You have to eat beefsteak. And fried in butter, to boot. Add two or three drops of soy sauce. That's the sort of nutrition we need.'

As he said this, plates of steaming beefsteak were brought in.

The company president had worked his way up in life and had been through a lot, but having made his fortune, he had gone on a trip to the United States to observe how things were done there and had as a result become a major Americophile.

'Americans are an extremely friendly people. They behave as though they've known you for decades, even when you've only just met. Even I was given the nickname Shu right away. It's things like that which make you feel how strong their country is.'

Then:

'Professional baseball started with a fanfare in Japan last year, but compared to the American Major League it's like the difference between a yokozuna and the lowest ranked sumo wrestlers. I went to a game myself and everything, even the cheerleading, was on another level altogether. But if it takes off here there'll be a number of advantages. It's exciting from the point of view of a toy maker.'

And so on.

'I have to say there's no lack of inspiration for toys in America.'
'Well, it *is* the home of Mickey Mouse,' the Master dutifully put in, straight-faced, as the Mistress smiled brightly. Young Master Kyoichi had finished all the sweets and was beginning to get bored, so I took one of the wrappers and started to make some origami for him.

At that moment the company president's wife showed a man into the reception room. He was young, not far in age from myself, with thin, silver-rimmed spectacles, and he greeted the company president cheerfully with a wave and 'Hallo!'

'Hirai, this is Shoji Itakura, who'll be joining our design department. I snapped him up straight out of art school. I'm sure he'll be a real asset to us.'

Mr. Itakura bowed lightly and sat down in the armchair indicated to him. Unlike the Master, however, he made no attempt to go along with the president's talk, looking entirely uninterested. Eventually he got up and came over to the table in the corner where the young Master and I were seated, plopped himself down on a chair and started drawing aeroplanes, automobiles and characters from the *Norakuro* manga to entertain young Master Kyoichi. The impression he gave was of an artist who knew little about business.

The Mistress kept glancing over at us as though worried about the young Master making a commotion in someone else's home.

'Oh dear me...' she mumbled, her hand over her mouth, although I'm not sure what she meant by that.

The company president and the Master had business to attend to in Tokyo, so returned home. I accompanied the Master, but it was decided the Mistress and young Master Kyoichi would stay on for another two weeks to keep the president's wife company.

The Mistress took over massaging the young Master's legs in my stead. From what I heard later, she warmed her hands in hot water before starting.

My only task during those two weeks was to look after the Master. Every morning he had coffee with toast and eggs for breakfast, and when the company car arrived he would put on his fedora, pick up his briefcase and packed lunch, and say, 'See you later,' as he left for work. He always came home in time for dinner, and I would look through the reception room's glass door at the appropriate time to see the black car coming up the hill like clockwork practically every day. I went outside to open the gate and took his briefcase and empty lunch box from him. The chauffeured car had been a fixture ever since he was promoted to executive director.

The Master was not at all difficult to look after. He said it was tiresome for me to have to deal with his clothing, so he chose his outfits himself, right down to his necktie and shirt, and only put out what needed washing for me to collect. So as long as I did what I was told, I couldn't go wrong.

When it came to taking a bath, too, all I had to do was inform him when it was ready and he would take care of it all himself. He never summoned me to massage him and when it got late, he would tell me to just finish what I was doing and then turn in, taking himself off to bed. He would tell me in advance if he was going to have lunch or dinner with a client. I must say, he was an exemplary Master to work for.

Yet with my girlish instincts, I knew there was something that was somehow different about the Master. If forced to pinpoint what it was, I would say it was something like a smell.

The Master lacked the smell naturally given off by the tradesman that came to the door, or even by Master Konaka, although perhaps it's odd for me to give him as an example. It was only during those two weeks that I noticed it: the Master did not smell like a man. So *that* was it, I realized for the first time. There was a reason the Mistress had not been blessed with another child since remarrying.

The Master never made eyes at me, not even once. He probably hadn't looked at any other women that way either. This sort of thing could affect his reputation, so I never mentioned it, and have no intention of ever mentioning it to anyone. I intend to take it to the grave with me, along with many other things. So even if you do read this behind my back, you mustn't tell anyone.

Apart from anything else, it didn't mean that he didn't cherish the Mistress. The word 'love' wasn't the word that came to mind with regard to heterosexual relationships in Japan in the old days, but he did absolutely cherish her, and was proud of his young wife. Just, that sort of thing wasn't there.

I've worked as a maid or servant in numerous households in my life, and every single family had secrets they didn't wish anyone else to know about. Couples especially had problems they hid from everyone. I really couldn't say there was any family that was normal.

What I have learned from doing this kind of work over many years is that if there are a hundred families, there will be a hundred different types of couples. Anyone such as a maid, who enters the inner circles of a family through their work, should not go spreading gossip about the family situation for their own amusement. Making a particular issue about the Master's situation was unnecessary. There are also men who don't go in for that sort of thing. That's all.

But just between you and me, it was then that the penny dropped that this could possibly have something to do with why the Master doted on a boy who wasn't his own son, never once raised his voice against his family, and always treated his beautiful young wife kindly.

***

On Sunday two weeks later, the Master sent me to Kamakura to meet the Mistress and the young Master. He had also planned to go, but some work came up making it impossible and he told me to go alone.

As I alighted at the stylish Kamakura Station, the company president's chauffeur was just pulling up with the Mistress and the young Master in the shiny black Buick. I hoisted the deeply tanned young Master onto my back and held out a parasol for the Mistress as she emerged from inside the car, dressed in a simple Korean cotton frock.

'I went to the beach every day!' the young Master told me happily.

With his crippled legs, it was really fun to float on a rubber ring in the sea. I had the feeling he had put on a little muscle since I'd last seen him, too.

The Mistress tried to give the chauffeur a tip, but he refused on account of having already been paid by the Master. As she watched him drive away, Mistress Tokiko at last relaxed and said, 'I'm so relieved to see you, Taki.'

No sooner had the company president left, apparently, his wife had suddenly opened up and grumbled to Mistress Tokiko how she wasn't cut out for that life. She had been with him all the way as he worked himself up out of poverty to be president of a small factory in town. Frankly, she really wasn't suited to the holiday villa type of lifestyle and would be far more comfortable at work making meals for the factory workers. She couldn't bear being told to stay behind and relax while her husband was on his own in Tokyo and probably fooling around with other women. Nobuko Yoshiya's *A Husband's Chastity* had been adapted to film, had she seen it? The Mistress had been bombarded with such exchanges on harmless topics one after another for the entire two weeks.

'Even so, she said that next year they would probably have another holiday villa in Karuizawa, so I should visit them there, too,' the Mistress said, slightly exasperated.

If she wasn't cut out for the holiday villa lifestyle, then surely she shouldn't own two or three of them, but after the latest incident in China foreigners were going back home in droves and selling off their properties at virtually give-away prices, so it was a good time to buy. You couldn't lose by having them as assets, she said, showing herself to be a wife with a good head for business who had always supported her wheeler-dealer husband, the Mistress told me.

Everyone loved Mistress Tokiko and she would have handled the conversation well, but apparently she hadn't felt comfortable. 'What with one thing and another, it wasn't like staying with a friend and was quite exhausting,' I recall her saying.

'I'll just take a little rest with Kyoichi here on this bench, so would you go to the Nirakuso and buy some dumplings?'

Miss Mutsuko had said that if we were going to Kamakura to be sure to try some dumplings from the Nirakuso. Leaving Mistress and the young Master at the station, I took the map she'd drawn and headed for Komachi Street to buy some as a gift to take back to Tokyo. I had them wrap the large, white, delicious-smelling dumplings, and returned to the station to find someone talking to the Mistress and the young Master.

It took me some time to realize that it was Mr. Itakura, who I'd met two weeks earlier at the company president's villa. I found it odd that he had stayed behind in Kamakura while the Master and the company president had rushed back to Tokyo on account of being busy at work.

Catching sight of me, the Mistress bowed to Mr. Itakura and said goodbye.

'Are you going back to Tokyo now?' I heard him say as I reached them.

'Yes. It's fun being on holiday, but I've had enough now. I'm longing to get home.'

A lightbulb seemed to turn on in Mr. Itakura's head. 'You live in that red-roofed house on top of the hill, don't you?'

'Yes, that's right. At the top of the narrow lane leading up from the station.'

'My lodgings while I was at art school were quite close by, so I know it well. I took the liberty of sketching it too.'

'Oh my, you did?'

'I'm sorry.'

'There's no need to apologize. I hope you were able to paint it well?'

'My painting isn't all that great, but I really took a fancy to it. It would look good however poor the painter himself was.'

'You are being far too modest. I am pleased that you like it. I will tell my husband, so please do visit us.'

Mr. Itakura grinned broadly and again took a piece of paper from his pocket, drew something for the young Master, and gave it to him.

'Aren't you coming back to Tokyo, Mr. Itakura?' the young Master asked.

'I've only just got here. I have a friend here in Kamakura, so I come as often as I can in summer. Until last year I freeloaded on them all summer, but now I'm working for a company I can only come at weekends. Being a company man really cramps your style!' he said, laughing, then waved us off as we went into the busy Kamakura Station building.

I'm sure Takeshi will be annoyed with me for noting all these random nostalgic memories, but I really don't remember much about the start of the war with China. I do of course clearly remember going with the Master, Mistress and young Master to see the lantern procession celebrating Japan's victory towards the end of the year.

Nevertheless, I don't remember anything in particular before that. About the only thing I can recall is the Master looking pained, saying how sales of toys were as strong as ever but the price of tin plate had soared, making things difficult for the company. Even so, at the time he was still saying that once things calmed down again, business would be back to normal.

The one who was really in high spirits, more than ordinary people, was Miss Mutsuko. Having made a big splash with Helen Keller, from that autumn she lost no time in going on about the importance of everyone on the home front showing support for the soldiers on the frontline. The first thing she did was to change her hairstyle. She had always been super stylish with her Modern Girl permed bob, but now she put her curling tongs to the opposite use, straightening her hair and tying it back in her self-styled plain 'home front bun'.

Working at the magazine, she apparently had to be ahead of the trend. Indeed, the home front bun did take off after some time, but in the meanwhile Mistress Tokiko and others continued to use their curling tongs and spray their hair with camellia oil to create a pretty chignon, and it did seem like Miss Mutsuko was taking things a bit too far with her hair pulled straight back into a plain bun.

I recall how, when Miss Mutsuko came to visit and I showed her into the reception room and poured her a coffee, I caught the fashionable Mistress Tokiko making fun of her.

'Come on now, what's this all about?'

'You don't approve? This is a home front bun, you know.'

'What on earth is that? Even the name is odd.'

'Oh well, I can't help your lack of awareness. But really, modern warfare is all-out war.'

'My husband says the same thing: modern warfare is all-out war. What does that even mean?'

'Well in the past, war meant men shooting it out between themselves. But this twentieth century war means intelligence warfare and economic warfare and propaganda. In other words, war is now part of daily life.'

'I don't really get it, but anyway, what has that got to do with your hairstyle?'

'You see, the whole population gets caught up in an all-out war, not just the soldiers. Prices have gone up since July when the war started, haven't they? That sort of thing affects everyone. So, the home front and frontline are basically the same thing, and we all have to fight hard. Apparently the reason Germany lost the last big war was that the women succumbed to hunger and neglected to defend the home front. We mustn't allow that to happen, so this plain hairstyle is a sign of our determination to keep our country safe, see?'

'I kind of understand, I think… but anyway. If that's the case, how about just adding a little touch, a fringe or something? I mean, really, you look like, um…' Mistress Tokiko couldn't suppress a giggle.

'Like what? Come on, out with it,' Miss Mutsuko said, frowning.

'Like Miss Hill.'

'Who?'

'Miss Hill. From P.E.'

'What? No way! I look like her?'

The two of them abruptly burst out laughing as if possessed, doubled over clutching their stomachs and tears streaming down their faces. 'Miss *Hill!*' they screamed, thumping the table.

I had no idea who they were talking about, but I suppose it must have been the physical education teacher from when they were at school together.

After they had recovered themselves, the Mistress suggested another cup of coffee. Miss Mutsuko opened up the package of Western-style cakes she had brought with her, and the young Master joined them for an afternoon snack.

Sometimes when she was with Miss Mutsuko, Mistress Tokiko would become extremely animated and enjoy herself so much that she looked like a girl again, as if taken back to their schooldays.

'You're only being like this because of your work. Lately *Housewives' Delight* is full of the war with China. All the newspapers tell us about is how we've occupied this and that place, and how now six brave soldiers and now ten brave soldiers made themselves into human bullets. That's all we ever hear about. There's nothing to read. The only thing of any interest are the advertisements for Wakamoto medicines.'

'Oh, come on, Tokiko. You're altogether too frivolous.'

'Not at all. Even I've made thousand-stitch sashes to send to soldiers here and there. I put a lot of effort into that sort of thing, you know. But that doesn't mean I want to read about it all the time. I think I might start reading *Women's Choice* instead this month.'

'So, what's so good about *Women's Choice*?'

'"Marriage is Happiness" by the former president of France, or "The Transience of Maidenhood" by Yvonne Matsubayashi, that sort of thing. "Diary of a Matrimonial Swindler" was good too. I could have done without your "Diary of Tears by Wives of Soldiers Killed in Battle" and the like, and that "Widows' Reader" supplement when the war had only just started, of all things.'

'Huh. Their issue next month will be about the current situation there too, you know. Better late than never, I suppose.'

'Really? Look, rather than that, how about an article on the efficacy of lait face cream?'

'Oh, for heavens' sake. I suppose the Chujoto traditional remedy for women would be more to your liking. What do you think?'

'No need to get so upset! I heard somewhere that when Setsuko Hara went to Germany for *The New Earth* film, she was praised everywhere she went for her smooth white skin and said it was thanks to Lait Creme.'

'That sort of thing is made up by someone like me. It's not that Setsuko Hara actually said it herself.'

'What? Really?'

'Yes, really.'

'I thought she really said it.'

'If you want something for your skin, I'll tell you what works well. Grind up some oatmeal in a mortar and pestle until it's fine, add a pinch each of powdered milk and boric acid, put it in a small plastic bag, add a little water, and knead it. Once it starts getting a bit slimy, rub it on your face. It's a steal. I heard about it when I interviewed the gorgeous wife of a famous personage.'

'Okay, I'll give it a try.'

'You never change, do you Tokiko? Still determined to find ways to be beautiful,' Miss Mutsuko, with her Miss Hill-style bun, said in exasperation.

'Since you're here, stay for dinner!' the Mistress said to stop her independent, career-woman friend from leaving.

The Mistress once told me that it was strange how well they got along, despite being so utterly unalike.

It was true. Just observing them, they were complete polar opposites of each other, but got along so well I felt envious just being around them.

In the end, the only thing I could recall about 1937 and the war in China were the victory celebrations for the capture of Nanking in December.

From around the start of December there was a bright atmosphere, as though a ray of light was dispelling the tension little by little, and a feeling of anticipation for the end of the year floated in the cold, crisp air as everyone busied themselves with preparations for the new year.

That day I accompanied the Mistress and young Master to Ginza. We went out onto the main road and hailed a taxi, and the driver too was cheerful as he informed us pleasantly that the fare would be only fifty sen.

People hadn't yet received their New Year bonus payments at work, but that year the stores were holding victory sales in addition to the usual grand year-end sales, and Ginza was thronged with people.

As we got out of the taxi, the young Master let out a cheer. All the buildings along the main shopping street were decorated to the nines, with large Japanese flags hanging on the corners of the department stores, and advertising balloons with the message: 'Grand Year End Sale to Celebrate the Fall of Nanking' hovered over the rooftops, while the crowd on the street waved hand-held flags.

There was a festive atmosphere, with a brass band and cheering voices loud enough to shake the imperial capital. The Mistress set off at a good pace through the crowd, saying, 'We'll never be able to buy everything I was planning to with all these people. We must get year-end gifts and comfort bags to send to soldiers, but we'll leave it at that for today. We can't go to the restaurant either, Kyo, we'll never get a seat. I'll take you to the lantern parade after dinner to make up for it.'

And so the shopping was quickly despatched. She bought gifts for the company president, Master Konaka who had been the go-between for their wedding, her family, and the Master's family, selecting items that would be either liked or at least not a burden, or that looked appetising. Once everything was ready, she went out onto the street saying that since we had so much to carry, we would get a taxi home too.

More than twenty aeroplanes flew overhead one after another trailing red-and-white streamers, and bills upon which were written: 'Celebrate the Imperial Army's triumphant entrance into Nanking' fluttered down all around like snow.

The young Master was so exhausted by the time we returned home to the suburbs that the Mistress decided he should have a nap. She herself was busy with sorting out the purchases and recording them in the household accounts, so I think it was left to me to prepare dinner.

That day we had dinner earlier than usual. The Master came home a little earlier from work and was in good spirits.

'Maybe tonight I'll have a little hot sake too.'

I remember this because it was so unusual for him.

'Oh my, has something happened?'

'Of course it has! The Imperial Army won, didn't it?' the young Master said, and the Master and Mistress laughed.

The Mistress signalled me with her eyes, and so I went back into the kitchen and poured some of the Master's favourite Kikumasa sake two-thirds full into a serving bottle and took it back through, together with a sake cup. I put the bottle into the iron kettle on the brazier.

The Mistress would serve him the warmed sake, so in the meantime I went back to the kitchen to prepare some snacks to go with it. The Master was not one to drink alone at home usually, but when he did, he preferred snacks rather than regular meals. I didn't have anything prepared, so I used what was on hand, chopping up some fried tofu and mixing it with wasabi pickles and a dribble of soy sauce, and dicing some canned corned beef and toasting it lightly with some green onion, and took the tray of food through just as the sake was ready to serve.

'Hopefully this will put an end to the trouble in China,' the Master said, downing a cup of sake with satisfaction.

'Yes indeed.'

Even I, as a woman, found the Mistress bewitching as she smilingly poured him some more. She was extremely beautiful with her slightly flushed cheeks, especially on the odd occasion when she joined him in a drink.

'It's essential for the war to end if the Tokyo Games are to go ahead. I was worried about it dragging on any longer. They were saying the Games would be safe if the war was over by March next year, but at this rate it'll be going that way in the New Year.'

'Oh, do you mean the Olympics? I thought they were already settled.'

'Well, yes, the decision itself has been made. In reality, though, given that it would take two years to build the stadium, it's possible it won't happen unless the government makes up its mind and allocates the budget for it by spring. Tokyo City is raring to go, but it can't go ahead without government funding. The company president is influential in the City Council and is pressing them to make it a grand occasion.'

'But since you're drinking sake like this, I suppose it means you're no longer worried about it?'

'Well, it'll probably be alright.'

'So, what will we do about Atami this New Year?'

'What?'

'Last year Kyo's legs were really bad and we had to cancel, didn't we? I was wondering what to do this year. I do really want to go.'

'I wonder if we'll be in time to make a booking?'

'As long as it's after the third, a booking for two nights or so will be fine. Let's go!'

'Maybe we should. It could be good for Kyo's legs, too.'

'Can you take time off work?'

'I'll see if I can arrange it.'

'Oh, I'm so happy! One more thing. The Grand War Victory Sale will continue to the end of the year, won't it? I'm thinking of having a kimono made for New Year.'

'Didn't you already?'

'I heard someone say on the radio this morning that since the summer, many people have tightened their purse strings due to the time of crisis, but with the recent victory in Nanking it's only human to want to have just one piece of clothing made and it should be okay as long as it's not too ostentatious a pattern. So, I almost placed an order at Mitsukoshi today, but then I thought I shouldn't go ahead without consulting you first.'

Mistress Tokiko was extremely good at wheedling and the Master found her so adorable that there was never any question she might not get her own way.

After dinner, the Master was in such high spirits even after a small amount of sake that the family went out again to watch the lantern parade and took me with them.

The young Master was so excited that he went to sleep that night cuddling a Japanese flag.

This year too is coming to a close, but I feel the end of the year is getting drearier as time goes by. Out on the street *Jingle Bells* is playing and buildings are gorgeously decorated, but I haven't felt that joyful bustle leading up to New Year for a long time. I don't really know whether it's because I'm old now, or whether the world has changed.

The other day I was invited over for dinner at my nephew's place, and my nephew's wife informed me, 'We won't be in Japan over New Year, you know.'

Apparently they'll be leaving for Hawaii on New Year's Eve. They've been invited to go with their daughter and son-in-law who married last year, and she's over the moon about it. At times like this they never think of saying I should come along too. Not that I would go, even if they did.

Takeshi isn't going to Hawaii, but he's going out with some biker friends to see the first sunrise, and so it seems settled that I will see in the New Year on my own. I don't feel particularly lonely. You don't have to be with someone else not to feel lonely.

After dinner, Takeshi brought me home by bike. Every time I put on that heavy helmet and sit on the bike with my arms wrapped tightly around him, I'm terrified.

He said he had to go straight home, but when I told him I'd stocked up on sweet bean-jam buns he came in, lured by food. I poured some tea, put two buns from Bunmeido on a tray and went back into the sitting room, to find Takeshi reading the notebook that I'd carelessly left lying around.

Young though he was, he said irritably, 'It's a nightmare.' When I asked what he meant by that, he exploded. 'It's a total nightmare, Nan! There was this huge massacre going on in Nanking, yet in Tokyo they were flying advertising balloons for a grand victory sale. Like they do at Seibu Department

Store when the Seibu baseball team wins. It's outrageous! I don't need your bean-jam buns. I've lost my appetite. I'm going home.'

I was disappointed, but there wasn't much I could do about it if he said he was leaving.

He paused by the door as if he'd just remembered something. 'Mum said that if you want to have some special New Year food, I should order a single portion at the convenience store for you. What should I do?'

I thought I would write about why the end of the year always used to be such a busy time.

For one thing, we did a thorough house cleaning, starting with changing the paper on the sliding doors, washing the curtains and seat covers, sweeping and cleaning the kitchen floor, the ceiling and the board that ran around the wall below the ceiling, wiping down wall hangings and ornaments, and everywhere that never normally got touched.

It was quite a task, as we used vinegar mixed with water for glass, warm water with boric acid on tatami, and for grease stained kitchen utensils and glass doors we first wiped them down with soap powder dissolved in water, then again with vinegar water, and finally with a dry cloth.

Ordering rice cakes, dry goods, vegetables and so forth from the tradesman on their rounds in time for the New Year menu was my job too. I remember the knack to managing this. You had to really consider everything carefully before ordering just enough so that you would use up everything over the New Year without any waste, while not being put out by running out of anything. Meat and fish went off quickly, so you got them delivered the morning of New Year's Eve.

Of course, the Mistress went again to the Victory Sale and ordered a formal kimono in figured satin. She apparently pressed a friend in Mitsukoshi's kimono fabric department to ensure it was delivered by New Year's Eve. Apart from that, there were many other items she had to buy like shirts and underwear for the Master, so she devoted herself to these tasks outside the home while I took care of things inside. There was also the matter of paying courtesy visits before the end of the year, so the Mistress was briskly doing the rounds.

As Christmas approached, the programme for the Tokyo Olympics was formally decided, and the Master looked conspicuously more relaxed. On Christmas Eve, a joyous party was thrown for the young Master, for which Granny and Grandad Suga came over.

As the year end grew ever closer, the preparations went into full production. The salted herring roe had to be soaked in water from the morning of the 27th to remove the salt. We would season it on New Year's Eve, but if it wasn't soaked long enough it would be too salty to eat.

Doing everything on New Year's Eve would have been too difficult, so on the 29th rice cakes had to be cut, on the 30th black beans and small dried sardines boiled, and preserved dishes like pickled vegetables made. Then I also accompanied the Mistress when she went out to buy the big round decorative rice cake and entrance decorations, and the New Year flowers and bonsai.

From the morning of New Year's Eve, we were in top gear. Sheets, futon covers, underwear and socks all had to be scrupulously washed. The Master instructed the handyman on the position of the New Year's decorations outside the front door.

In the afternoon, the cooking really got underway, with the Mistress and I working together. After making the various delicacies, including rolled omelette with fish paste and fish wrapped in konbu seaweed, and egg roulade and mashed sweet potatoes with chestnuts and so forth, we left them to cool down before arranging them in layered boxes. Meanwhile we placed the fern and false daphne leaves, and konbu on the offering stand and topped them with the large, round, white rice cake and single bitter orange, hung the pine, bamboo, and plum-painted hanging scroll in the tokonoma alcove, and the Mistress arranged the flowers for the reception room, teaching me about ikebana as she did so.

The Master went out to have his hair cut and would be expecting to have an early bath upon his return in the evening, so I couldn't neglect to prepare that for him, too.

If I failed to place the order for New Year soba noodles early, they didn't just bring them late but by the time they arrived they would be soggy, so I had to ensure they would be delivered in time for dinner. Once we had eaten the soba, we would arrange the prepared food in the layered boxes, being sure to make everything look colourful and appetizing.

Once the kitchen work was finished, it was time to finish the cleaning. It was considered particularly unlucky for the bathtub and lavatory to be left dirty, so I made sure to clean them thoroughly.

I then made sure the family's clothes were ready to wear the next day: I brushed the Master's morning suit and hung it up, placed the Mistress's gorgeous kimono in the wardrobe basket, and hung the young Master's sailor-collared best clothes to ensure they wouldn't be crumpled.

On New Year's Day we didn't use the living room as usual, but rather celebrated with spiced sake in the Western-style reception room, so I set the dining table ready for that. In between running around like a headless chicken placing a bonsai pine tree in the entrance hall and a tray for the visiting cards of people who would come over the New Year, I also had to massage the young Master's legs.

After I had finally finished putting the house in order I said goodnight to the Master and Mistress, then went back to my little room and gently opened up a cloth bundle.

Inside was the hand-me-down meisen silk the Mistress had given me. For the past few days I had been steadily working on getting it ready to wear on New Year's Day. I wanted to wear a new kimono for New Year too. The hand-downs from the Mistress were good quality and felt really good to wear.

I was just putting the finishing touches when I heard the temple bells beginning to toll. Sometimes they could last until two or three o'clock in the morning, but I liked this time that I had just to myself.

And so 1937 drew to a close. It was in the new year, on New Year's Day, that Mr. Itakura first visited the Western-style house with the red roof.

Chapter 3

Tinplate Toys

My nephew's family are all away on holiday, so I don't have anywhere to go this New Year. I don't know anyone here in Ibaraki, having moved here simply to be close to my nephew. None of the people I knew back up north where I'm from are alive now, and I can't summon any enthusiasm to go to Tokyo.

I made a simple soup with rice cakes to eat by myself, but that was my only nod to New Year tradition. The soup was made the way we do up north, with a lot of burdock root, and the added rice cake was toasted in the Tokyo style. I suppose I was the only person in Japan eating the traditional New Year dish prepared this way.

With Takeshi away, it would be a good time to write down more of my recollections, I thought. For some reason, though, when he was reading it behind my back I had plenty to write about, but when I thought that perhaps nobody would ever read it, I began losing the urge to put pen to paper.

Still, I steeled myself and decided to try and remember things from the past so that I could write my first words of the year.

1938... 1938 was the year the young Master started elementary school.

I kept repeating this over and over, like a mantra, until suddenly a particular song started playing loudly in my head.

Lo! Above the Eastern Sea
Clearly dawns the sky
Glorious and bright the sky
Rideth up on high

Yes, the Patriotic March! That year, you only had to turn on the radio to hear it blasting out. I'd been made to memorize it for the first entertainment day at the young Master's elementary school. Suddenly I had the urge to stand before the mirror and see if I could still do the dance. It was funny to think that I was the only person in the whole of Japan to be doing that on New Year.

I bowed to myself and sang an exaggerated version of the prelude *La-la-lalalalalala,lalalala,* then launched into *Lo! Above the Eastern Sea,* swinging my arms energetically left and right. At *Glorious and bright the sun,* I marched on the spot, and on *Rideth up,* I bowed and crossed my arms in front of me, then stretched my arms up to the ceiling and stepped forward with my right foot for the *on high.* How did it go for *Spirit pure of heaven and earth fills the hearts of all*? And what about *Hope abounding springs—O sweet Isles Imperial*?

I was surprised to find I couldn't remember, even though I'd practiced it so much back then! The young Master had found it hard to remember the dance, probably because his legs were crippled and he had grown up without doing much exercise. He lagged behind all his classmates and came home crying. And so I studied the mimeographed copy of instructions he had been given at school, learned the dance moves, then trained him arduously until he could do it.

He had already learned the song from the radio, and now the two of us sang it together. Our voices rang throughout the Hirai house from the upstairs room, now converted into a dance studio.

As I write this, the melody comes back and embeds itself in my head. I'm glad I was able to remember it, but now I'm stuck with the earworm, just like I was back then.

That New Year's was a merry occasion. Gates were adorned with pine leaf decorations, Japanese flags were raised, and people dressed in their Sunday best came and went, clutching cloth bundles as they went about their courtesy visits.

The trip to Atami that the Mistress had been so looking forward to ended up being cancelled because they couldn't find anywhere to stay. They had been too late in phoning to make a reservation, and in the end the Master was unable to take any extra time off work and had to start back on the fourth.

Instead, they spent the first two days of the New Year visiting their local temple and doing the rounds of courtesy visits. The Mistress loved gaiety, so was exceptionally animated. Generally, she wore Western-style clothes, but for this occasion she attired herself in a formal kimono of silk satin damask with the traditional New Year pine-bamboo-plum motif, along with black haori jacket and a decorative ball-shaped scent bag. She attended her hair more carefully than usual with the curling iron, and made it glossy with camellia oil. Just seeing her going out dressed up like this raised my spirits too.

On 3rd January there was a steady stream of the Master's clients coming to pay courtesy visits, and even Mr. Itakura put in an appearance, so I was rushed off my feet in the kitchen.

Of course, New Year's was always like that. The front door was always open and everyone who came to visit was welcomed in, so I had prepared a lot of food in advance. Since the rich traditional fare grew tiresome after a while, I had made other dishes like duck broiled in soy sauce, sweet sake with green onions, and deep-fried fresh mackerel marinated in spicy sauce. These dishes kept well and were quite novel, which went down particularly well with male guests.

The clients all greeted the Master with serious faces and talked about work. They were all feeling positive following the fall of Nanking, and the Master, whose motto was: 'Looking to the future is the key to business,' talked fervently of the products that should do well on the market following the victory. For anyone outside the world of work, however, his determination was of little interest.

That's what men do when they gather, I suppose, but the Mistress looked a little bored of the endless work-related talk, and went up to see the young Master who had taken his New Year gift money upstairs, or wandered into the kitchen where I was at work and said cattily, 'There's really no need for that kind of talk during the holidays, is there? They'll be talking about that sort of thing in the meeting room at work tomorrow anyway.'

When Mr. Itakura suddenly turned up later that afternoon, the atmosphere completely changed. He had apparently just come from paying his respects to the old couple with whom he'd lodged during his art school days, and in some ways he hadn't quite shed his student aura. He brought with him a gift of Shiseido Hanatsubaki biscuits, saying, 'I don't eat sweets myself, but I can't resist buying these because they're such a great design.' That much was fine, but after enjoying a cup of spiced sake with the Master, he didn't seem able to relax and looked on edge.

'If the situation in China stabilizes now, we can't just capitalize on the victory with domestic products. We'll have to devise a strategy to launch our products to children on the continent too. The market there is huge. Practically limitless. The continent covers such a vast area. We have to always prepare two years in advance, of course, so naturally we'll be relying on the youthful energy of the likes of you, Itakura. There's one thing in particular I want you to do.'

'Oh?' Mr. Itakura responded unenthusiastically.

The Master was of course referring to the need to research and manufacture toys that would go on sale at the time of the Olympics and the Grand International Exposition of Japan to be held two years later. But just then, Mr. Itakura caught sight of the young Master coming downstairs with a tinplate aeroplane in his hand.

'Hey, nice plane!' he called out, with the air of having been saved. 'How about showing me around? I've wanted to see inside this house for ages.'

'You should have said so. I'd have shown you around myself,' the Mistress said, looking highly amused.

Mr. Itakura flushed bright red. 'No, no, that's alright,' he said hastily. 'I want Kyoichi to show me.' He headed for the stairs while pushing the young Master on ahead of him.

Having roped the young Master into showing him around the rest of the house too, Mr. Itakura was just coming downstairs when he again caught sight of the stained-glass window in the front door. He stood staring at it, transfixed.

It was a stunning piece that would stop anyone in their tracks. Even now, if I close my eyes I can see the evergreen magnolia and large white blossoms radiant with the light shining through from outside. The large leafy tree was on the left, and in the bottom right a little blue bird sat quietly on the end of a branch.

Mr. Itakura took out his small sketchbook and knife-sharpened pencil, and began drawing it with such astonishing speed that the young Master let out a loud whoop of delight.

Designers somehow focus on details that ordinary people don't notice, and are able to accurately capture them with just a few simple lines; the wickerwork ceiling on the veranda, the light fitting on a globe lampshade, the metal fixtures on a sliding door. He had already sketched the outdoor porch, sloping roof, and even the ridge tiles in this manner.

I was a bit taken aback when Mr. Itakura next said he wanted to see the bathroom and the kitchen, but Mistress Tokiko smiled amiably and said she didn't mind. She even offered to show him the blueprints if he liked, and he responded seriously, 'Yes, I'd love to see them.' His eyes shone. 'Actually, I originally wanted to do architecture.'

As he drank a little sake and snacked on the New Year dishes, his tongue loosened up and he began to talk about himself a little more.

'My grandfather on my mother's side was a traditional carpenter working on temples and shrines, so I was always interested in buildings. Although, gradually, my interests tended more towards design.'

He was originally from Hirosaki or somewhere far up north but had come to Tokyo to study at a higher technical school and had stayed on afterwards, enrolling in art school. His last visit home, the first in a long time, had been a few years ago to take the medical for the military, he said.

'Ah, the medical. Good for you.'

The Mistress seemed to have undergone a complete transformation from when she had been with the other visitors that day, and animatedly joined in the conversation, whereas the Master started nodding off, maybe tired from the day or having eaten and drunk too much.

'Oh, but as you can see, I don't have much of a physique. My eyesight and bronchial tubes are weak too, so unfortunately I was classed as C.'

'That means you can't be a soldier, doesn't it?' young Master Kyoichi said scornfully, and I recall the Mistress shot him a reproving look.

Once Mr. Itakura had loosened up, he proved to be a skilful conversationalist and amused the family until dinnertime with his stories. He was fond of music and the cinema, and spoke about the film *One Hundred Men and a Girl* that had been released at the end of the year to great acclaim.

'I always thought Shirley Temple-type films were just for kids, but somehow this one brings tears to my eyes. You really should take Kyoichi to see it.'

'The girl who played the part of Patsy had a beautiful voice, and Sto-what's-his-name, Stokoivich or Stokovsarekov or something—anyway, a famous conductor—played himself in the film, and hearing the orchestra play with him conducting was amazing. It really was a movie that everyone from adults to kids could enjoy,' he explained with ridiculous enthusiasm.

'My, is that Sto-what's-his-name really that good? You know a lot about it, Mr. Itakura.'

'I like classical music better than jazz, myself. In fact, before I was trying to choose between architecture and design, I was even thinking of being a violinist.'

'Really? Oh my!' the Mistress exclaimed, opening her eyes wide in surprise.

Mr. Itakura laughed mischievously and added, 'Although I've never picked up a bow in my life,' and the Mistress and the young Master burst out laughing so loudly they woke up the Master.

The Mistress and I exchanged glances, and choosing the right moment, I brought in steaming rice and miso soup, pickled vegetables, and freshly grated daikon topped with sliced herring roe and bonito flakes. Everyone generally craved simple fare after all the sweet, rich New Year dishes and sake.

Mr. Itakura often visited the Hirai household after that. Looking back, it's quite amazing to think that was the first occasion he ever visited the house.

After the fifteenth, when we'd finally put an end to the New Year festivities with some traditional red bean porridge, the Mistress made sure to give me a day off, telling me, 'Taki, you need to relax too.'

The servant's holiday was called yabuiri, or 'into the bushes', since it signified going home to the countryside, but at the time 'home' was a long way away. When I first went into service, I would go to a great deal of trouble to go back up north, or visit relatives in Kasukabe just outside Tokyo to hear news of home, but it was far from relaxing.

Eventually I stopped bothering to go away anywhere, but even so the Mistress would give me an entire day off and send me out to enjoy myself.

That year I arranged to meet a childhood friend, who was also in service in Tokyo, at a wholesaler's in Kappabashi, and we went to eat sweet red bean soup in Asakusa. My friend wanted to go and see a sword fighting drama performed by an all-woman cast, but I didn't really like that sort of thing, and I recall we argued about it.

She was quite taken aback when I said I didn't want to go. She'd always been a bit bossy, and was used to getting her way in everything. I didn't want to upset her, and had always gone along with her without saying what I thought. For some reason, though, this time I suddenly couldn't take it anymore, and dug my heels in.

She asked me irritably if there was anything else to do. I wanted to see the movie that Mr. Itakura had recommended to the Mistress and the young Master, but I thought she'd say I was getting too big for my boots wanting to see something like that, so I didn't say anything. In the end, she went off in a huff after we'd finished our soup to watch a drama by herself.

A Hundred Men and a Girl was a huge hit, and after the Mistress took him to see it, the young Master announced that he wanted to become a world-renowned conductor when he grew up.

Tickets for the Grand International Exposition of Japan two years later went on sale that spring.

It was in mid-March, a cold day as I recall. The Master stood in a long line in the freezing rain to buy a set of twelve tickets for ten yen. Ten yen was two thirds of my salary, so I don't think it was all that cheap, but it did include a lottery. The first prize was something like two thousand yen, enough to build your own house, so everyone was falling over each other to buy tickets and they all sold out in no time at all.

The Master put the set of tickets into a paulownia wood box, wrapped it in a purple silk cloth, and put it on the household altar. They could all look forward to the grand draw in May. Just the fact he'd made a show of putting it in a box to stop the young Master, and even the Mistress, from touching it was quite amusing. The Exposition would be taking place only two years later, and he'd apparently bought more tickets than he needed to have a better chance of winning the lottery, thinking that he could always resell them later.

In the end, the Master didn't win the May draw, but he wasn't all that disappointed and seemed to find it amusing. Even someone like myself could get some inkling of the joyous sensation of buying dreams.

Making tickets to enter in the draw became the favourite game of the young Master and his friends at the time.

At around the time the tickets went on sale, it was formally announced that Tokyo would host the Olympic Games. They would be held some six months after the Grand International Exposition.

'The festivities the year after next, marking the Empire's 2600th Anniversary, will involve the whole world, you know,' the Master said. 'It'll be a major occasion!'

Not long afterwards, he joyfully informed the Mistress that Sapporo had also been formally announced as the host for the Winter Olympics.

'What, really?' the Mistress screeched in surprise. 'But I thought the Tokyo Olympics were to be held in Tokyo?'

'That's right. The Tokyo Olympics will be held in Tokyo.'

'Oh. So what will be held in Sapporo, then?'

'The Winter Olympics.'

'But I thought the Olympics were going to be in Tokyo…'

'They are! Just, the Winter Olympics will be held in Sapporo.'

'Um, so what's being held in Tokyo, then?'

Sometimes the conversation between the Master and the Mistress was like a comedy act. Although to be honest, I was just as confused as the Mistress.

When the mistake was cleared up, the whole family had a good laugh about it. Indeed, that was perhaps the happiest of times in the Hirai household. At least, it felt as though the Master had been longing for something good, and that soon it would happen at last.

The Master was no doubt much better informed than I was, but it had never occurred to me that bad things were soon going to befall us. All I felt at the time and subsequently was a vague notion that the economy wasn't in such great shape, but that was about it.

But so much time has passed since then, and now looking back I realize it was quite an extraordinary year. From around that time, various things began to change in the Hirai household. The Master was busy with the trade association and started coming home late more often. He was on the whole an optimist, but he was beginning to wear a frown more and more frequently.

That summer the Olympics the family had been looking forward to for so long were cancelled, soon followed by the postponement of the Grand International Exposition. A new date wasn't set, however, and it seemed that the ten yen spent on the tickets—placed on the family altar with such ceremony—had been wasted.

'I don't get it,' Takeshi said.

He was back from his bike tour and had come over to cadge the customary New Year gift of money from me. To butter me up, he'd brought me some gourd-shaped chocolates that my nephew had brought back from his trip to Hawaii.

I'd gone to look for the special decorative envelopes for money gifts that I'd put away somewhere, and came back to find him reading my notebook.

'I just don't get it. It must have been four years after the Berlin Olympics, so in 1940? They were planning to hold the Olympics in Tokyo and Sapporo in 1940?'

'That's right.'

'Seriously?'

'Yes, seriously.'

'So why didn't it happen?'

'Because the war started.'

'Oh, right. Yeah. I suppose you wouldn't be able to host the Olympics if you're at war.' He squinted at the envelope to check I'd put some money inside. 'Thanks,' he said, grabbing it from me, then left.

***

Thinking back to what happened after that, it isn't hard to understand why the government did a U-turn and decided not to hold the Olympics after all. But at the time I didn't understand at all. All I knew was that the Master had set his heart on them, and I was upset by the announcement.

'In this time of crisis, we shouldn't be throwing money around like that. It's just not possible when the country is preparing for war,' Miss Mutsuko said angrily. But while her magazine was full of articles about the time of crisis, it didn't really feel much like one to me and deep down I wasn't convinced.

Having put so much effort into something only to see it come to nothing, I thought the Master would kick up more of a fuss, but he didn't say much at all when the decision was taken that summer.

That really surprised me, but I suppose he must have known more about the general situation and just couldn't find it in himself to say anything. At any rate, the Olympics, once such a frequent topic of conversation in the family, were never mentioned again.

And then war broke out all over the world and it wasn't just impossible for Tokyo to host the Olympics, but also Helsinki and Rome too, and ultimately the Games themselves were cancelled, so what I'd said to Takeshi wasn't exactly wrong either.

In any case, I didn't really understand the Master's work, let alone that of important politicians. I didn't understand it then, and I still don't understand it now.

More importantly, Mistress Tokiko had to make an extremely significant decision that year. To cut a long story short, she was constantly fretting about which elementary school to send the young Master to.

It's true that she'd considered her sister in Azabu a fuss pot for getting in a tizzy over young Master Masato's education, but when it came to her own son it was a different matter entirely.

'Look, the best option is to get your child into one of the top elementary schools affiliated with a high school. But those have all filled up while you've been here with your head in the clouds, going on and on about having built a nice house. He'll never get into a good school now,' the Mistress Azabu had scolded her. 'It's all very well having delayed his entry into school on account of his legs, but I'd thought you were at least spending that year making adequate preparations.'

Stung by the thought that her mistaken choice of elementary school might have a negative impact on her own son's future, Mistress Tokiko all at once changed her tune and became an ardent follower of her sister's example.

'Masato didn't take an exam to enter elementary school, did he?' she asked, sounding as though she was clutching at straws.

'He didn't take an exam, but I put in the application at the earliest opportunity. The popular schools fill up quickly, you know,' Mistress Azabu said, cool as a cucumber. 'The top five are Seishi Elementary in Hongo, Seinan Elementary in Aoyama, Kojimachi Elementary, Bancho Elementary. And Shirogane Elementary, the one Masato attended. If he doesn't go to one of these, he'll never get into a decent middle school.'

At any rate, it had taken a Herculean effort, Mistress Azabu said, but she'd finally managed to get young Master Masato into an elementary school affiliated with the prefectural high school, which meant he wouldn't have to face the major hurdle of a middle school entrance exam. This was already something to be terrifically proud of. She sounded rather like a forceful fortune teller warning Mistress Tokiko that her son wouldn't have a chance unless she listened to her.

Mistress Tokiko flinched and mumbled, 'Oh my, but they're all so far away from home.' So that was what she was really worried about.

'What an irresponsible thing to say! Masato's classmates at Shirogane all lived far away and had travel passes, you know.' Mistress Azabu looked like an angry, snorting bull about to charge.

After that, Mistress Tokiko mobilized all the connections she could think of and started a campaign to get the young Master into a prestigious elementary school. But it turned out that the timing was hopelessly bad, and of course she had started too late, so all the schools were filled to capacity and he would just have to go to a different school until a place opened up.

It just so happened that the newly established elementary school two stations east of the Hirais' house had a fairly good reputation, and the proportion of students getting into middle school was quite high, so the Mistress decided to send the young Master there.

It was in a relatively recent residential development that had emerged over the past decade or so, unlike the old fashionable districts near the Seishi or Shirogane schools; but still, many of the residents were doctors or professors, and the area had a reputation for being stylish and cultured.

The young Master was a year older than his new classmates, but he was small for his age. His cap and jacket with gold buttons on the collar were too big for him, and his little body strained under the weight of the heavy leather satchel on his back. Still, he seemed thrilled to be going to school at last.

The Mistress was pitifully anxious that he might not fit in, since he hadn't been to kindergarten either. For a while she hardly ate a thing. He still dragged his leg a little as he walked, and to begin with she was so terribly worried about simply giving him a commuter pass and making him take the train alone that she chose to accompany him. When she was unable to go, she would always ask me to go in her place.

Even now I can still feel his little hand in mine as we went down the hill, waited at the station then rode the train, chatting about this and that until we alighted two stations later and went up the street to the school gate.

But the time came when the young Master would look embarrassed as we reached the station near his school and would refuse to hold my hand as we walked up the hill to school. It must have been when he was in about the fourth grade that he eventually told me he didn't want me to come with him anymore.

I don't have any children of my own, and still feel a special fondness for the young Master, having looked after him from when he was a baby. I was still so young myself back then. I've worked in a good number of other households since, both with and without children, but I never felt the same closeness and affection that I felt for young Master Kyoichi in any other family. He was like my own child or little brother, irreplaceable. He was a cheerful boy, and not such a worrier as the Mistress, so I made friends with him right away.

His friends would come round to play at the weekend, and the tinplate toy collection he was so proud of was the envy of all. The Master would bring him toys from his own company, and also the toys of rival companies that he bought for research. Not only did the young Master have the Arawashi and Kamikaze fighter planes, but also a Zeppelin and a tinplate Mickey Mouse wearing the uniform of the Imperial Japanese Army.

He also had a loop-the-loop plane, a seaplane, a wind-up plane hanging on a thread that went around and around, and machine-gun toting soldiers wearing gasmasks and helmets. All in all, the young Master's bedroom was like a showroom for the toys that all boys coveted.

Having had an indulgent upbringing, the young Master wasn't possessive about his toys and let his friends play with them to their heart's content, so he quickly became popular. And that meant he could get them to show him things too. He would do things with them on the way home from school, such as the time he went with them to see a kamishibai.

The Mistress had heard somewhere that these open-air picture-card theatres were not only terribly unhygienic, with everyone sucking loudly on candies on the dusty streets, but furthermore filled children's heads with nonsense. She didn't want him watching hair-raising stories about a dead child that came back from the grave for revenge, or a spiteful mother-in-law who forced her daughter-in-law stark naked into a water jug and bullied her to death, so she banned him from going. However, he would end up being shunned by his classmates if he broke his promise to go, so I secretly slipped him some money to pay for the candies they had to buy as admission.

I hid behind a tree to watch too, but they weren't at all the sort of scary stories the Mistress was so worried about. Instead they featured soldiers and were more like text books for moral training, not very interesting at all.

The young Master, too, seemed satisfied after watching once and didn't show much interest in kamishibai after that. However, he said that all his friends had bamboo-copters and wanted me to buy one for him. Apparently they were sold in regular candy stores. 'Why do you want something cheap like that when you've got so many tinplate aeroplanes?' I asked him, but he just pouted and said, 'Everyone's got them, so I want one too.'

He was overjoyed when I did buy one for him, and was playing with it in the street by the house until it got dark. It seemed to catch the breeze just right and fly really well. When I went outside to tell him it was time to come in, I saw the car bringing the Master home from work pull up at the bottom of the hill.

The street was narrow, and the Master would often get out and walk up the hill instead of making the car come all the way up to the house. That day he was just getting out of the car when the cheap bamboo toy caught the breeze, flew unsteadily down the hill and crashed into the feather adorning his fedora, landing at his feet.

He bent down and picked it up and stood looking at it for such a long time that the young Master started looking worried that he might be about to get a telling off, and I too began to feel uncomfortable.

Then the Master tucked his briefcase under his arm and, holding the bamboo-copter in one hand, adjusted his hat with his free hand and came up the hill.

The young Master glanced at me, unsure what to do.

'Is this yours, Kyo?' the Master asked, putting the plane back in the young Master's small hand. The young Master nodded, still looking as though he was about to cry. 'Where did you buy it?'

The young Master went bright red and looked at me.

'I bought it in the candy shop. I'm sorry, I shouldn't have done that.'

The young Master kept looking fearfully from me to the Master. In his child's heart, he probably felt he had betrayed his father, a top executive in a toy company, by buying such a cheapskate toy.

'How much was it?' the Master asked.

'One sen,' I answered.

'One sen, is that all? What good business sense!'

Finally he sighed, patted the young Master on the head, and went into the house.

That summer, the same summer the Olympics were cancelled and the Grand International Exposition postponed, the domestic sale of metal toys was banned and the Master's company had to shut down the factory they had opened only two years previously.

To be honest, I didn't really understand the reason why metal toys were banned. Apparently, since the war with China was dragging on, all metal was needed to make arms and ammunition and shouldn't be used for toys. In any case, it was really tough on the Master's company, and many of the staff had to be laid off. The factory land and facilities were sold off too, I heard.

I remember the Master and Mistress arguing about it after dinner one night. I was in the kitchen doing the washing up, but

I could hear their raised voices in the living room. It apparently started after Mistress Tokiko's father, worried for what would become of the toy company now, had suggested the Master should move to another job, which he had refused.

'It's not like you started your career there. You used to work in a department store, so surely you shouldn't feel such a sense of obligation,' the Mistress said. 'Father told me there are any number of companies prospering on munitions, so if you are of a mind there are opportunities out there for you.'

It was true that the Master had been employed in a department store, and the toy company president had poached him when he decided to expand his business and needed someone who knew about distribution. The Mistress had apparently heard that the toy company, which had started as a small local workshop, was now shrinking its business back to size, and was worried.

The mild-mannered Master sounded like he didn't want to argue about it, and had been talking in a subdued voice, but then I heard him say decisively, 'Look, stop making a mountain out of a molehill, will you?'

He had never raised his voice before and, shocked, Mistress Tokiko stormed into the kitchen.

'I've had enough! If he's going to be like that, then I'll take Kyoichi and leave home and set up business as a stationer's,' she raged.

Subsequently, on the few occasions the Mistress and Master ever quarrelled, the Mistress would always have the last word with, 'I'll set up business as a stationer's.' At the time, a stationer's was considered a proper business for respectable widows.

Sitting in the kitchen, she blew her nose and continued, 'Come with me too, Taki. We'll get by, the two of us. I'll be able to cope with a small shop. Just so long as it's near Kyoichi's school.'

The Master waited a while, then came to get her. 'Look, it's just that we can't sell to the domestic market. We haven't been told to stop making metal toys altogether, you know. They want us to focus on exports instead. Raw materials are in short supply, but there are ways of coping with such shortages. I like having a job making the kind of things that make Kyo happy,' he said, and led her away, still sobbing.

In fact the Master really did have a positive outlook. He'd seemed quite depressed when the large factory was closed, but he eventually picked himself up and got good at pulling strings to purchase materials on the black market. And he also threw himself into making wooden toys and the like for the domestic market.

I think it must have been in Kamakura that year when I heard him and the company president talking together: 'At this point, we'll have to somehow come up with a toy that makes the most of rayon's poor tolerance of water.' What strange things they cooked up, I thought.

Rayon was the artificial silk that had emerged on the market and dominated during wartime. It was a natural fibre fabric that didn't do well in water. It was used a lot for socks, but if it happened to get wet it would fall apart, and rip even if you sweated. What on earth could they mean by a toy that made use of that weakness?

It was the one cloth that maids disliked most. In order to make it last a long time, you had to perfect the art of working quickly to wash it while not getting it too wet. Even so, I was really good at it. It's a pity it doesn't exist anymore, as there's no opportunity to show off my skill.

At the end of summer, there was another small incident. It had started raining in the afternoon, and gradually the wind picked up, making conditions frightful.

The Master had gone to Yokohama on business and was due back in time for dinner, but the meeting had perhaps dragged on, for there was no sign of him. Eventually the Mistress and young Master gave up waiting for him and started having a late dinner, while a terrible storm raged outside. The wind rattled the windows and whistled through the trees, which made us feel quite anxious.

After the young Master went to bed, the rain and wind grew even more intense. The house was on high ground, so there was no fear of flooding, but the urban development was located on the Musashino Plain with nothing to obstruct the wind, and the roar as it mowed down trees was terrifying.

There was a crash upstairs as what sounded like a branch torn from a tree slammed into the storm shutter over the young Master's window. Moments later a bucket or plant pot rolled furiously past the front door and smashed into something outside.

The Mistress was so worried about the Master that she couldn't sleep, and she must have felt terribly nervous alone. She was unwilling to let me withdraw to my own room, and said she wanted me to stay up with her in the living room, so I occupied myself with mending clothes.

Suddenly there was a loud knocking on the front door.

'Oh, he's come home at last!' the Mistress exclaimed, and together we gathered some towels and went to open the door. A man in a pitch-black raincoat traipsed in, accompanied by wind and rain.

'Mr. Hirai has been forced to stay in Yokohama tonight,' he said.

Just then there was a loud bang upstairs, as though a tree had fallen against the house.

'What the heck was that?' the man said, taking off his raincoat and hat. It was Mr. Itakura.

'Oh, but why?'

'It appears the Tokaido Line has stopped. Mr. Hirai called the office to say he was unable to return tonight. I wanted to let you know right away, but in these conditions it wasn't certain that even a telegram would get through, so I thought I'd better come myself.'

'Oh, but…!'

'More importantly, we'd better do something about upstairs.'

I looked up to see the young Master standing at the top of the stairs in his pyjamas looking as though he was about to start crying. 'The window in the other room is going "bang bang",' he said.

It sounded as though the guest-room window was flapping about hard enough for the glass to break. The guest room had a semi-Western design, and the window was covered in fashionable wooden shutters that opened out in the foreign style. The other rooms all had traditional sliding storm shutters, so even in strong winds there was little to worry about.

As I'd expected, when I went upstairs to check, the shutters were dangling open, the glass broken by a stone whipped up by the wind so that rain was coming into the room.

'This won't do,' Mr. Itakura said. 'Taki, is there a ladder in the house?'

'Yes, behind the kitchen.'

'What about some kind of board we can nail over it, and carpentry tools?'

'I'll go get them.'

'Make sure the Mistress and the young Master are safe, then get changed into some old clothes and come help me.'

'You're not going up onto the roof, are you?' the Mistress said. 'It's much too dangerous! You'd better leave it.'

'Better while the wind's still like this. It's going to get much worse later on. We have to nail that window up now.'

The lightbulb sputtered and went out.

'What's that?'

'A power cut. Don't worry, the storm will have passed by morning and it'll be sunny tomorrow.'

And so I left the Mistress and the young Master in the house and went out into the raging wind and rain with Mr. Itakura.

It was hard enough just to stand the ladder up, and it would blow away if I took my attention off it for one moment, so I had to put my foot on it to hold it firm.

Mr. Itakura put some nails in his mouth and climbed up the ladder carrying a hammer in his right hand and the board under his left arm. He nailed the board over the broken shutter.

I had to struggle to stop the ladder from falling, and was nearly hit on the head when Mr. Itakura dropped the board, which took all my strength to pass back up to him. Looking up I couldn't see a thing for my rain-soaked hair, but I couldn't take my hand off the ladder to push it out of the way or dry my eyes. Still, working out in the storm soaked to the skin was somehow exhilarating, and gave me the strength to keep the ladder firm until finally Mr. Itakura came down it carefully, one rung at a time.

'It's done, Taki. Thank you,' he said, and patted my shoulder.

The smell of rain-soaked human skin reached my nose. In that moment, I suddenly remembered something unexpected. And for some reason felt guilty.

The Mistress brought lots of handtowels into the kitchen, and thanked him over and over again. 'You're wet through! You'll catch cold like that, so please wear one of my husband's kimonos,' she said. 'And you must have some warm tea.'

But Mr. Itakura just replied, 'If I borrow a kimono, it'll just get ruined in this rain. Anyway, I'd better get going before the trains stop running, so please just relax and get some sleep now. It'll be a fine day tomorrow, and Mr. Hirai will be home right away.' And with that he exited via the kitchen door.

But I hadn't even finished drying myself off when the Mistress was opening the front door for him again. It turned out the train that serviced the station at the bottom of the hill had also been stopped due to the rain, so Mr. Itakura had no option but to come back.

That night the Mistress took the terrified young Master into her bedroom, while I slept in my maid's room. The upstairs guestroom was already soaked from the rain and even now rain and wind were coming through the cracks in the board nailed over it, so I tidied the living room and lay out some bedding for Mr. Itakura in there.

The terrible storm that night was a typhoon, second in strength only to Typhoon Kathleen that came just after the war. It was terrifying. To give you an idea of just how awful it was, some poor bear drowned in the Tama River.

The next morning the wind was still strong, and since the newspapers said it was dangerous to go to school, the young Master's elementary remained closed for the day.

I made breakfast for Mr. Itakura. He lived a fifteen-minute walk from the station near the young Master's school, and could probably get a lift in a car along the way or even walk, so he said he was going home right away without waiting for the trains to start running. I recall that he went home wearing a kimono borrowed from the Master, not his soaking wet suit.

That night of the typhoon was when I learned that the Mistress and Mr. Itakura had met again that summer in Kamakura. After changing into the Master's summer yukata and thick padded over-kimono, he was warming himself by the charcoal brazier in the living room drinking tea with the Mistress and they were chatting about it.

It was an innocent story, about nothing really, but the two of them seemed to enjoy reminiscing about a summer's day spent together.

I'm writing down my memories of the family, so I don't feel any particular need to write about myself, but I've decided to mention something here in passing.

That autumn I received a marriage proposal.

It was eight years since I'd left my family up north, and I had already turned twenty-one. The proposal had come through one of the Master's customers, and concerned a middle school teacher.

It could only be said that such a proposal to a mere uneducated maid like myself, coming from a splendid man who was a middle school teacher and part time advisor to a national policy corporation, was entirely thanks to being in service to the Hirai household. I was quite taken aback, having only ever expected to be summoned by my family to return to the north to get married.

'My dream is to get you into a really good marriage, Taki,' Mistress Tokiko would always tell me. She seemed to enjoy the role of getting me ready for marriage. 'It doesn't mean that we won't have anything more to do with each other, you know. You can keep coming here to work until you have your own children. I'm not of a mind to employ another maid. After all, we've always been together.'

Hearing the Mistress talk like this, I gradually began to feel more enthusiastic about the idea, but when I saw the photograph and personal history statement I felt utterly deflated.

The man was over fifty years of age. What's more, this would be his third marriage. He had four children, all of whom were older than me, as well as grandchildren already!

Considering his social standing, it was a better opportunity than I deserved, but I couldn't bear the thought of being a bride to a man more than thirty years older than myself. I cried myself silly whenever I was alone.

I was crying in my maid's room when the paper door suddenly slid open and the Mistress came in.

'You don't like the idea, do you?' she said quietly. I looked down, unable to speak. 'Of course you don't. It's only natural. You don't need to worry. We'll turn him down.'

'But what about the Master?'

'The Master can't force you, and anyway, it's really not a good proposal at all. I had no idea he was so old! I don't care what anyone says, it's absolutely shameless of him. I'll find someone better than that for you.' She grimaced in vexation, turned smartly on her heel, and left the room.

The next day, after dinner, she talked it over with the Master. Having sent the young Master upstairs to bed and me to the kitchen, she asked him to turn the marriage proposal down.

'Say what you like, but it's absolutely impudent of him!'

'Really? I thought it was a good offer. He's a school teacher, you know, the intelligentsia. Taki would be able to have her own maid and become the Mistress of her own household.'

'Becoming the Mistress of a household is all well and good, but there's an age difference of over thirty years! Poor Taki. And she'll find herself with grandchildren to look after all of a sudden!'

'But young men are all getting their draft calls now, you know, even those employed in our factory. I'd intended to find someone of an appropriate age, but there just aren't any. Even if there are, it won't be long before they're taken off to fight in the war, so what would she do then? That would be worse for her, wouldn't it?'

'Some of the men taken off to fight do come back though. With a man of that age, the future's uncertain even without the fear of being hit by a bullet.'

'Stop going on about his age, will you? He's not that much older than I am.'

'Taki is a lot younger than me, though. She has her whole life ahead of her. Apart from anything else, who knows if she'll even be able to have children with someone as old as that.'

All of a sudden they fell silent. The next thing I knew, the marriage proposal had been dropped and was never mentioned again.

The reason I wasn't all that disappointed by the failed marriage proposal was probably because I truly enjoyed being in service in the Hirai household. If it would be more of a hardship to marry someone I didn't want to, then I would prefer to stay with the Hirais for the rest of my life.

Unlike now, people at that time didn't have high hopes for marriage. It was unusual for a man in his fifties to take a bride of twenty-one, it's true, but then I knew a number of women who were treated worse than a maid after getting married.

The fact I didn't receive any more good proposals after that was probably due to my own lack of enthusiasm, although the fact that times were hard no doubt also had something to do with it.

More important to me at the time was my new role, as the Hirais' maid, of being in charge of local fire prevention. The Master had told me to forge close links with the fire prevention squad and civil defense corps. Taking part in air raid drills and so forth was challenging and fun. These days you might call me something of a career woman, I suppose.

Since the Olympics had gone down the drain, there had been more talk of the need for air raid drills and preparing for bombing raids.

Even so, Tokyo wasn't actually hit by an air raid until the year after the start of the Greater East Asia War, or what we now call the Pacific War, so for the four years until then we were simply training, a bit like being in rehearsals. Making blackout covers for light bulbs out of cardboard, and stitching emergency clothing for the Master, Mistress, and young Master Kyoichi was an opportunity to make full use of my skills, and was also fun.

That was also the year the Master called in a builder to construct a splendid air raid shelter in the garden using concrete. It was big enough to keep a small table and chairs inside, and the Master said that as long as we took in some blankets, we would be warm enough there in winter, too.

'As long as we're prepared, we don't have anything to worry about. If you think of it as an extension to the house, it's extremely economical.'

This was at a time when no other houses yet had an air raid shelter, and it was just like the novelty-loving Master to have one built, the Mistress Azabu said somewhat uncharitably, and others agreed with her.

'Nan, that's not right,' Takeshi said. 'You don't use the term "career woman" like that.'

He'd chosen to read my notes, and I wish he wouldn't keep on griping about things I'd written. I'd just wanted to get across, as clearly as I could, what a bold figure I cut in baggy pants and sleeved apron as I got everyone, even the men, together and instructed them what to do, diligently working on fire prevention activities.

Food and luxury items were gradually beginning to be scarce, and in order to provide the family with the meals they were used to without running short I had to use my influence with the tradesmen, too. An ordinary maid wouldn't have been able to do this so well.

I'll stop boasting now, but really the difficult times gave me the opportunity to hone my abilities and show what I was capable of.

Chapter 4

Ouverture de Fête

Writing things down as they come back to me, I smile as I recall how adorable young Master Kyoichi was when he started at elementary school.

He made friends with two boys from school, Sei and Tatsu, and would be out all weekend playing at the house of one or the other. They often came over to play at the Hirai household too, and I went out of my way to make tasty snacks for them.

Under his friends' influence, he started subscribing to *Boy's Club* instead of *The Elementary School First Grader*, and before we knew it he was a fan of the manga *Norakuro*, about a black-and-white dog who was a soldier in an army of fierce dogs. 'When I grow up, I want to be an Army General,' he announced.

Of course the next day he was going to be a scientist, and the day after that a builder, and many other things too, but one of the many futures he came up with was, 'When I grow up I want to marry you, Taki!' So sweet!

I was the young Master's unwavering candidate for a bride until the third grade, when he fell for a new girl in school, Mitsuko. Naturally I never expected to actually marry him, but I couldn't help imagining myself as Lord Tokugawa Iemitsu's wet nurse, the virtuous Lady Kasuga who was all the rage in women's magazines at the time.

Every morning it was my job to fill his small lunch box with attractively colourful foods, and I felt supremely happy as I washed the empty box he brought home in the evening.

Remembering the young Master's lunch box reminded me of Patriotic Services Day. This was a system introduced when the young Master was in the second grade, in the second semester of 1939, whereby the first of every month was decreed Patriotic Services Day, which meant he had to go to school even if it fell on a Sunday.

On that day, his lunchbox had to be a plain bed of white rice topped with a single pickled plum so that it resembled the Japanese flag. This gave me an opportunity to show off my skill, lining the bottom of the box with a thin layer of rice, then spreading some finely chopped dried bonito with soy sauce, or tiny shrimp simmered in soy sauce and mirin, covering it with a sheet of crisped nori laver, and concealing it all beneath another layer of rice topped with the requisite pickled plum.

The decree had stated that we should not indulge in luxury during wartime and the first day I'd followed the instructions to the letter. However, Sei, Tatsu and all the other children had tastier lunches hidden away in their beds of rice, and the young Master had come home with his face flushed red with rage like a little devil, so from then on I followed this method.

Incidentally, I don't suppose Takeshi has a clue what Patriotic Services Day was all about. If he were to ask me straight up what it was, though, I would be in quite a fix. I myself don't quite know.

On the first day of every month, the entire population was to remember all our soldiers were doing for us and abstain from luxury. More concretely, I think we did things like disaster prevention drills and making comfort bags to send to soldiers, but other than that I can't really remember.

What I do clearly recall is how that summer, the Mistress suddenly told me, 'Taki, when they start the Patriotic Services Day in September, be sure to take yourself out somewhere every first of the month, won't you?' She went on, 'It was in the newspaper this morning, in an article by Tsuneko Hirai. Maids should do only the basics of household chores that day and refrain from social contact,' she said. 'Instead, housewives should do the work and send their maids out to visit Yasukuni Shrine, or to see a national policy movie. Servants should have one day in the month where they have time to educate themselves, at least. That made quite an impression on me. What an amazing writer she is! So, Taki, I want you to go out, please.'

The Mistress said she would see the young Master off to school and meet him afterwards, and so I took a train into town, changing onto a tram to get to the Yasukuni Shrine. I don't recall ever taking a day off and going to the shrine or to the cinema after that, though. Perhaps it was just that once.

When I got back to the house, the young Master was back from school and furious about having been given such a plain lunch, and so it was decided that I would make him a tastier, concealed lunch every first of the month from then on.

Almost everybody believed there was plenty of food in Japan, but since government controls were making it hard to get hold of things it was necessary to start stockpiling some supplies, just in case.

I suppose we did occasionally hear talk of someone somewhere-or-other being arrested by the Special Police, and it wasn't as though we were unaware of troubles, but we had never heard a thing about having been routed in China, and the department stores were still holding pretty good bargain sales.

My knowledge about the war with China was pretty much limited to what I learned from Mr. Torazo when I went to purchase germ rice at his shop.

'The war's really dragging on, isn't it?' I grumbled.

'Look, Miss Taki,' he retorted. 'The Imperial Army has already achieved a great victory, so the war's practically over, isn't it?'

'Really? Then why are we still in a time of crisis?'

'Oh, come on, they're working on it, that's all. Establishing a Greater East Asia, that is. It's a huge area, you know. Things are a bit different over there, but the government decided they should still go ahead with it.'

That was probably true for the most part, I thought. And people like Miss Mutsuko of *Housewives' Delight* were making a whole lot of noise about how 'a frugal housewife is the cornerstone of the home front', and how we should be 'doing whatever we can to economize on rice and meat', so I felt obliged to somehow stock up on things and learn how to make bread.

And when I really put my mind to it and applied myself to researching how to make bread, I got so good at it that the Master would even request it, saying, 'Taki's bread is just the best thing to go with stew.'

My copy of *The Maid's Handbook*, published in 1934, said that 'stew should be served with pickled vegetables,' so I invariably made those two things together. However, the Master said it was the worst possible combination, as the sweet vinegar clashed with the milky taste of the stew. When I thought about it, it did make sense, but Western-style food like stew just didn't come naturally to me, and when I got something into my head I could be really stubborn.

And so, stew with bread became a standard in the Hirai household. I added grated carrot and chopped greens to help make our frugal meals more nutritious, and the bread I baked looked appetising too. Chicken stew was the tastiest, but even the shelled clams that were then flooding the market could make a really fine dish if done well. If I recall, stew and bread often graced the dinner table on Patriotic Services Day.

Milk was rarely available, so I tried using soy milk in the stew. However, it had a distinctive smell and lack of depth to the taste, which I compensated for by adding white miso and fried bacon.

One type of substitute food that went down really well with the Master and the young Master was peanut butter. Some relatives of the Mistress had sent some peanuts from the neighbouring Chiba prefecture, so I roasted them in an earthenware pot until fragrant, then ground them up in the pestle and mortar and added a little rice bran oil, salt and sugar.

I was in the middle of making it when the young Master came into the kitchen and asked if he could try it. 'It's bad manners, so don't tell your mother,' I told him, then the two of us stuck our fingers in and licked them clean.

When I served it the next morning with golden brown toast, the Master savoured it with a smile and commented, 'It tastes even better than real butter. And it's so much better than that artificial stuff.'

My efforts were so well received that Miss Mutsuko asked me to share my knowledge, and a number of my recipes for meals economizing on rice were published in *Housewives' Delight*. A letter was sent in from an ordinary housewife asking, 'Miss Taki, think up some tasty dishes for us, will you?' and so after a lot of thought I came up with menus for things like steamed sweetcorn bread, and steamed rice with lotus root.

To the steamed rice I added reconstituted dried shrimp and the liquid they had soaked in, along with lightly toasted lotus root for added flavour. To make it especially appetizing, I garnished it with soaked root ginger and chopped white chervil. It was so good that I still sometimes make it even now.

There were rumours going around in those days that sugar was running out, and that we wouldn't be able to get hold of soy sauce and so forth, but that's precisely when the benefits of having a good relationship with the door-to-door tradesmen paid off. When they pressed me to buy something, if I diligently did as they wished, paying the price they asked for or offering to take something off their hands for a cheap price, in return they would go out of their way to bring the things I requested.

I had always used the paper bags from the grocer's and dried goods shop for lighting the fire to heat the bathwater, but when I realized that they were getting to be in short supply, I neatly folded them and handed them back. To show their gratitude, the next product they brought me would be of better quality.

'It's the thought that counts' really is the basis of being effective as a maid.

And just when the newspapers and magazines were full of how you couldn't get hold of white rice anymore, Mr. Torazo told me, 'I don't know what they're talking about. We still have plenty, so I'll bring you as much as you like. It's more nutritious and economical if you don't mind having a bit of germ rice mixed in. But according to the powers that be, we'll have to start selling all rice seventy percent polished this winter, so best buy in now. Seventy percent polished rice is rough, and it's no good for making sushi since it falls apart. Sushi's our national food, right? It's the taste of our heart. It's vital to building a Greater East Asia! As a rice merchant, the very idea of rice as useless as that is just not right.' And so I bought a lot of white rice mixed with germ rice.

Even the fishmonger brought me some super fresh fish, telling me bashfully, 'As long as it's you Taki, I don't mind,' as he gave me a discount.

It was much later that supplies of food in Tokyo really did hit rock bottom.

The Master's company's toy vehicles made from paper or wood proved a hit, and he and the company president regained some of their former confidence, albeit not fully. Their staff was still much reduced, but the forward-thinking, energetic company president recovered his bounce.

The Master once forgot to take an important document with him, and a telegram arrived at the house saying, 'SEND IMMEDIATELY', so the Mistress told me to take it in to him. After closing the big factory, they had moved to a much smaller neighbourhood place. The Master's sales department and Mr. Itakura's design department were in one corner of the factory floor there.

I opened the wooden door with frosted glass panels to find myself in a reception room with brown arm chairs. The office where the company president and the Master had their desks was partitioned off by a wickerwork screen.

'Ah, this is it. Thank you, Taki. Wait here a moment, will you?' the Master said, so I sat nervously on a chair and was staring at the wall when a slogan caught my eye: 'All toys are national defence toys!' It was written by hand and finished off with the company president's seal.

Around that time, there were some advertisements for a brand of cookie that read: 'Cookies aren't just sweets. They're a national defence food!' and: 'Today's children will be tomorrow's soldiers on the frontline, so we mustn't neglect the nutrition of infants on the home front', and so forth. The company president was probably just following their example. However, without any explanation of what the 'national defence' actually was, it didn't strike me as being as convincing as the cookies ad.

Inside the office the Master and company president were talking loudly about how strong the sumo wrestler Futabayama was.

'He might have fallen short of his dream of seventy wins, but still, he set a new record of sixty-nine wins that's unlikely to be beaten any time soon. I can't help thinking that the ordeal our valiant toy export business is going through is somehow like Futabayama falling to Akinoumi at the spring tournament,' the company president boomed.

'You're absolutely right. Everyone suffers a setback sometimes. It's how they pick themselves up afterwards that counts,' the Master responded.

'But losing those four bouts in the spring tournament! Futabayama was trounced and looked like he was finished, only to rise again like a phoenix and win all his bouts to take the championship. He's really lit up my fighting spirit! What a wrestler! The toys business has to be like this, too, you know. An indomitable spirit is a must!'

It was painfully obvious that they hoped to take strength from Futabayama's example following the major surgery and reconstruction of their company.

'Sorry to keep you waiting, Taki. We just got a new product through. It's fresh off the factory floor, so I wanted to get you to take it back to Kyo as quickly as possible. We have the Toy Makers' Guild meeting tonight and I'll be back late, so I won't need dinner. I told the Mistress about it this morning, so she should already know.'

'Yes sir, I'll take it to him.'

I said goodbye and left the factory, and made my way home carrying the new toy very carefully so as to be sure not to break it.

'I brought you a present from your father.'

The young Master was used to this and took the paper bag from me as though it were the most natural thing in the world, just like a little prince.

'Oh!' he gasped as he opened it, apparently impressed.

'Oh my, what is it?' Mistress Tokiko asked, going over to take a look.

It was a small yacht made of elaborately put-together thin sheets of plywood. It was painted with a thin coat of celluloid to make it waterproof and had rayon sails printed with the national flag's vivid red rising sun.

That summer the family was again invited to the company president's summer villa in Kamakura. The Master, Mistress, and young Master Kyoichi all left together, and as usual the Master came back early, leaving the Mistress and young Master at the villa.

As the summer vacation was drawing to a close, the Master sent me to meet them and accompany them back to Tokyo. As he was leaving for work that morning, he told me, 'You should go early and enjoy some sea air yourself, Taki. It's good to have a change of scenery.'

I was due to meet them in Kamakura at three o'clock, so it would be enough to take the train from Shinagawa just after two, but the Master was being kind enough to tell me that I should go earlier to make the most of my time there.

After seeing the Master off, I did the cleaning even more conscientiously than usual, then left the house before noon. I made some rice balls with the leftovers from yesterday's dinner and put them in the sleeve of my kimono, thinking I would have them for lunch on the outbound Yokosuka Line train.

It was barely an hour's ride, a rare trip outside the city for me. I opened the window, and a cool breeze blew in.

Even the Mistress, who had complained that spending time with the company president's wife was tiring, now often said what a wonderful place Kamakura was, which made me long to go there too.

I only had to hear the Mistress talk of her experiences for me to feel as though they were my own. Her account of the Kabuki actor Uzaemon playing the part of the unfortunate lover Yosaburo in the play *Kirare yosa* made him sound positively seductive! It was so vivid I almost felt like I'd seen him play the part myself. And she made bathing in the sea on the Shonan coast sound like so much fun that I felt like I'd experienced being in the water. If I ever had the opportunity to do any of the things the Mistress spoke of, those were the things I didn't want to miss out on.

I took the Master at his word and left a little early, feeling quite as though as I was on a pleasure trip as I pondered whether to ride the Enoshima Electric Railway, go to the seaside, or visit the Great Buddha in its grove of trees.

The train was crowded with students looking fresh in summer blouses, elegant women carrying parasols, and small children going to the beach. Elderly men wearing Japanese-style clothing puffed leisurely on their pipes.

Topics of conversation included how strong Futabayama—or alternatively Minanogawa—was in sumo, or whether shares or bonds gave the best returns on investment. I had the feeling that all of them were doing quite well out of both, and that none of them were short of cash.

'Iron for reinforcing concrete might be in short supply right now, but here in Japan we know how to get the job done with bamboo instead. After all, we have the best knowhow in the world, right?'

'All the shortages lately don't mean that things aren't available. The thing is, the government sets the official price so ridiculously low that nobody wants to sell it at that price, and everyone ends up selling it overseas instead.'

'Rayon is useless, really.'

They all sounded as though they were just exchanging pleasantries about the weather.

Having grown up in the countryside, I'd first seen the sea only after coming to Tokyo, and the smell of the sea and the majesty of Mount Fuji were inextricably linked to the modern Tokyo lifestyle for me.

I got off the train at Kamakura, and transferred to the Enoshima Electric Railway. I had decided to visit the Great Buddha, which I had heard of only once from the Mistress. As I recalled, she had recited the latter part of a famous poem by Akiko Yosano that went: *A good-looking man amidst the green trees of summer*. She laughed, and added, 'Although I can't say I find that portly Buddha particularly good looking!' Still, I thought his figure sitting there in the trees must be beautiful, even though I'd never seen it.

I alighted from the train at Hase Station and started following other people heading to the temple. The air shimmered over the road in the humidity rising from the sea, and wind chimes tinkled outside the souvenir shops lining the street.

I entered the forested temple precincts to find them bustling with people, the voices of fathers admonishing their children to keep still as they readied cameras to take a photograph.

A parasol in front of me twirled. It was made from linen embroidered with silk thread, held by a woman in a jade green dress. I thought I heard her murmur the beginning of Akiko Yosano's poem, 'Kamakura has Shakyamuni the Buddha' and stopped in my tracks.

I retreated to the shade of the trees and quietly looked around. A small boy in shorts was running towards the Great Buddha. I gasped, unable to move.

Even though I had the Master's permission to be here, I didn't want to be seen walking around Kamakura on my own enjoying myself. I had felt that it would be fine to take advantage of being in Kamakura to let down my guard and do a little sightseeing. However, a maid is bound to only act under instructions from her mistress. The Master gives orders to the Mistress, and she can instruct me to run errands for the Master. It has to be like that to prevent the chain of command from getting mixed up.

For example, the novelist Master Konaka did as he pleased, giving orders to the maids and spending money at will, and as a result the Mistress lost her position and was put in a fix. The maids looked down on her and would no longer do her bidding. I recalled how Master Konaka's wife had once said that, and suddenly felt ashamed. I hadn't thought I was being lazy behind the Mistress's back, but I felt as though I'd been proved wrong.

I didn't want to be seen by the Mistress, so I took to my heels, trying not to get in people's way. As I was doing so, I crossed paths with a young man in a white shirt. I don't think he saw me. Of course, he wouldn't have been expecting me to be there. I kept my head down as I went past him.

As I did so, I thought I heard him murmuring a different poem by Akiko Yosano: *That day, that time, there were no words or poems; my feelings stayed within my heart.*

Suddenly I had the sensation of being transported back to the night of the big storm.

Sitting here now letting my mind wander, that's all I can recall. That scene amidst the shimmer of hot air is so long in the past, there is no way of confirming it now. Even at the time I couldn't. It was more like a divine revelation that I was somewhere I shouldn't have been. I didn't even ask the young Master where he had been before coming to the station.

Two hours later I went to meet him and the Mistress at Kamakura Station. The company president's black Buick pulled up, and the chauffeur got out to open the back door on the passenger side. A white parasol opened out, and the Mistress's beautiful, slim legs appeared from within the car. She was wearing her jade green dress and carrying her leather travel bag.

I took her bag, and the three of us went to buy some dumplings from Nirakuso. We then took our seats on the Yokosuka Line train, and sat listening to the young Master's bouncy chatter all the way home.

He talked mostly about the sea, how far he could swim, what shells he had picked up, that sort of thing. The Mistress watched him, smiling. There was nothing at all to suggest this summer, their third spent in Kamakura, had been different in any way from the previous years. It was as though I'd imagined the scene amidst the summer foliage.

Yet the reason I could remember that poem so well is because after returning from Kamakura, the Mistress put a collection of poems by Yosano Akiko on the display cabinet in the reception room. When I took it out to dust it, I saw a small piece of coloured paper used as a page marker.

Opening it up, I read, *That day, that time, there were no words or poems; my feelings stayed within my heart.*

The Mistress and Master began quarrelling the following year. It was mostly about money. The Mistress was not very enthusiastic about putting money into savings, but in view of the situation, the Master tried to persuade her to economize and to set her sights on investing in government bonds.

I had just seen the young Master off to school and came back into the house through the kitchen entrance to find the Mistress sitting absently on a round wooden stool.

'This time I really am going to set up a stationery store,' she said glumly.

'Oh dear, whatever happened?'

'The Master keeps going on about The Honda Method this and The Honda Method that.'

'The Honda Method?'

'The savings method promoted by that man Seiroku Honda with an honorary doctorate from the Imperial University!'

'Savings method? You mean how to save money?'

'He says one quarter of all income should be put into savings, as if it were any of his business.'

'I see.' I made a point of always agreeing with the Mistress, even if I didn't really understand.

'All I said to him was, "Perhaps if you get another suit made," that's all,' she went on indignantly. 'Then he goes and says, "Maybe we should do the Honda Method too." "What's that?" I ask, and he says, "You should try reading the newspaper sometimes." That really got up my nose, I can tell you. I read the newspaper every day, I'll have you know.'

'You do.'

'So just now I was looking for an old newspaper that has an article in it, "Stand-up collars good for both summer and winter".'

'So this Honda Method, it's not only about putting money away, then?'

'That's right! It says that in winter you should layer your underwear. That way, if the layer next to your skin gets sweaty, all you have to do is move it to the top layer and keep wearing it for longer. That sort of thing. I mean, really! Isn't that unsanitary?'

'It is a bit…'

'And that's not all. It says to make social occasions as informal as possible. Really. I mean, how can you possibly replace a wedding ceremony with a tempura party?'

'What's a tempura party?'

'It's when relatives get together and eat tempura. It says to hold that sort of party sometimes.'

'Oh, a party for eating tempura.'

'And that's great. It's lovely, relatives all eating together, very nice. But he's saying that when your daughter or son gets married, you should just hold a tempura party and announce that your darling baby is now married. That it's the kind of economical, simple lifestyle suited to the times. It does make me feel quite miserable, I must say.'

'Oh my. It does sound rather sad.'

'It *is* sad, Taki! For the bride, a wedding is a once-in-a-lifetime experience! Replacing it with a *tempura party*, whatever next!' the Mistress spat as though it were something utterly detestable.

And if her husband was now demanding that she, too, live the 'tempura party' lifestyle, she went on indignantly, then there was nothing for it but to leave this house and open a stationer's shop. 'Taki, you must come with me too when I do,' she finished angrily, arching her eyebrows.

Up north where I was from, I secretly thought to myself, you never held a fancy wedding ceremony unless you were considerably wealthy, and it would be quite a luxury in itself for the relatives to get together for a tempura party. But at any rate the Mistress certainly didn't seem taken with the idea.

'It's not as though I want so much luxury as to be called an enemy of the people,' she said, patting her prettily waved hair.

I suppose she was referring to the 'Luxury is the enemy!' signs that had recently appeared in the streets. She had never been one for the perms that were banned the year before, had always used curling tongs to do her hair and was keeping up this custom for as long as she could, despite the war.

'Even I don't agree with luxurious lifestyles. But on the one day in her life that a girl will become a bride, is it so wrong to hold a celebration just for her—for the young couple's—sake? Surely it's not a luxury to spend a bit of money on blessing them? We shouldn't lump everything in together as a common old tempura party!

'And it's not like I told him to have a luxury suit made, you know. We can't afford that anyway. But we're not even allowed to wish for an all-purpose stand-up collar anymore, you know. It's not about money. It's about sentiments. Really, I hate that sort of thing.' She then abruptly squared her shoulders and stood up. 'Taki, will you make some tea and bring it to the reception room for me?' she said, and stalked out of the kitchen.

'With sugar?' I asked to her departing back.

'No, no sugar,' she replied.

I took out the blue can of Lipton's from the mouse-proof cupboard, shook it slightly to check how much was left inside, and opened it with an aluminium one-sen coin. Then I warmed the Mistress's favourite teapot, put in some tea leaves and fresh hot water, and took it through to her in the reception room with a small sandglass timer, to find she had lit the gas stove. Yes, at that time it must still have been the gas stove. It changed to charcoal a little later on.

'Taki, come and join me too, will you?' the Mistress said, smiling.

'Oh dear, that would be far too extravagant.'

'It's fine. It's the sentiment, you know. Once you make a pot of tea, it's enough for three cups anyway. Bring some more hot water, would you? Enough for two.'

I went back to the kitchen, put some water in a teapot and took my own teacup, then went back to the reception room. Ah, it tastes so good, the Mistress said, her breath white in the cold air.

'The Master has changed lately,' she said abruptly. 'Don't you think so, Taki?'

'Um, I wonder.'

'He was never like this before. He was much more magnanimous.'

Better not say anything out of place, I thought, and took a sip of tea without responding.

'I know he's busy with work. And I know he's taken on a lot more responsibility. But he used to be so much kinder.'

'Kinder?'

'He used to take me out to exhibitions or to see a movie, saying it was good research for toys, and we used to eat meals together. Lately he always eats dinner out at the Toy Makers Guild.'

'But Ma'am, these days, even if you go to a restaurant rice is banned, so there's nothing to do about it. I don't know what they eat at the Guild's meetings, but I'm sure it's not all that good.' I didn't think it was a very good counterargument, but I had to say something.

'It's not banned. It's only that in order to conserve rice they're only allowed to serve it between five and eight o'clock. What's more, depending on where you go, they'll certainly serve you the tastiest.'

'Hmm, I suppose so.'

'But Taki, it's not that I want to eat out. Maybe I didn't express myself very well. The Master said the same thing.'

'I'm sorry.'

'No need to apologize. I just want peace of mind, that's all,' she said a little shamefacedly, stroking the colourful metallic rim of her cup.

After we'd finished our tea, she gave me a few things to do and told me she would remain here for a while, so I should come back if I needed anything, then opened up a magazine that she had to hand. It was an arts magazine called *Mizue*, a special issue on an art exhibition that had opened around that time entitled 'Celebrating the Empire's 2600th Anniversary'.

'Here,' the Mistress said, noticing that I was looking at it, and held it up for me to see. 'I want to go to the exhibition, but

I don't have time, so I just bought the magazine instead. The colours are beautiful, aren't they? Just looking at it is like food for the soul.'

The reason I remember this is that I have a copy of that issue of *Mizue* to hand even now. The colours really are beautiful, and I feel enriched by gazing at its pages. I came across it in the display outside a local second hand book store some years after the end of the war.

It brought back vivid memories of days spent with the Mistress, and I had the urge to buy it even though it wasn't something I would usually do.

That was the one and only time I ever bought an art magazine.

'Show me that magazine, will you, Nan?' Takeshi suddenly came out with yesterday.

I'd been writing in my notebook thinking that Takeshi would read it, and even passed it to him whenever we happened to meet, but he had stopped responding to me and just looked bored. I hadn't realized he was actually reading it.

Apparently he's smitten with a girl at university who wants to be a picture book illustrator and is a fan of *Mizue*, so he wanted to show her his Nan's old issue as a way to strike up a conversation with her. The more I listened to him the more it sounded like an unnecessarily roundabout way to get a girl's attention, but still, I fetched the old magazine out of my wicker trunk.

'Wow! It's in full colour!' he exclaimed, impressed by all the beautiful photos.

The next day he took the magazine to university. When he came back, he was so excited that I knew his girlfriend must have been delighted with it.

'All of the paintings are by famous artists! She knew a whole lot about them. Ryuzaburo Umehara, Morikazu Kumagai, Tsuguharu Foujita, Ryohei Koiso, Sotaro Yasui, Kazumasa Nakagawa, Shohachi Kimura… and what's more, it's not just a few of them. There's over a hundred, isn't there? If they held an exhibition like that now, it would be huge, she said. She also said that the paintings weren't about war at all. She'd always thought pictures painted in Japan during the war were all like Foujita's *Final Fighting on Attu*.'

Takeshi was all worked up about this, but for the life of me I couldn't see why. The battle on Attu Island happened in 1943, whereas the exhibition had taken place in 1940, so neither Foujita nor anyone else could have known about it, and they were hardly going to depict a future scenario.

I don't know much about art, and didn't even know all the artist names that Takeshi mentioned. But that didn't matter. I might be uneducated, but even I knew that these were good paintings.

White snow piled up on the roof of a hot springs inn.

People on a wharf.

Children playing in the sand.

A boy climbing a tree.

Puppies frolicking.

A mother holding a child at a night stall at a festival.

A Noh stage.

A woman in a kimono with her face half hidden with a black fan.

Buddha.

A bamboo grove.

A street corner in a foreign country.

All of the people depicted in the pictures looked tranquil, and they were all gentle, beautiful, peaceful scenes.

In all senses, 1940 was the year of 'Celebrating the Empire's 2600th Anniversary', marking the founding of the nation by Emperor Jimmu, the first in the imperial line.

Marking 2600 years

Ah, a hundred million

Hearts sing

Even now, the anthem's words still flow spontaneously from my mouth.

A ceremony to mark the occasion was held in November. On the same day, the young Master's elementary school held a sports day. Since it was a very special occasion, we were instructed to make a lavish lunch box, so I put in the young Master's favourite *sukeroku* sushi, frankfurter sausages cut to look like little octopuses, omelette, and apple bunnies.

Schools and companies were off for the day, so all of us, the Master included, went to watch the young Master valiantly compete. The event kicked off in the morning, and concluded with a short ceremony near to lunchtime. We then listened to Prime Minister Konoe's address on a radio placed on the morning assembly dais. As usual, the open air radio broadcast was barely audible other than the usual expressions of gratitude, but it was a live broadcast of the commemorative ceremony held in the Imperial Palace Plaza. Everyone followed Prime Minister Konoe's prompt of 'Long live His Imperial Majesty!'

with a chorus of *banzai*. And then the sports day's activities were resumed.

The young Master lost in the foot race, but did quite well in the ball-throwing event, in which two teams throw red or white balls into a basket on top of a tall pole.

'With that kind of control over the ball, he should write his name on the ball before throwing it. He's bound to get the Outstanding Performance Award,' the Master said.

The Mistress really looked as though she was enjoying herself that day and seemed to have recovered her good humour. She had always loved festivities and was apparently delighted to be out as a family again for the first time in so long.

Now that I think about it, that autumn in 1940 was when we should all have been watching not just the young Master's elementary school sports day, but the whole world competing against each other at the Tokyo Olympics. Nobody remembered that any more, however, least of all the Master as he placidly watched the young Master compete.

The next day, or maybe it was the day after that, the family headed for Ginza, and took me with them. During the celebrations, restrictions on restaurants and bars were lifted and alcohol and rice were served from lunchtime onward, so the Master took us out to eat for the first time in ages. I had curry rice, as usual. The atmosphere that day was light hearted and gay, and after lunch we went out into the flag-lined main street.

'Taki! Taki, look! The tram's been decorated,' the Mistress called out excitedly. She had always talked nostalgically about the decorated tramcar she'd seen in the Reconstruction Festival many years earlier. 'I always wanted to show it to you, Taki!' she was fond of saying, and now her dream had come true she was so happy, she rested her hands on my shoulders as she spoke.

That day the family had a commemorative photo taken in the studio. This was the photo the Mistress gave me when it was decided I should go back up north. The Master was wearing a very good quality wool suit, the Mistress an elegant dress with white collar and cuffs and a hat. The Master standing between them was wearing a cute bow tie.

Afterwards, the young Master said he wanted to go and see *The Monkey King*, so we went to the cinema. I thought I would go home ahead of them, but the Mistress stopped me, saying, 'It's a festival! Stay with us.'

With the comedian Enoken in the lead singing and dancing, the movie was really fun. I don't think that kind of film could be made in Japan today. We'd only gone to see it because it was for children, but even the Master was impressed by the magic wand that transformed into an aeroplane so that Son Goku's party could fly to a country of the future.

'Hah. We really must watch children's movies for toy research, of course. I'll have to recommend it to the guys in the R&D department,' he said, stroking his chin.

I recall that even after we got home, the young Master made me play with him for some time, he taking the part of the Dragon King and myself as Pigsy, singing, *Fly through the air, bury through the earth, dive into water*.

I'll never forget that we also had a special delivery of sticky rice for red bean rice, and I made a splendid spread that evening.

***

It must have been about a month later, around mid-December as the year-end approached, when the Master and Mistress had another spectacular row. I say spectacular, but both were gentle people and it wasn't as if there were any bowls flying, or anything. It was an extremely civilized quarrel, but it was loud enough to shock myself and the young Master.

Furthermore, it wasn't about the household finances this time but about whether to go to a concert at the Kabukiza or not, and I did wonder why the Mistress got so worked up about it.

It all started after dinner, when the Master said nonchalantly, 'I have an Association meeting on Saturday.'

'But that's the night we're going to the Kabukiza,' the Mistress said reproachfully, her voice unusually sharp.

'The Kabukiza? Oh, that. A concert, wasn't it?'

'That's right. You can't have forgotten, surely. It was at the company president's invitation.'

'The president has an important connection there. I decided to go to the Association meeting instead.'

'Oh, but that's really too bad. You're always out at Association meetings lately.'

'This one's a gathering of companies making toys for export. The ones I've been busy with lately are the Toy Makers' Guild meetings.'

'Either way it's the same thing.'

'It's not the same thing.'

'So, what to do about the Kabukiza?'

'To do? Nothing. In any case, it's a Saturday afternoon. I've got work, so I can't go.'

'But we've got two tickets for it!'

'It can't be helped. Shall we give them back?'

'*What?*' The Mistress's eyes almost popped out of her head.

Wondering what was up, I'd come running out of the kitchen and exchanged a look with the young Master, who was eating his dinner with them.

'We got them some time ago, you know.'

'Yes, this came up at the last minute. Can't be helped.'

'So, you're saying you'll give them back, are you?'

'Well, we shouldn't waste them, should we?'

'Oh, is that so? Right. Fine,' the Mistress said in a tone that made it clear it was anything but fine and sat staring fixedly at a point in space.

'What's up with you? You can be so difficult sometimes! So, you're saying I shouldn't return them?'

'No, I'm not saying that. If you say you're returning them, then go ahead and return them.'

'What are you angry about?'

'I'm not angry. Not in the slightest.'

'You *are* angry! What a way to behave in front of Kyo,' the Master said disdainfully.

Hearing this the Mistress's blood drained from her face. 'So please go ahead and give them back!' she shot back at him, then ran down the hallway and shut herself up in the reception room.

'What was *that* all that about?' the Master said in displeasure, then went back to his newspaper as an icy silence descended over the living room.

After a few moments, as if he'd suddenly thought of something, the Master stood up and went to the reception room.

'I didn't say anything about returning two tickets. You can go by yourself, can't you?'

He'd managed to keep his voice relatively calm, but the Mistress responded shrilly, 'I couldn't possibly do that! Going alone without you, whatever next?'

'But I don't mind. Something came up at work stopping me from going. There's nothing I can do about that now, is there?'

'If you're not coming, then I can't go either.'

'How about inviting someone else, like Miss Mutsuko? I'm sure the company president would rather that than the tickets be wasted.'

'Oh, really! I can't go foisting something you were given onto someone else like that. Apart from anything else, it's far too short notice.'

'Well I don't know. You're so stubborn. Try and act your age, will you? You can't go on acting like a young bride forever, you know.'

'So now you're saying that my judgement can't be trusted, are you?'

'It sure looks that way.'

'Look, it's just common sense. I am not offloading your ticket onto someone else.'

'I simply thought that you wanted to go.'

'It's not a matter of whether I want to go or not. The company president invited us, so I thought I had to attend as the executive director's wife!'

'Well you don't have to shout about it.'

'Just go ahead and give them back.'

'All right, I will!'

The Master slammed the reception room door behind him and strode back to the living room. He looked so furious that the young Master hurriedly took himself upstairs before he got yelled at to go to bed.

The atmosphere was still tense at breakfast the next morning, too, but in the afternoon the Mistress went out into the garden, cut some pink camellias, and brought them back inside. She trimmed them with her gardening scissors and arranged them in a bowl for the reception room, retaining a single blossom for the entrance hall. By the time she had finished arranging them and sat down to rest, she appeared to have completely forgotten the argument. Her face looked very tender as she arranged the flowers.

But that evening, when the Master came home, he brought the matter up again. As he loosened his necktie and removed his jacket, he took out a white envelope from his inside pocket and threw it down on the table.

'The company president said that it's a pity to waste them, so you should go even if it's on your own.'

'What is this?'

'He said he will give the other ticket to someone else. At this stage it'll be hard to find two people to go instead.'

'So I'm to go on my own?'

'Yes.'

'Are you sure it's okay?'

'I'm sorry, but that's the best I can do. It's the company president's invitation, so please do go,' he said, changing into his usual lined kimono and tying the sash around his hips. He looked completely exhausted, and even sounded quite chivalrous, not at all like his usual self.

'Is that so?' the Mistress said quietly, and that was the end of the matter.

On the day of the concert, the Mistress dressed up in a dark blue kimono and light grey obi with a snow lily pattern, together with a glossy velvet overcoat for her shoulders. She was in high spirits, the quarrel of a couple of nights before apparently forgotten.

'It's a long time since I last went to the Kabukiza. If you're a good boy,' she told the young Master, 'I'll bring something back for you.'

The young Master sneaked a look at me and screwed up his face. He probably thought it hardly worthwhile unless he could go with her and choose what he wanted, which would obviously be ice cream.

But he was quite taken aback when she came back later that evening and told him, 'Kyo, I brought you a special present,' handing him a book of manga.

'How did you know what I wanted?'

'I just did. I'm your mother, after all,' she said with a straight face, then burst out laughing. 'Actually, Mr. Itakura gave it to me. I bumped into him at the Kabukiza. He said the company president had given him your father's ticket, since nobody else in the company listens to classical music. He'd hastily taken half a day off and rushed to the theatre, quite out of breath, but still he hadn't forgotten to bring a present for you, Kyo. What a nice man he is.' Her cheeks were somewhat flushed, and her eyes glistened a little.

'Sei has it and I wanted it so badly for myself. But you always say we don't buy manga in this house, so I didn't think you'd ever get it for me,' the young Master said as he gleefully opened up the brand new copy of *Expedition to Mars*.

'Oh my, it's in full colour too!'

'Yes! And it's really interesting. Oh, what a brilliant day this is! Never in my wildest dreams did I expect this day to come.'

The young Master was being so melodramatic that the Mistress laughed out loud, and stayed in a good mood for the rest of the day.

When the Master came home, she reported simply, 'I went to the concert and met the company president and his wife, and Mr. Itakura was also there from the company.'

But Master looked uninterested and just nodded and said, 'Hmmm,' and that was the end of that.

Looking back, it must have been a really difficult time for the company, but it wasn't as though we would have known about that, and the Mistress couldn't have known about the details.

The Mistress's good humour continued for a while after that.

The Kabukiza's program for the Concert Celebrating the Empire's 2600th Anniversary, printed on beautiful Japanese-style paper with a flower pattern, now adorned the display cabinet between the poetry anthology and the issue of *Mizue*. The ticket stamped with the date 14th December 1940 and admission price of 2.5 yen was there too.

When Miss Mutsuko dropped round to say hello at the end of the year, the Mistress took the programme off the shelf and proudly showed it to her.

'Richard Strauss's *Japanese Festival Music* was good, but Ibert's *Ouverture de fête* conducted by Kosaka Yamada outstanding, you know.'

'Oh, you went to the concert at the Kabukiza? How on earth did you manage to get tickets for that?'

'I was given one. I ran into Mr. Itakura there too. I've told you about him, haven't I? He's in the design department at my husband's firm. He knows a lot about classical music and says that the revered old Mr. Strauss has lost some of his earlier shine, perhaps because of his age. But for the Ibert piece, the composition, the conductor, and the performers were all really world class.'

'Of course they were! The very best of world-famous composers from France, Germany, Italy and Hungary took the trouble to compose pieces especially for the celebrations of our Empire's 2600th anniversary. That's what's really amazing about the whole thing, you know. More than amazing, if you think of our long history. I could shed tears of gratitude for having been born in this "Land of Abundant Reed Plains and Rice Fields".'

'It's not so much that I feel like crying, but Ibert's Ouverture is cheerful and has a good rhythm to it. Even Mr. Itakura said that's what's so good about it.'

'Tokiko, really! The whole world is celebrating the 2600th anniversary of the Great Japanese Empire, you know, and a number of the world's most prominent musicians performed pieces for us. Are you not filled with emotion for the importance of this happy occasion?'

'Well, yes,' the Mistress said automatically, as if bowing to Miss Mutsuko's insistence. She absentmindedly reached for the copy of *Mizue* in the display cabinet, as if something had just occurred to her. 'Mr. Itakura said he also went to the art museum in Ueno.'

'Oh really?' Miss Mutsuko said disinterestedly, her mind still set on the importance of the 2600th anniversary having attracted attention from around the world.

In my own head, I was recalling Mr. Itakura in his white shirt, standing in the shimmering hot air in Kamakura.

Chapter 5

War Starts

*T*he celebrations are over and it's back to work!

This was the slogan posted around town once the 2600th anniversary events had all finished.

But Mistress Tokiko was entirely unsuited to work. She was far more cut out for social activities like celebrations and festivities, going out and welcoming guests, that sort of thing, and was at her most attractive when having fun. She grimaced whenever she heard slogans like: 'New year decorations outside every house is too much of a luxury!' and: 'Abolish the custom of posting New Year cards!'

Relatively affordable meisen silk was in fashion and widely advertised by department stores at the time, but the Mistress turned her nose up, saying, 'Meisen kimonos made a long time ago are really good quality, so why should I have any new ones made?' Instead she bought some Western-made fabric. 'You know, Taki, I really do prefer the blouses, dresses, and suits that you make for me. That way I can have things the way I like them.'

I'd learned how to use the sewing machine from the Mistress. And then I started designing my own clothes, imitating the slim, girl-style sketches by Junichi Nakahara, and making my own paper patterns. The Mistress praised them highly, and when I finished making something she was really excited and said how good it was.

'Taki, you really take care over the concealed parts, don't you? That's the most important thing with needlework. I can make things look good at a glance, but there are always some surprisingly sloppy bits, so seams quickly come apart and things like that. I was obviously right in asking you to do it, Taki!' In any case, it was fun to see such a lovely model wearing my creations.

The other women in the neighbourhood also praised me, saying, 'Taki, you make everything so well!' In those days, good workers were all snapped up by factories, and nobody was willing to work as a maid, so the Mistress often commented how lucky she'd been to find someone as efficient as me. 'After all, you've been with me since before I married. We've been together all this time, and you're far more experienced than the usual run-of-the-mill maids, so there's really no comparison.'

The Mistress smiled in delight, the way she did after being praised for her fine clothing and jewellery, and I felt so proud I could burst.

New Year came around again, and the Mistress wore a beautiful kimono as always. Since the rule of the day was to avoid luxury, she avoided wearing anything too ostentatious, but still her outfit was elegant and had an air of quality about it.

Unfortunately, the Master was out when Mr. Itakura came to pay his respects at New Year. He had accompanied the company president on a courtesy call to an important client and Mistress Tokiko had been in a bad mood, grumbling how he'd gone out before the third day of the New Year. However, she brightened up the moment Mr. Itakura turned up on the doorstep.

'I'd better leave if Mr. Hirai isn't home. I just thought I'd drop by since I was in the area,' he said, holding out a box of cakes.

'My, you're always so attentive. My husband will be back soon, so do come in. Please have some dinner. After all, you don't have a wife to cook for you.'

What was memorable for me was how warmly the Mistress spoke to him. Young Master Kyoichi, too, came running downstairs carrying *Expedition to Mars* when he heard Mr. Itakura arrive.

'This is my favourite manga, you know. I like it even better than *Norakuro*. I love the bits where Tentaro goes to Mars and he gets ill when a tomato starts growing in his tummy, and the cat Nyanko explains the importance of whiskers.'

'That's right, it's great isn't it? Well, *Norakuro* is good too, but everyone dreams of going to Mars, right? And the artist Noboru Oshiro is a genius. How good of him to draw such fine pictures for us.'

The Mistress looked amused when Mr. Itakura replied so seriously, and said teasingly, 'My, Mr. Itakura, have you really read so many children's manga?'

'Well, I now have the excuse of having to read them as part of my research for designing toys.'

'What a fine excuse that is!'

'Actually, I had thought of becoming a manga artist myself while at art school.'

'Oh? I thought you wanted to be an architect? How fickle you are!' she laughed brightly and rolled her large eyes, making fun of the younger man.

Both Mr. Itakura, who had been caught out, and the young Master, who didn't really understand what was going on, laughed along with her and the atmosphere suddenly became cheerful and lively like a typical New Year.

'Well, don't just stand there! Do come in. Taki, bring us some tea in the reception room, please.'

I went back to the kitchen, put some green tea and Japanese sweets on a tray, and took it through to the reception room. The Mistress and Mr. Itakura were looking at the *Mizue* issue about the celebratory art exhibition.

With one hand, Mr. Itakura was skilfully sketching the manga characters Tentaro and Nyanko on a piece of straw paper for the young Master, and with the other he was holding the magazine open and displaying his specialist art knowledge to Mistress Tokiko sitting at his side. The Mistress looked just like a young student with her teacher, commenting now and then in a serious tone of voice. Her expression was one I'd never seen before, and it's still etched on my memory.

The conversation moved from the exhibition to the concert, and then to Kazuo Hasegawa's role in the movie *The Man Who Disappeared Yesterday*, and finally to a book by some French author called Martin de Gaulle, titled *Le Chibault* or something of the sort. The Mistress put in the odd word here and there and seemed dazzled by the speed at which he kept changing the subject.

I had known the Mistress since she was twenty-two, but I had never seen her look like this with the Master. Maybe she'd once looked like that with her first husband, who died that rainy night?

I suddenly wondered what the age difference between Mistress Tokiko and Mr. Itakura was. I was twenty-four that year, and the Mistress thirty-two. The Master must have been about forty-five or six, but had white hairs due to the stress of work and was already looking old. The Mistress was still young, and it was possible to imagine them being mistaken for father and daughter.

Mr. Itakura was twenty-six, as I found out just an hour or so later when the Master came home with the company president.

The important New Year's call had turned out to be in the neighbourhood, so the Master had invited the company president home with him. He didn't appear be particularly taken aback at coming home to find Mr. Itakura there. He was young enough to be his son, so it probably felt like having a student drop by.

The company president, on the other hand, did seem rather put out. 'Oi, Itakura. Getting your New Year visit in early, are you?' He probably wasn't too pleased to find Mr. Itakura paying his respects to the Hirais before having visited the company president's own home.

The Master hastily informed him that Mr. Itakura had lodged close by while at art school, so was in the habit of dropping by from time to time. Mr. Itakura seemed nervous now that his superiors had turned up and tried to excuse himself by saying he had to be going, but the company president said he wasn't about to let him escape so easily.

'Indeed,' the Mistress said. 'I'm delighted it's turned into a festive New Year. We'll be having dinner now so you must stay, Mr. President, although I can't offer you the usual seasonal delicacies this year. And you too, Mr. Itakura.'

The Mistress signalled me with her eyes to start preparing dinner, and I was just leaving the room when the company president boomed, 'Incidentally, Itakura, how old are you now?'

'Twenty-six.'

'So young,' the Master started, but the company president cut him off, saying, 'So it's time for you to be getting married, then.'

'Oh, I'm fine for the moment.'

'Nothing fine about it. You might think so, but the world around you doesn't. There's a shortage of good men in war time, and men like you are in high demand. There are beautiful women graduating from women's universities just itching to get wed, you know.'

'I would prefer to stay single a little longer, really. I'll consider getting married once I'm thirty.'

'Out of the question, my man. Last year the average age for getting married in our country was twenty-five for women, and thirty for men.'

'So it's normal for men to stay single until they're thirty.'

'Absolutely not. Up until 1923 the norm was twenty for women, twenty-five for men. Medically speaking, the best age for women to give birth seems to be between twenty and twenty-four. The fertility rate drops dramatically once they pass twenty-five. What with building a Greater East Asia, the government is urging everyone to have as many children as possible, to produce future leaders for our blessed land. Medical doctors insist this means we need to reduce the marriageable age to what it was in the 1920s. You can never be too young. Although I suppose men can make babies at any age, unlike women.'

The company president had apparently started drinking at the client's place. He let out a vulgar laugh, but I don't know how the Master responded, since I left the room and went to the kitchen.

'What on earth is he talking about?' the Mistress snorted as she put on her sleeved apron. 'Mr. Itakura is far too young to get married.'

'Ah, I suppose he is,' I said, without much conviction. Up north where I was from many men took a bride at a much earlier age, so I didn't think he was too young at all.

'He's much too young,' the Mistress repeated firmly, apparently dissatisfied with my response.

'He is rather, isn't he?'

'He *is* too young! Definitely too young,' she nodded in satisfaction, and then briskly started issuing instructions as we set about preparing the food.

While the guests enjoyed a drink with a couple of snacks of vegetables simmered in soy sauce and whitebait boiled in sweetened soy sauce, I steamed some rice together with shellfish preserved in mirin, ginger, and soy, and cut up some sardines marinated overnight into bite size pieces, coating them in potato starch before deep-frying them.

'Oh my, Taki, what fantastic ideas you have!' the Mistress said delightedly. I had always been adept at making do with what we had.

The Master told me to open one of the precious cans of corned beef we had in reserve. The company president was partial to American food, and openly professed to liking meat better than fish. He often said, regretfully, that he had to eat less meat now that it was more tightly controlled, so the Master decided to treat him.

Every time I took some food into them, I heard the company president speaking openly about whether we should go to war with America or not. On that New Year's in 1941, at least, he was adamant, 'It'll never come to that.'

That night, the company president was drinking a lot, and I was worried the sake I'd managed to procure on the black market would run out.

Once the young Master had finished eating, I took him up to bed. When I came back down again, I found the dinner party in full swing. All talk of war with America had ended, and the subject of the difficulty of marriage in our blessed land had been revived in a different form. When I went in to serve them, I found it was my turn to be on the chopping board.

'By the way, the Assistance Style Beauty in this household isn't married yet, is she?' the company president said, by now completely drunk and red-faced.

Since Prime Minister Konoe had formed the Imperial Rule Assistance Association the previous autumn, the term 'Assistance Style' had been all the rage and was used for anything and everything, from Assistance Style Economy to Assistance Style Lifestyle, to indicate something was serious, good and proper.

'I suppose Taki will have to be married off before long, too,' the Master, sitting at his side, answered.

'So you've heard, then? It seems The Imperial Rule Assistance Association are about to announce the standard for Assistance

Style Beauties. Young people's idea of beauty is the fashionable slim and pale willowy figure, but this doesn't fit in with national policy. I suppose you're the same, are you, Itakura? You like the willowy type, do you?'

The company president had evidently made up his mind, so Mr. Itakura merely said with distaste, 'Not at all.'

'The powers that be have apparently decreed that wide hipped women ideal for childbirth are the true beauties. The Association is leading the way in making this the fashion. The willowy type of beauty like Mistress Hirai is in the past, and the new standard of beauty is the wide-hipped type, like your maid.'

'So, I have both old and new beauties here in my home.'

'I'm quite envious of you.'

Hearing the company president and the Master go on like this, the Mistress frowned.

Mr Itakura seized the chance to say that well, then, he'd see the president home, so I ran to the station to use the telephone to call a black cab.

While waiting for the taxi to arrive, the company president continued coming up with his theories, but Mr. Itakura seemed to have completely sobered up. Apart from anything, he couldn't be the meek subordinate before his superiors while also parading his knowledge before the Mistress.

When the taxi came up the hill, Mr. Itakura bundled up the company president and pulled him out into the entrance hall.

'Of course, if it comes to war, Japan will win, obviously,' the company president babbled, red-faced, as if suddenly anxious about a war between Japan and the US. 'However, I simply can't hate everything about America. Better not to start a war in the first place, is what I think.'

'Well, I'm sure Prime Minister Konoe is of the same opinion, so it probably won't come to war,' the Master said soothingly, but Mr. Itakura impatiently pushed him into the waiting cab and took him away, fully aware that he could easily stay chatting all night in his inebriated state.

When at last the door was closed behind them, I went back into the kitchen to find the Mistress there.

'I don't want to get married yet,' I blurted.

She looked at me strangely, as if wondering what had prompted me to say that, but then remembered the earlier subject of conversation. 'It won't do, Taki, we have to get you married off as soon as possible.'

The reason I recall all of that is because the marriage issue was a hot topic that year, and I was caught up in proposals that amounted to nothing. Two in particular were unforgettable due to the major upheavals they caused. Indeed, you could hardly call them auspicious events.

Come to think of it, nothing good at all happened in the run up to the war in 1941. The Master was in an unusually bad mood, which meant the Mistress also tended to be on edge.

It must have been around that time, too, that the young Master heard a particularly terrifying ghost story, popular at the time, that kept him awake at night. It was about a toilet spirit known as the Red Cape. Children going to the toilet alone would hear a voice ask them: 'Would you like a red cape or a blue cape?' If they answered 'red cape', they would be sliced up and die in a pool of blood, but if they answered 'blue cape' all the blood would be sucked out of their body until they turned blue. Either way they would be dead. The poor boy was completely traumatized by this.

As soon as the holidays were over, there was a sudden crackdown and food rations were introduced. Coupons were needed to eat out, rice shops were closed down, and various restrictions were introduced. It was around the same time that the use of gas was limited. It goes without saying that I had to use all my ingenuity to ensure the kitchen didn't seem so forlorn.

My first marriage literally fell on me out of the blue. I wasn't even given a chance to meet the prospective groom, I was simply married off. Even now, my nephew and his family don't know about it.

The Mistress had always dreamed of arranging a good marriage for me, but this proposal came from back home in Yamagata. My parents had been scolded by their local neighbourhood association for having an unmarried twenty-four-year-old daughter, so they had scrambled to find someone for me. The groom was a soldier guarding the border between Manchuria and the Soviet Union and was due to reach the term of his service that summer. The neighbourhood association had decided to set him up with a wife and home ready for his return.

The photograph they sent me was so dark all I could make out was the whites of his eyes, and having never met him I neither liked nor disliked him. Nevertheless, since my parents had ordered me to come home I had no choice but to comply. I would be given no say in the matter; the marriage had already been decided.

I was distraught at having to leave the Mistress and the young Master, and couldn't stop crying. The Mistress was upset too, having intended for me to marry someone close by so that I could continue working as a maid for her.

However, the Master barked at her, 'It's a luxury for a small household like ours to have a maid. We can't stop Taki from serving the country by having at least three or four children of her own just for our own convenience.'

'What are you saying? That you want Taki to leave?'

'No, that's not what I'm saying. I myself would love to have her stay on forever. What I'm saying is that we cannot stop her from helping the country. Soldiers don't choose to get sent to the frontline either, you know!'

And so, I had no choice: I would have to marry whoever the neighbourhood association back home decided for me.

'What? Were you married, Nan?'

Takeshi had come over to bring me some rice from my nephew's home, so I had him read my notes. As expected, he was quite taken aback. I had planned to go to my grave without telling anyone about my marriage, but I'm glad I wrote about it after all.

'When was that?'

'It was in April, around the time when elementary schools in Japan were made national schools for young patriots. April 1941.'

'I had no idea.'

'It was decided I would go back up north in June, and I said my farewells to everyone in the neighbourhood. I'd been quite involved in the local fire prevention and the like, and they all said they were going to miss me. When the day approached for me to leave the Hirais, I was crying so much I couldn't even see to thread a needle to mend clothes. I'd hoed the soil in the garden to grow vegetables, so that I could at least feed the family. But when I thought how I'd never be able to cook the fresh vegetables, even if they did grow well, my heart hurt so much I thought it'd break.'

Just remembering all this brought tears to my eyes, but Takeshi didn't seem the least moved. 'I never heard about that, Nan, are you sure it's true? I keep saying this, but you really shouldn't go making things up, you know,' he said, lecturing me as always. That's what happens when you try telling people the truth.

Several days before I was due to leave, my prospective husband suddenly died. The cause was said to be a heart attack while on sentry duty. I also heard that he was hit by a stray bullet, but there wasn't supposed to be any fighting on the Soviet-Manchurian border at the time so they'd probably cobbled together a story to make it an honourable death in action.

Nobody ever actually referred to me being a widow as such, but when the Mistress heard that my marriage partner had died, she exclaimed, 'Oh no, you poor thing!' The Master, too, said that as long as there weren't any more good proposals, there was no need for me to go back home, and so I continued on as maid of the Hirai household.

That summer, another marriage proposal caused a much bigger hullaballoo.

The Master never really talked about his work so even the Mistress didn't know much about it, but the national shortage of metal had been a topic of conversation in the Hirai household for some time. It was becoming increasingly evident as even metal benches and riverbank fencing around town were gradually replaced by wooden ones. The Master's company had long since stopped making metal toys for the domestic market, replacing them with mostly wood and paper, but they'd managed to negotiate with the government and procure enough supplies on the black market to continue making metal toys for export.

One day, the Master brought home photographs of two women.

'These are from the company president,' he told the Mistress. 'One is the daughter of a relatively influential person in the Imperial Rule Assistance Association's Lifestyle section. The other is the daughter of a relative of a government official pulling the strings. Neither family is likely to make unreasonable demands. He's thinking of one of them for Itakura.'

'Mr. Itakura?'

'There just aren't any marriageable young men around these days, since they've all gone off to war. However, the country is pushing marriage as part of its higher productivity policy. Families with young daughters are desperately seeking sons-in-law. Luckily, Itakura is of a good age, and isn't bad looking, either. He apparently failed the military medical because he wears glasses and has weak bronchial tubes, and now being a company employee and twenty-six, he will not have to go to war. There are hardly any men with such favourable terms to be found. These days even wounded soldiers are in great demand! If he can settle on one of these two women, it'll benefit the company in all sorts of ways. Itakura is rather unrealistic and quite immature sometimes, so it would be good for him to settle down, don't you think? So, how about it? Will you mediate the marriage with him?'

Mistress Tokiko looked at him blankly. 'You're asking *me* to arrange it?'

'Women are much better at this sort of thing.'

'Are we now?'

'Oh, come on. You two get along really well with each other, don't you? Surely you have some idea of his taste in women? His parents died when he was young and his only relative is an older brother up north. I'm more like a parent than executive director to him, and as my wife you're like a substitute mother. Do this one thing to take care of him, will you?'

The master rolled his neck and shoulders as if to impress on her how exhausted he was and how he relied entirely on her to take care of the matter henceforth, washing his own hands of it.

The Mistress looked uncomfortable as she took the photographs from him. Both were of young ladies just graduated from women's college. She glanced briefly at them and put them on top of the chest of drawers in the living room.

A few days later, the Master told her, 'I've called Mr. Itakura over, so I want you to talk to him about it.'

It was a Sunday afternoon, and the Master had gone out somewhere with the company president.

The Master seemed deeply uncomfortable with the idea of having to arrange the marriage. He was zealous about his work, but had no interest whatsoever in the subtleties of relationships between men and women and had himself married relatively late, so it was likely too much trouble to have to lecture the younger man on the matter. He'd had no choice about it, since the company president had foisted it on him, and had probably assumed he could palm it off on his sociable wife and get her to deal with it.

The Master had said there was something immature about the younger man, and it was true that Mr. Itakura was rather boyish. He wasn't good at talking about work, the state of the war or the economy, but excelled at drawing manga and making paper planes. When the older man was around he was as quiet as a mouse, but at other times was lively and engaging. When they drank together, each would inevitably doze off when the other was talking animatedly.

The Master probably only saw him as an exceedingly well-behaved young man, which was quite a miscalculation on his part.

It was an extremely hot and humid afternoon when Mr. Itakura climbed the hill to the house, his shirtsleeves rolled up. He came around to the garden and presented himself at the veranda. Apparently emboldened upon hearing the Master was out, he said, 'It's hot,' and took off his shirt so that he was wearing only his undervest. With his upper body exposed, showing slight muscles on his skinny frame, he started a paper plane battle with young Master Kyoichi.

The Mistress had planned to have a formal talk with him in the reception room, but gave up and had me take a hand-towel and some melon out to him on the veranda.

'Mr. Itakura, listen,' the Mistress started, watching him put the hand-towel around his neck and sink his teeth into the melon. 'I've been given some marriage photos to show you.'

He glanced at her then quietly stood up, still chewing on some melon, and sent another of the planes he had made out of old newspapers flying to the end of the garden. The chirr of cicadas rang out through the hot and humid summer garden.

Mr. Itakura watched the young Master run after the paper plane, and said, 'I don't want to get married.'

'You must.'

'Not yet.'

'Please agree to it.'

'I never thought I'd ever hear you say that.'

'After all, at your age it's about time, isn't it?'

'Not yet.'

'Look, just agree to it.'

'Why are you telling me to do that?'

'Because!'

It seemed as if their exchange, against the garden greenery, the yellow melon and chirring of cicadas, would keep going around and around in circles forever.

'Look, just agree to meet one of them, whichever takes your fancy most. I'll give you the photos when you leave,' the Mistress said, her eyes downturned, while Mr. Itakura fiddled sullenly with the old newspapers. The pair of them looked wan and agitated sitting there on the veranda.

Later, when the Master came home, Mr. Itakura joined them at the dinner table as usual. The only reference the Master made to the marriage issue was to say simply, 'I'll leave the choice up to you, so please just accept whichever you prefer,' and with that the topic of conversation turned once again to the pros and cons of war with America.

It was well known that negotiations between the two countries weren't going well, and the Master's nerves must have been on edge given the implications for his company's exports and imports.

'Ordinary Americans don't want war at all,' he said. 'Lindburgh, the hero of transatlantic flight, made that clear when he stated his opposition before Congress. The company president is probably right that we'll avoid war. Even if America does join it, they'll probably be so busy supporting Britain fighting on Germany's strong European front line that they won't be able to deal with the Pacific arena too, especially knowing that Japan is a formidable opponent. They'll likely take the path of peace. However you think about it...'

Mr. Itakura and the Mistress, who had absolutely no interest in war, only made desultory comments now and then, to be polite as he droned on and on.

When it was time for Mr. Itakura to leave, he tried to refuse the marriage photos but was forced to take them with him.

As time passed with no answer from him, the Master eventually said, 'Look, he has to make up his mind. The company president wants to pass on the other photograph to someone else. I mean really, I'd thought he was a bit more savvy of the ways of the world, but he's just a child. If he could just make a decision, we could move things along. We can't have him snivelling like a little girl. Go see him and give him a piece of your mind, would you?'

I think it was at the beginning of September that the Master ordered the Mistress to do this.

***

'Well, then, I'll see you later.'

The Mistress went out dressed in a dark green-brown striped summer kimono with a light summer Nagoya-style obi, carrying a linen parasol and four tomatoes we'd grown in the garden wrapped in a furoshiki cloth. Her expression was a complex mix of vivacious and somber as she set out to persuade him to accept the marriage.

I was sweeping the porch as she left. Halfway down the hill to the station, I saw her stumble on something and almost fall. I was about to run to her aid but she managed to keep her footing, then straightened up again and carried on her way. I watched her go.

Several days earlier she had sent Mr. Itakura a postcard saying that she intended to visit him to talk about the photographs, and a few days later received a reply saying that he understood and would be waiting for her. The young Master said he wanted to go with her, but she replied soothingly that they had to talk about a grown-up matter, so he couldn't come this time, and went alone.

Mr. Itakura's apartment was two stops away on the train, followed by a fifteen-minute walk. The Mistress would have to ask for directions to the address on the postcard. The chirring of the large brown cicadas had by now given way to Walker's cicadas, as the air shimmered in the heat and humidity. Even now the vision of the Mistress in her persimmon-coloured obi as she made her way forlornly down the hill is burned onto my retina.

The Master was out that day, and the young Master's friend Tatsu came over in the afternoon. The two boys read books in the young Master's bedroom, then went out into the garden to play and climb trees.

It was unusual for their friend Sei not be with them, but when I asked after him the young Master pouted and answered disagreeably, 'We don't play with Sei anymore.'

'Oh dear, did you have a fight?'

'No, it's not that. We just don't play together anymore.'

'But why, if you haven't fallen out?'

'Sei's father was an enemy spy, you know. The police came and arrested him. So we don't play with him anymore,' he said. His eyes were stony and he shook his head to put an end to the matter, before climbing back up the tree to join Tatsu.

The Mistress came home just as Tatsu was leaving. She had the two photos in her hand.

'It's no good,' she said. 'Mr. Itakura says he doesn't want to meet either of them.' Her cheeks were flushed, maybe from climbing the hill in the heat. 'Taki, would you be so good as to bring me a glass of cold water?'

She sat on the tatami floor of the living room with her legs folded to one side, fanning her neck.

When I brought her a glass filled with water, she was hugging her fan to her chest, gazing into space.

'Are you all right?'

'What? Oh, I'm fine. It's just so hot I was distracted.'

She drank down the glass of water in one and gave a heavy sigh. 'Oh, how long is this heat going to continue? I think I'm going crazy.'

It was most unusual for her to come home and sit languidly like this in the living room without even changing out of her clothes. She wearily pressed a hand to her temple.

The Mistress's attempt at persuasion had failed. If, indeed, she had actually attempted to persuade him. It did not mean that was the end of the matter, however. When the Master came home and heard what had happened, he was extremely displeased. It was preposterous at this stage to spurn both girls, and if Mr. Itakura couldn't decide then the Master himself would do so for him. He would be married off to the daughter of the relatively influential person in the Imperial Rule Assistant Association's Lifestyle section, a plump young woman with a fair complexion.

'I would have thought the wife of an executive director could be relied on to take care of marriage arrangements, of all things,' the Master went on. 'You need to hone your skills, my dear.'

'But Mr. Itakura was adamant that he is absolutely not interested. I'm not his mother, so how am I to force him? Surely there's someone else in the company better suited to them, a younger man. What about Mr. Tachibana, or Mr. Akagi?'

'Both have already been conscripted. Mr. Itakura is the only young man who hasn't yet been sent off to fight. I don't know what you're talking about in this day and age. Really, that's enough. I shall give this directly to him tomorrow. This marriage is a company order.'

'Wait!' The Mistress snatched the photograph from the Master's hand as if something had just occurred to her. 'Wait. Arranging a marriage isn't something you do without listening to the other party. I will try talking to him again. Let me try once more, okay?' she said quickly.

'But that's what I asked you to do initially,' the Master grumbled. The next morning, however, he went to work with only one photograph. In the living room, the Mistress started writing another postcard with an extremely displeased look on her face.

That afternoon, I was just off out to collect the household rations when she called after me, 'Taki, post this for me, will you?'

Written on the postcard was, 'Mr. Itakura, I want to ask your real feelings on the matter, so I will visit once more on Sunday.'

A few days later, the reply came: 'I also wish to convey my true position, so please do come.'

The following week, the Mistress set off again carrying her parasol. 'Well then, I'll see you later.'

I was sweeping the porch, as I usually did in the morning, and saw the Mistress off as she went down the hill.

I will never forget that day.

The Mistress went out wearing a plain splash-patterned kimono and Hakata weave obi with a narrow, patterned strip along one side. This was an unusually spirited outfit for her, reflecting a certain determination on her part.

She came back that evening without the photo. 'He said he wants to think about it,' she mumbled, 'I've left the photo with him. If we don't hear soon, I'll call on him again.'

'For goodness sake! How much does he have to think about it?' the Master exclaimed in exasperation.

'I'm going to get changed,' the Mistress said, and went back to the couple's south facing bedroom.

And that's when I noticed her obi. Even now I can clearly remember it. Seen from behind, it had clearly been retied the wrong way around. The Mistress always tied the obi so that the patterned strip was on the right, but now it was on the left.

I'm sure people will say I must have been seeing things. Someone so well accustomed to wearing this obi would never tie it the wrong way around, you would think. I was young at the time and must have made a mistake, I can hear you say. But what if, for example, she'd had to tie her obi in a hurry. Or when she was flustered?

'The veranda's so damp from the humidity. Would you wipe it again for me?' she asked, so once again I wrung out a cloth and wiped the veranda for the second time that day.

Behind the closed sliding paper door, I could hear the rustle of the Mistress's clothing as she loosened the obi. The very idea that it probably wasn't the first time that day she'd loosened the obi with the patterned strip set my heart aflutter.

Suddenly, I accidentally kicked the bucket of water and knocked it over.

'Oh my, Taki, it's not like you to make a mistake like that,' the Mistress said with a smile, sliding open the paper door, now dressed in a white blouse and doing up the hook of her sky-blue pencil skirt.

The Mistress went over to Mr. Itakura's apartment twice more after that. Both times she wore Western-style clothes, and the first time she said it looked as though he had finally agreed to go forward with the marriage proposal, and that she had arranged for a photographic studio to take his photo to send to the girl.

The second time it was already autumn, and the garden was enveloped in the heady perfume of the blooming osmanthus. The Master and the young Master were both out that day too, and I was left to look after the house.

Since that fateful day, I had been terribly concerned about the Mistress, but I couldn't possibly ask her outright and so was constantly anguishing about it.

I was alone when I heard a bright voice say from the veranda, 'Hello there!' It was the Mistress's friend Miss Mutsuko.

'I'm afraid the Mistress isn't in, but she should be back shortly so please do come in and wait,' I told her.

'The garden smells so heavenly I couldn't help coming in this way. Will she really be home soon?'

'Yes, I believe so.'

'Well, in that case.'

A working woman, Miss Mutsuko was drearily dressed in a khaki suit with her hair pulled back in a tight bun. She had a black leather bag like that of a bus conductor slung across her chest.

I apologized for not having any elegant sweets to go with tea and instead served her some toasted, pickled plums with konbu that had been boiled in sweetened soy sauce. 'Your pickled plums are my absolute favourites, Taki!' she said with a smile.

It was to be the only time I ever had or ever would mention the matter to anyone.

'Lately the Mistress has been acting a little strangely,' I started as I poured her some tea.

'Oh? What's up?' Miss Mutsuko asked, cradling her tea cup.

'She's gone over to Mr. Itakura's place again today.'

'Mr. Itakura. Is that the young man who works in Mr. Hirai's company?'

'Yes. She's gone to meet him several times in order to broker a marriage for him.'

'Tokiko isn't really cut out for taking care of marriage arrangements.'

'No, she isn't. But the Mistress is acting a bit strange.'

'How do you mean, strange?'

'The Master mustn't hear about this.'

'Oh? Are you sure it's okay for me to hear something not for the Master's ears?'

'But I don't know what to do.'

'What on earth's going on, Taki?'

'The Mistress has gone to see Mr. Itakura again today.'

'Um, so what? Has that young man done something?'

'Yes. Probably.'

'What has he done?'

'I, er… that sort of thing.'

'*What* sort of thing, for heaven's sake?'

'Mr. Itakura is in love with the Mistress.'

That's all I said, but I felt terrible. Suddenly I felt the blood rush to my head and felt dizzy, as if I'd stood up too quickly. Before I knew it, I'd flung my upper body flat on the reception room table and was in floods of tears.

'So that's what it's all about,' Miss Mutsuko said, rubbing my back. 'She's fallen in love with someone she shouldn't.'

'Yes,' I answered. 'She has.'

Of course, I was referring to the Mistress and Mr. Itakura, but what Miss Mutsuko started saying then was extraordinary. Even now it leaves me with the strange sensation that she was misconstruing the situation—or maybe she wasn't. Why on earth Miss Mutsuko talked about such things that afternoon, I'll never know.

'Tokiko was really gorgeous when we were at school, you know. She was the prettiest girl in the school, and everyone was in love her. That's how it was back then. One girl in particular was really obsessed with her and wrote her a love letter every day and hung around her on the way to and from school. She was so in love that she couldn't concentrate on her studies and even had to change schools the following year so eventually she was able to graduate and go on to women's college. When Tokiko got married, she went out and got stinking drunk and sank into despair, making a huge scene generally. Beautiful women are cruel, they say.'

Then, as if reading something aloud, she went on, 'The ideal path in life for humankind is certainly that of a man and woman loving each other deeply, but there must also be a second path. And even a third path must be open to those unable to find someone to love and who are lonely, so that they may dedicate their life to their work. I think it's fine to follow either of these three paths, as long as you follow it wholeheartedly, with the desire of giving back to the universe, so that the self may flourish and thrive. And I believe those who follow these three paths have no option to live their lives in any other way.'

'What's that?'

'A passage from a story by Nobuko Yoshiya. I have diligently lived my life according to this, as though it were my Bible. This just between you and me—you mustn't tell anyone. We, you and I, will probably end up following the third path,' she said, and gave my hand a squeeze.

I felt even more confused.

I was still holding Miss Mutsuko's cool, dry hand when we heard the front door open and the Mistress call out that she was home, and I hastily pulled my hand away.

I rose to go and greet her, but she exclaimed, 'Oh, Mutsuko, you're here?' and rushed into the reception room and collapsed on a chair. I quickly went to get some tea.

'It's no good,' the Mistress blurted out. 'Really, we can't go on like this or we'll never get anywhere. We have to stop now, really we do! I keep telling him I won't come again.'

'What are you talking about, Tokiko? What's happened? What do you have to stop?'

'What? What do you mean, what? It's no good, you know. Impossible. Of course it's wrong!' the Mistress groaned and picked up her teacup. 'Ouch, that's hot!' she shrieked, and quickly put it back down again. Abruptly she pulled herself together and said, 'I'm talking about this marriage thing, of course. Mr. Itakura says he absolutely won't contemplate accepting the marriage. Really, if he's going to be so obstinate, then that's enough. I told him I wouldn't come again.'

'Really? Is that all?'

'What do you mean, "is that all?"'

The Mistress slumped in her chair, apparently exhausted. Miss Mutsuko also seemed weary after her earlier speech, and I was in a state of confusion, so the three of us sat there for a while in silence.

The Master and the young Master arrived home together, having met at the station. Finding the three of us sitting despondently in the evening gloom, the Master said, 'Whatever happened to the lights? Is there a blackout?'

After the war I found the passage that Miss Mutsuko had recited from memory in Nobuko Yoshiya's story *Black Rose*. She had recited it almost exactly as it was, only after 'but there must also be a second path' she had left out, 'permitted to the small number of people who follow the path of same-sex love.'

Now I can no longer ask her whether she had deliberately omitted it in consideration of the times.

It was already November by the time Mr. Itakura's marriage was settled.

During that time, he and Mistress Tokiko did not meet even once, and neither did a single letter pass between them. The Master looked grave and asked no questions, and the Mistress didn't mention the matter either.

In the space of that month, the Mistress visibly lost weight. Her pale face grew even paler, so pale in fact that one might suspect the blue cape of the ghost story that had terrorized the young Master had sucked out her blood. When I commented on it to the Master, though, he apparently hadn't noticed. His head was probably too full of company matters.

And the Master wasn't the only one who was despondent: a gloomy atmosphere hung over the whole of society. Everybody was feeling fed up.

A letter from home arrived, the first in a long time. My mother had written in her clumsy handwriting, 'I felt so sorry for you when your marriage came to nothing after he died in action, but there's a reason I wanted you to marry. Unmarried daughters over twenty years of age are now being conscripted and sent to work in munitions factories or farms, so you shouldn't expect to be exempt. It's just awful being conscripted because it's too late to marry, and as your mother I wanted to avoid that fate for you, so wanted to get you married quickly, but we haven't received any more proposals. You will probably have to work in a factory or farm after all, but it's your patriotic duty, so you should prepare yourself for it.'

If I was really going to be conscripted, then better in Tokyo than back up north, I thought. Maybe I'd be able to work in the factory during the day and serve in the Hirai household early in the morning and at night. My heart sank when I saw the students and maids that came to work for the neighbours disappearing one after another.

The branches of the persimmon tree in the garden were beginning to sag under the weight of the late autumn fruit when Mr. Itakura paid a visit one Saturday evening. It was unarranged, but the whole family happened to be at home. Mr. Itakura stood in the chill of the entrance hall holding out the offending marriage photo.

'Don't stand out there in the cold, come on in,' the Master said, but Mr. Itakura refused and remained standing by the front door.

'It was such a good offer that I dithered about it and took so long to answer that I thought it expedient to come here and talk about it properly,' he said.

'I see. So you're rejecting it after all, I take it?' the Master said mockingly, having discerned the situation from the grim look on the younger man's face.

'Sorry to have held onto it for so long. It's just that, as was reported in this morning's newspaper, it appears that even those of us who failed the medical are to be conscripted into this righteous war.'

'What?' the Mistress exclaimed in surprise from behind the Master.

'The conditions attached to the proposal were that the groom be a company employee, young, and would not be sent to war, so that means I am no longer eligible.'

'Oh, don't worry about that. They'll have to relax their conditions anyway. If they insist on that sort of thing at this stage, they'll never find anyone.'

'Even if they do relax their conditions, I'm not suitable. I don't want to make anyone wait or weep for me. When I've completed my service to my country, I will settle down.'

'Is that so? A fine resolve indeed. All right then. Please return the photo to me,' the Master said with unexpected good grace. 'Well then, since you came all the way here, Itakura, let's put formalities to one side and have a drink,' he added amicably.

He had rarely invited Mr. Itakura to drink with him, and probably just wanted someone to drink with. As the Master drank, he became even more morose and started droning on about all his troubles.

'We've tried absolutely everything. The shop floor manager and company president were desperate, you know. We developed springs made from both bamboo and celluloid, and used paper to imitate the feel of tinplate. We even collected sawdust from a local carpentry workshop and came up with ways we could convert it into a solid to use for something. I put everything into getting hold of what little metal we could, and had to do all kinds of things in the process. Well, there are some things I really can't talk about in front of my wife and child.'

Mr. Itakura tried to refuse any more sake, but the Master insisted on pouring some more him anyway.

'But we've really come to the end of the line now. We haven't even been able to get hold of any scrap iron since last year due to the economic blockade. And what little does get through won't be wasted on toys. As for exports, both Europe and America are boycotting Japanese products, so there's no market there. And there isn't a big enough market in China yet. There's really nothing more we can do.'

The Mistress's gaze had been fixed on Mr. Itakura the whole time.

'I had thought that if your marriage worked out, it might give us some advantage, but even that slight hope has gone. So, it doesn't really matter any more.'

'I'm sorry,' Mr. Itakura answered, also sneaking glances at the Mistress.

'Oh, how frustrating it all is! This sake is a bit watery, but drink it, won't you?'

The Master was already drunk, but I felt anxious when I heard him say this. Given that rations were limited, I'd added a little water to the sake before serving.

Meeting for the first time in a month, the Mistress and Mr. Itakura both looked dispirited. They only had eyes for each other, but the moment their eyes met they immediately looked away. In contrast to the Mistress's pale appearance, Mr. Itakura was flushed bright red right down to his neck from the sake, again reminding me of the red cape/blue cape ghost story.

The Master tried to detain Mr. Itakura further saying the night was young, but the younger man brushed him aside and left.

As I watched him make his way down the hill, his thin figure doubled with the image of the Mistress.

And then the war started.

Pearl Harbour Day. 8th December.

It was just an ordinary day. The radio had broken two or three days earlier so the Mistress and I missed the ongoing afternoon broadcast, and only finally heard the news that evening.

The young Master, who had been going alone to school since the fourth grade, came running up the hill as fast as he could, shouting, 'We did it! We started the war! Japan bombed the naval base in Hawaii!'

The Mistress went placidly outside and asked, 'Oh really? Is that true, Kyo?'

'Yes! This afternoon, the headmaster gathered the whole school together and told us. Didn't you hear it on the radio?'

'No, I didn't. Whereabouts in Hawaii? The Dutch East Indies? French Indochina?'

'What are you talking about, Mummy? Hawaii's in the western Pacific!'

'Geography's not my strong point.'

'It's not Holland or France we've started a war with, it's America!'

'Oh my, really?'

'Is that all you can say? Women are so useless,' the young Master said angrily and ran upstairs.

The Mistress sighed and muttered, 'But your father said only the day before yesterday that the Tojo Cabinet's policy was not to fight America.' The sharp-eared young Master overheard her and yelled down from upstairs.

'It's because America is so awful, and Japan put up with them for the longest time, but couldn't bear it any longer. Don't you even know that? Oh, that's why I hate women!' he yelled as loud as he could.

This time the Mistress was careful to whisper so that he didn't hear, 'The war with China lasted four years, and now they're starting another one! I'm really getting a bit fed up with this.'

I can't say whether women are useless or not, but certainly the two males in the Hirai household were singularly excited, and made quite a racket until late at night, singing in chorus: *Tens of thousaaands/of enemies/may coooome!*

Somehow the Master too had completely transformed into the pro-war faction. 'Now America will have to realize they can't make fools of Japan any longer. Well done Japan! Banzai!' he boomed. 'That's what the company president and others say too. The Americans and British have always considered East Asians to be a lower class of people, and have kept on forcing unacceptable conditions onto us one after another. When the company president went to America, he was embarrassed to find people he'd never met before insisting on calling him Shu this, Shu that, as if he were a dog.'

'Oh, but he always used to give that as an example of how friendly the Americans were!'

'That's what's so nice about him. He always tries to put a positive spin on everything. That's one of the merits of Japanese people generally. But thinking back, he said, even when white people were addressing each other as Mister this and that, he was always just Shu.'

Personally, I never heard the company president tell the story, so I can't say what spin he gave it at the time, but one thing was certain: in the Master's own mind, the story of Shu had transformed into a completely different anecdote.

To be honest, I couldn't summon any enthusiasm for the celebrations that night. But when I saw the headlines in the newspaper the next morning, it was as though something in me had changed and I felt I was beginning to understand. So, it's actually starting, I thought. A new age is starting.

Until then, the newspapers had been decorously reporting daily how negotiations between Japan and the US hadn't been going well. Dark photos of Prime Minister Tojo's sober face and Secretary of State Hull's spiteful one were shown day in day out as we were informed there had been no progress in the peace talks. I'd hated reading the newspapers, as they were just full of how America and Britain were making fools of Japan, or despising Japan for being cowardly, or forcing unreasonable demands onto us and not listening to what we had to say.

But on the morning of 9th December, we were greeted with rousing headlines in big fat letters: 'US Pacific fleet wiped out!' and, 'War declared on the world's strongest navy!'

I went outside and took a deep breath.

Chapter 6

Muddling Through

'We're going skiing!' the Master boomed the moment he arrived back home.

It was the end of December 1941, and ever since Japan had declared war against America everything had suddenly brightened up.

Food had become a little scarcer, but not to the point where there wasn't enough, and shares for rubber companies in the south had soared providing huge returns for investors, so the streets became a little livelier and people were calmer, too.

The company president had invited the family to go skiing. They were to stay for two nights somewhere like the North Japan Alps, where the snow was deep. Mistress Tokiko had apparently been an expert skier in her student days, but she'd given it up since getting married because of the young Master's illness. Now soon to start the fifth grade, the young Master no longer dragged his leg and was a healthy, growing boy.

'It's time we taught Kyo too,' the Master said, poking the boy's arm as though sharing an in-joke between men.

'I want to try. I'm sure I'll be good at it!' the young Master said, gripping his hands into fists and adopting a crouching pose, while clumsily swinging his thighs from side to side.

'Skiing? Oh, but when?'

'When? Over the New Year break, of course. Two nights from the second, probably.'

'Oh, but...'

'What's wrong?'

'Someone might come over. New Year's visitors, for example.'

'So let them come! We have to be away sometimes. You've been dying to go to a hot spring for ages, haven't you? There are some great hot springs in snow country.'

'But really, when I think there might be an air raid...' she muttered, maybe thinking of how the blackouts had become stricter than ever since the start of the war.

'Ha ha ha!' the Master laughed agreeably.

'Ha ha ha!' the young Master joined in.

'First Hawaii, then Guam, then Hong Kong,' the Master went on. 'The Imperial Army is really giving the enemy a good kicking. As if any country is strong enough to meddle with Japan! It'll end with America groaning and wailing in the Pacific. There won't be any attacks on the mainland. It's impossible!'

'Impossible!' the young Master mimicked.

The Mistress's expression was enigmatic. The men were clueless, but I knew what was on her mind. The thought that Mr. Itakura paid a visit to the house on 3rd January every year was enough to bring a faraway look into the Mistress's eyes.

And so the family went skiing in the New Year of 1942. I stayed behind in Tokyo to look after the house, but Mr. Itakura didn't appear.

On 8th January the young Master saw his first Imperial Rescript Day. Patriotic Services Day, which had been held on the first of every month since the outbreak of the Pacific War, had now been renamed and switched to the eighth of every month in commemoration of Pearl Harbour.

'The Imperial Rescript Day is way better than Patriotic Services Day. It's really very solemn, you know,' the young Master said excitedly when he came back from school.

The Mistress had been looking dejected, but she recovered some of her usual cheerfulness after the kimono fabrics dealer turned up at the front door on the fifteenth, commonly known as Women's New Year, as women finally had time to pay their own New Year's calls by then. Clothing was soon to be rationed and the dealer had to sell his stock within the next few days, so he was doing the rounds of his valued customers.

Most were practical cloths like meisen silk and poral worsted, but it was a joy to see the dealer skilfully unroll and reroll each one on the doorstep, while the Mistress issued him with brisk instructions.

'This is something you can rarely get your hands on,' the dealer said, unrolling an undyed silk crepe. 'It's the sort you want to purchase while you still have the chance, ready for the right occasion. I'm only showing it to you, Madame,' he added, clearly flattering her.

The Mistress's eyes gleamed. 'I'll take it,' she said immediately.

After the dealer had left, she turned to me.

'Well then, Taki, I'll be going out now,' she said, clearly in high spirits. 'Oh, but why are you looking so surprised? Now that the fabric dealer's been, there's not a moment to lose. I must stock up on socks and underwear for the Master and Kyoichi before rationing kicks in.'

The Mistress changed into a kimono and oiled her hair before heading out.

By February Singapore had fallen, and even the Mistress was excited. Young Master Kyoichi was really adorable when he came home from school and ran straight to me to show off his new blue rubber ball.

'Look what I got! Look what I got! Taki, look! Look at this!'

The balls had been distributed to all elementary school children throughout Japan to commemorate the victory in the Naval Battle of Malaya.

'Oh, how lovely! Go now and show it to your mother, too.'

Mistress Tokiko bounced it a few times on the flagstones in the porch.

'It's thanks to Lieutenant General Yamashita, you know. He says that the Japanese army is great and good, so from now on our country will become really rich. We'll get lots of sugar, too.'

Tomoyuki Yamashita's ultimatum of 'Answer "Yes" or "No"!' to Lieutenant General Percival had been widely publicized throughout Japan, and the young Master was fond of pretending to be Yamashita while I had to be Percival and surrender unconditionally to him.

'It was worth finishing Percival off, wasn't it?'

'Yes or no?'

'Yes. I give in.'

That night the young Master went to bed hugging the rubber ball. He dreamt he was alone, sitting on an armchair beneath a palm tree on a South Seas island, wearing the uniform of the Imperial Japanese Navy. South Sea islanders their ears and noses decorated, were fanning him with big leaves, so he felt pleasantly cool. South Sea islander girls brought lots of flower garlands and placed them around his neck and on his head. Then boys brought him trays laden with bananas and sugar cubes, coconut milk and more, and urged him to feast, he told me jubilantly when he woke up.

'And you know what? Da daaaa, the music started, and they all started dancing and enjoying themselves. They all said: "Japanese soldiers are so strong. Thank you! Thank you!" In the dream, I had already grown into a fine young man and a soldier of the Imperial Army, so I said things like, "Oh, it was nothing, really," and laughed and pulled on my beard like this.'

'Goodness, did you already have a beard?'

'I did!'

'Your dream is mostly true,' the Master said. 'In Sumatra and Java and Mindanao and Cebu and Panay and Corregidor, everyone is dancing and welcoming the Japanese troops! Oh, this war is so encouraging. We were right to search out a new way in the South Seas after all.'

Even the Master was in a good mood those days. A big load had been removed from his shoulders that spring when the Metal Toy Industry Association had been disbanded. Until then he had been stressed out as he frantically ran around trying to secure metals or suitable substitute materials, but after this he completely gave up on making toys and devoted himself to the company president's campaign to be voted onto the municipal assembly.

The factory, too, had switched over to manufacturing aeroplane parts. The company president was still the president, of course, but now that he wasn't able to make what he wanted to, he had come up with something else to pour his energies into.

He began by helping in the elections for the Diet, which preceded the municipal assembly elections. The house on top of the hill began to fill up with pamphlets with titles like: 'The Mission of the Imperial Rule Assistance Political Association', 'Do the right thing: vote for IRAPA!' and: 'A General Election during Wartime'.

Instead of going to the company, the Master would often go to the Greater East Asia Hall in Hibiya. The Greater East Asia Hall was the building that had hitherto been known as the Tokyo Kaikan. In fact, it was only called the Greater East Asia Hall for a few years during the war to reflect the name the Japanese government had given to what elsewhere was generally known as the Pacific War.

Before the war, it had been really popular for its rooftop garden, where one could enjoy the cool summer evenings. I had once accompanied the family there too. The building was home to a splendid conference hall, but the summer rooftop garden was where families could get together and enjoy a cheerful atmosphere. And the beef hotpot in the Japanese-style room on the third floor was reputed to be the best. There had been talk of celebrating the young Master's entrance to middle school there, but by the time he went to middle school the restaurant no longer existed.

The Greater East Asia Hall had been made the headquarters for the Imperial Rule Assistance Association. The Mistress had often dressed up to go to the Imperial Theatre next door, but that had been requisitioned even before the Tokyo Kaikan and now had a sign outside reading, 'Cabinet Intelligence Bureau'. Both had been established around the time of the Empire's 2600th Anniversary celebrations.

In 1942, when the Imperial Rule Assistance Association was moved elsewhere, it became the office of the Imperial Rule Assistance Political Association, so the Master was often there.

Even when Tokyo was hit by the first air raid in the middle of the Diet elections, the Master blustered, 'Until now the Americans had just been envious of Japan's advances. Now, though, they dare to enter the city during daylight hours, albeit cautiously. I almost want to congratulate them! Although it seems they quickly fled again without having achieved much.'

'That's going too far, Nan,' Takeshi said. 'Saying that the South Sea islanders danced and welcomed us, of all things! As if they would. And saying that Japanese soldiers are strong. Come on, what's that all about?'

But that's what everyone thought back then, whatever he says.

'1942 was the year of the Midway Battle, wasn't it? That was the battle in the Pacific when Isoroku Yamamoto attacked and got thoroughly routed, right? Anyone who watches movies knows that. I watch quite a lot of old films myself. Yamamoto was played by Toshiro Mifune. Henry Fonda was the enemy Admiral, what's his name? Minitz, wasn't it? After the Battle of Midway, the Japanese won hardly anything.'

Takeshi's nostrils flared proudly as he lectured me, but we hadn't been told about any of this at the time. The Battle of Midway had been reported as a major victory for Japan, as they sunk enemy battleships one after another, and the news films showed footage of children visiting the Japanese soldiers bearing fruit.

What's more, the enemy admiral's name wasn't Minitz, but Nimitz. The instant I recalled his name, the song that had been sung everywhere during the war began replaying in my head: *C'mon Nimitz and MacArthur, we'll plunge you into hell.* It had been popular later on, in 1944, when the military situation was more critical.

I thought about singing it for Takeshi, but he'd probably just make fun of me, so I didn't. He really was ridiculous, the way he criticized me for not knowing anything.

'What do you mean by the first air raid to hit Tokyo? You mean the bombing that flattened the city?'

The bombing that flattened the city, burning a great swathe through a densely populated area, wasn't until March 1945. As if that first air raid in April 1942 was even close to that kind of scale!

The first air raid on Tokyo took place in the afternoon of 18th April. The young Master was at school, while at home I was doing some gardening, and the Mistress was inside darning clothes or something.

I heard some muffled explosions like fireworks and looked up into the sky. Sleek black aeroplanes were flying from the east headed northwest, leaving a black curtain of smoke in their wake.

'Taki, what was that odd sound just now?' the Mistress said, coming out onto the veranda. 'Oh my, those planes are flying really low.'

She was speechless when she saw the black smoke left by artillery from the antiaircraft guns.

'Oh! I wonder if Kyo's school is okay?'

I rushed to turn the radio on, but it didn't make the situation any clearer. Having seen the American planes flying so low put me on edge.

A neighbour came out of her house and told us that there was an air raid warning in place. Even that felt surreal, and I couldn't quite grasp what she meant.

'Really, is Kyo's school okay, I wonder?' the Mistress repeated.

I told her I would go to check and went out, but when I reached the station I found the trains weren't running. Disheartened, I went back up the hill.

'The trains have stopped,' I called out to the Mistress. She was so worried she had come outside.

She nodded, and pointed up at some Japanese fighter planes. 'Look at those, Taki. Aren't they rather too high?'

I looked up at the sky to see Imperial Army planes flying in leisurely formation.

'Oh!'

'What are they doing all the way up there when those American planes were flying all the way down here?' the Mistress said, emphasizing the relative positions by moving her hand up and down.

That evening, the young Master came home extremely excited, and talked about how he'd watched the planes from the schoolyard. I was shocked to hear there had been fires in Toyama and Meguro, and the thought that this was not so far from the Master's school sent a shiver down my spine.

I had always been told that Japan's air defences were infallible, but I began to doubt this after watching enemy planes fly so close you could almost touch them. But the Master laughed it off, saying, 'Well we can congratulate the Americans for having made a good go of it, but it wasn't such a big strike after all, was it? It's not worth worrying about.'

He then started going on about how important these elections were to ensure they could make the nation's defence systems even stronger. And in order to ensure national unity in wartime, they would have to fill the Diet with the new candidates put forward by the IRAPA, and so on and so forth.

Even now I still don't quite understand what he was talking about. The Master generally became obsessed with his work, which was his strong point, but he tended to drone on, and bore us in the process.

That was the only air raid that I experienced in Tokyo. The next one wouldn't be until the autumn of 1944.

According to the newspapers, the nine enemy planes that had pulled off the April air raid had all been shot down by the Japanese military, and there hadn't been all that much damage. And so I decided to believe that the Master was right.

But I couldn't help secretly nodding in agreement when local people whispered among themselves about the planes having been so low that surely we'd have seen them being shot down.

Mistress Tokiko almost fainted when she heard about some poor elementary school child who had been killed by machine gun fire after waving at the enemy planes having mistaken them for Japanese planes.

'Don't you ever wave at a plane, whatever the circumstances, do you hear me?' she admonished the young Master, and made him link his little finger with hers to seal his promise.

After April's Doolittle Raid, as it came to be known, all I remember is the hullaballoo surrounding the company president's election to the municipal assembly.

The Mistress and Mr. Itakura's little fling seemed to have ended without being detected.

It must have been around that time, too, that it was decreed the person responsible for fire prevention had to be either the householder or his wife. Neighbourhood association meetings too should be attended by the wife, not the maid or anyone else. This role had mostly been undertaken by maids or students in the early days of the war, but now they had all returned to their hometowns, been married off or gone to war, and there was no one left to go to the meetings.

On top of that, the Master was so deeply involved in the Tokyo City Assembly elections that even the Mistress had to get involved with the Women's League for the Election of Imperial Rule Assistance. She was not exactly keen on this, and I don't recall ever seeing her tie back her kimono sleeves with the cords inscribed with the League's name in black ink that was part of their uniform.

With her face expressionless, she dutifully handed out eye-catching leaflets with slogans like: 'A vote for my husband is a vote for the Imperial Rule Assistance', and 'A vote for my husband shows love for your city' in the neighbourhood and to her old college friends.

For my part, I mostly tended to the vegetable garden, did the cleaning and cooking, and re-stitched old kimonos into new garments, that sort of thing.

Occasionally I would have to go to the Greater East Asia Hall on errands for the Master. Heading to the city centre after so long was exhilarating. By this time even department stores had been commandeered by the military, and the cityscape had changed considerably. Even so, the built-up neighbourhoods of Marunouchi and Hibiya were still my beloved Tokyo.

One day, on my way back from the Greater East Asia Hall, I bumped into Master Konaka on the street. Over ten years had passed since I had left the household of the great novelist, where I first went into service after leaving elementary school. I had seen his photograph in magazine articles from time to time, but it was the first time to actually meet him since I'd left.

Never dreaming that he would remember me, I bowed and walked on past when I heard him call, 'Taki? It *is* you, isn't it, Taki?'

'Yes, I am Taki.'

'The Taki who used to be in my house?'

'Yes, I'm Taki, who was in your service.'

'I couldn't believe my eyes when I saw you! How old are you now? You've grown into a fine woman, haven't you? Well I never.

Are you still in service with Suga's daughter?' Suga was Mistress Tokiko's maiden name.

'Yes, Mistress Tokiko married Mr. Hirai, a toy company executive, and I went with her.'

'Oh, is that so? She's called Tokiko is she, that beauty? Taki, do you have a little time?'

Surprised, I didn't answer.

'Having met like this, it would be good to talk a little, wouldn't it? I've known Tokiko since she was in nappies, so there's no need to be scared. All you need to do is tell her that you met Master Konaka in Hibiya and that I insisted you take her back a gift from me, so you couldn't refuse.'

'But...'

'Come now, just a short time. Thirty minutes at most. Won't you come with me?'

Master Konaka took me into the Fuji Ice café. I hadn't been there for a long time. I was served some tea. My heart was pounding. Master Konaka ate a sandwich or something, and kept rudely saying how terrible it tasted.

When I asked after his family and household, he said that whereas he had once had three maids, now he had just the one, a young woman who I didn't know. He gave a deep sigh, and said, 'There have been a few changes, you see.'

Then he suddenly started going on about that story. The one he told me when I first started working for him and was still a child, that story. The careless maid in England who had mistaken the manuscript of a difficult book her Master had received from his friend, and burned it in the fireplace. That's why I shouldn't clean the study, lest I carelessly burn an important manuscript.

'Did I tell you about this before?'

'Yes, you did.'

'Hey, are you telling me that I'm going senile?' he said, giving me a mischievous look behind his glasses.

'No, not at all. You told me that story many times, Master Konaka.'

'Ah, many times, did I? Well then, maybe I've been senile for a long time,' he said, and laughed pleasantly. His hairline was receding, but he was still the plump, amusing Master Konaka of old. 'Maybe you remember the other part of the story. The bit about whether the maid had really burned the manuscript out of carelessness.'

'Yes. How the maid had burned the manuscript so that her Master's friend couldn't publish his book before the Master could publish his.'

'You really do have a good memory. It's true, you always did have a good head on you, Taki. Out of all the maids in my house, you were the brightest. I shouldn't have let you go.'

Then he went on, almost as though he was talking to himself, 'Sometimes I wish I had a clever maid, you know. One who would know when to burn something I've written but deep down think I shouldn't publish, or when to mail something I'm dithering about sending, that sort of maid.'

'Can't you just instruct her to burn it, or to post it?'

'No, that wouldn't do at all. If a maid is as dense as all that, well then, there are plenty like that to be had.'

'So it's cleverer for her to go ahead and do as she pleases?'

'It's not as simple as all that. I'd be in a fix if she just did as she pleased. Look, it's like this. The stupidest type of maid is the one who burns something she shouldn't burn. The average type of maid is the one who burns something when she is told to do so. And an excellent maid is the one who can judge for herself without being told when to burn something that her Master, out of his own weakness, can't bring himself to burn, and then when she is scolded for it, apologizes for having done something wrong.'

'And it's okay when something that the stupidest kind of maid carelessly burns, and something that the Master can't quite make up his mind to burn, happen to be the same.'

'Oh, that's right. Absolutely right. You are a clever maid, you are.' Master Konaka impulsively reached out and gave my hand a squeeze. I was terrified of being seen holding hands in such a busy place as this.

'It's no big deal, but even I'm doing my best. Even me, even Kishida, even Kikuchi—we're all doing well. We're second to none in our love for our country. Even so, there are those who attack us. That's the terrifying side of the literary world. Somehow fanaticism even creeps into the intellectual world, and little by little everyone starts saying what they think others want to hear. And those who come out with a simple message loud and clear drown out the others. You can't protest. It happens so quickly that it takes over everything. If it continues like this, you'll be better off coming out with something strong before you're attacked. I don't want to do that. But if I don't, I'll be in danger. This sort of thing wears you down so much that your health deteriorates. I don't want to end up like that. I also have a family. This is the problem. I worry. I write. I think I should burn it. Either that, or I think I should send it. But I can't do either. Oh, dear me.'

Mumbling away to himself, Master Konaka took a sip of coffee and grimaced with distaste.

'It's called "muddling through" in English,' he said, to no one in particular. As well as being a novelist, he had translated children's books from English, too. There were a lot of Western books in his study.

'Muddling?'

'Muddling through. Just somehow managing to find a way through without having any specific plan or secret strategy. It's how they cope on the battlefield. It's a phrase I've been using lately. Muddling through. Muddling through. Not having any secret strategy, not thinking about anything.'

When I didn't say anything, he sighed slightly and gave a gentle smile. Then he stood up and purchased some sweets for me to take back to Mistress Tokiko.

'Take care of yourself, Taki. Be sure to look after yourself well. If you do go back home, be sure to come and say goodbye, won't you?' he said, patting me on the cheek.

The company president achieved a landslide victory in the Tokyo City Assembly elections, as a candidate for the Imperial Rule Assistance Political Association. As he filled in the remaining eye on the daruma doll, indicating that their wish had been fulfilled, the Master echoed the company president's slogan, 'For a bright society in support of Imperial Rule, with a municipal administration free of corruption!' and led a rousing chorus of 'Banzai!'

After the election, around the end of the summer I think it was, everyone was given an extra ration of coffee and tea to celebrate Japan having captured some islands in the south. The young Master remembered the dream he'd had following the occupation of Singapore in February, and wrote a composition about it that earned him top marks at school.

I wonder what position the Master was in at the time. Perhaps he was secretary to the company president, but I'm not really sure. Takeshi tells me off for making out things were so cheerful during the war, but as far as I can remember, we had been living peacefully ever since Pearl Harbour right up to the Tokyo City Assembly elections.

Of course, things were changing little by little: vegetables started to be rationed, all rice was unpolished, and it was hard to get hold of sweets. I remember the young Master being given some caramels at school during the harvest festival. It was rather flimsy paper-thin candy, but even so, that year children were given candy and a rubber ball, and the general atmosphere was still quite relaxed.

That all changed the following year. What shocked me the most was the decision that summer to merge Tokyo Prefecture and Tokyo City into a new body called the Tokyo Metropolis, which meant the company president abruptly lost his job. When Tokyo City ceased to exist, all the assembly members were fired just like that, despite having been voted in with great fanfare. It was quite awful.

The Master too was quite crestfallen and suddenly aged visibly. Now he no longer had anything to do, he started tending the vegetable garden himself.

And that wasn't the only change.

Something even worse was happening in that little house.

***

At the start of 1943, the loss of Guadalcanal followed by the death in action of commander-in-chief of the Combined Fleet Admiral Yamamoto and the honourable deaths of the Japanese troops on Attu Island were all widely reported.

By this time everyone knew that the war was entering its decisive phase. This was a phrase that Miss Mutsuko from *Housewives Delight* often used. It was commonly used in neighbourhood association slogans, too, along with phrases like: 'All-out war', 'Decisive battle' and 'Final victory'. Miss Mutsuko also provided instructions on how to make women's air-raid clothing and baggy work pants, the kind gathered at the ankles. I liked these as they were easy to move around in, but Miss Tokiko didn't seem to like them much.

Miss Mutsuko also started pulling her hair back into an even tighter bun and spouting idealistic fervour, such as: 'The key to victory in a major war is not science or weaponry, you know. It's the Japanese spirit. Even all the aeroplanes and guns, they're all foreign inventions. It's only through our fighting spirit that we make them strong.'

Not long after the young Master went into the sixth grade, a notice came around from the neighbourhood association to hand over rings and other jewellery. Mistress Tokiko sat still in the reception room reading the notice. She was extremely attached to her accessories.

'Darling, do I really have to hand them over?' she pressed the Master a number of times.

Each time his answer was the same: 'The country's going through tough times, so all we can do is comply.'

Dissatisfied, she pulled the corners of her mouth down. 'But dear, do I really have to do this?'

After hearing the same question several times, the Master roared irritably, 'Once we've won the war and everyone's calmed down again, I'll buy better ones for you. Stop dithering and just hand them over!'

Then a neighbour brought round the circular from the neighbourhood association and happened to comment, 'Everyone around here knows that the Hirais have tinplate toys at home, so you'd better hand them over too if you don't want to be seen as uncooperative.' The Mistress remained stony faced and avoided the neighbour's gaze.

When the young Master heard that he would have to let go of his beloved toys, he accepted it surprisingly readily. 'I'm sad, but it can't be helped. Now's a time when the Empire is pulling together with the fine objective of building the Greater East Asia. My teacher told us that even though we can't go to the front line as soldiers, us young citizens should always be thinking about what we can do individually. Mother, you too should stop looking so glum. You can spare your rings, can't you?'

All of a sudden the young Master had eschewed 'Mummy' for 'Mother', and had even started espousing praiseworthy opinions.

In fact, the one who changed most around this time was young Master Kyoichi. There was no longer any trace of the sweetness he'd had when he was little. Instead, he had a tough, mature resilience about him. Little by little, he was beginning to resemble his womanizing birth father in looks too. He'd always had weak legs and had been short for his age, but now he had a sudden growth spurt and was a head taller than his friends. Having started school a year late, he was a year older than his classmates.

He belonged to the Great Japan Youth Group, which swept the streets and collected the rubbish, and had been made a squad leader or something of the sort. This was a youth organization modelled on the Hitler Youth. Having trained for a role that involved issuing orders, it grated on him to see his own mother so grudging about handing over precious metals, apparently so unaware of her position as a subject of the Empire.

His grades at school were not at all satisfactory, but he became an extremely strong fighter. And then, one day he came home from school with a splendid black eye.

He greeted his astonished mother in a small voice and, avoiding meeting her eye, handed her a letter. It was from his teacher, and properly sealed. The Mistress watched in mute astonishment as he ran upstairs without saying a word, then pulled herself together, opened the letter with some scissors, and started reading it. Her face paled instantly.

I hurriedly went back to the kitchen, pretending not to notice the Mistress's agitation, but a short while later she came in herself, ashen-faced.

'It seems Kyoichi started a fight at school. The letter from his teacher says that we should chastise him at home, too, but I don't plan to say anything about it to the Master,' she said. 'I don't want to worry him. When he sees that black eye he'll know anyway, but all boys can be expected to have a fight once, right? Kyoichi's at a difficult age now, and I don't think it would be a good idea for him to be harshly scolded by a male parent who isn't a blood relation. Do you understand what I'm saying?'

'Yes, indeed.'

'I want you to keep quiet about the teacher's letter.'

'Of course,' I answered.

'I'm going to take a little rest. Would you bring me some water in the bedroom?'

She looked more unsteady on her feet than I'd ever seen her as she tottered down the corridor.

The Mistress had been so upset that she left the letter on the low dining table. When I saw it lying there, I didn't know what to do.

Anyone who watches TV dramas, especially ones featuring Etsuko Ichihara, would think that housekeepers and maids felt no compunction about reading their family's letters, but it was something we would never do. A long-serving maid who found such a letter lying open like that would instinctively feel that it should be burned, I recall thinking.

I remembered Master Konaka. It was definitely not something the Master, the young Master or anyone else should see, and by Master Konaka's standards it was something that a clever maid should burn, I thought.

However, that didn't mean that things would go as favourably as they had for the English maid in his story. If I took it upon myself to burn the letter or hide it, the Mistress would be troubled when she realized it was gone. But then I couldn't leave it lying around where anyone could read it.

It would probably be best to take the letter to her now, but then she would suspect me of having read it. Even if I told her I hadn't, she would still be left in doubt. And that would be the start of distrust between the Mistress and myself.

I really didn't know what I should do.

So I made up my mind and read the letter.

Young Master Kyoichi's teacher had felt it was his duty to inform the boy's father of what had happened.

The fight that had left his son with a black eye had been with a boy named Sahashi Tatsukichi, that is, the Tatsu who had been best friends with the young Master ever since he had started school. The young Master had apparently come across Tatsu crying and had made fun of him, saying, 'Boys don't cry.' Tatsu had responded by lashing out at him, and so the fight had started.

Tatsu had been crying because he'd had to give up his Shiba dog Taiyo the day before. Big dogs had already been commandeered for use by the military, but people had been allowed to keep their smaller Shiba dogs at home. Eventually, however, the order had come to hand them over, too. A strange rumour was going around that their meat would be canned and their fur used for military clothing to be sent to soldiers on the front.

Tatsu had been distraught at having had to hand over his beloved Taiyo. The young Master used to go over to Tatsu's house and play with the dog too, so he must have known how his friend felt.

The teacher thus suspected there might have been some other reason, and quizzed the boys on it. They hesitated to answer, but gradually it transpired that their relationship had soured somewhat after they had stopped playing with their other friend, Sei.

The boys had always been a threesome, but when Sei's father was arrested on suspicion of spying, the young Master had deserted him. However, Tatsu had secretly continued to play with him. The young Master was not pleased with this, and when he came across Tatsu crying for his dog, had taken his revenge.

'Ishikawa Seita's father is a dangerous character, so it's natural that your son would want to distance himself from the boy. What's more, it was clearly Sahashi Tatsukichi who threw the first punch, so your son got into the fight by responding. However, we cannot permit private fights at a time when we must pull together for the sake of our nation, so I made both parties to blame for the fight stand in the classroom. They have been punished by the school, so I don't think there is any need to scold them further.'

However, there was one other matter that concerned him. According to those who witnessed the fight, Tatsu had said something strange. It probably wasn't true, the teacher said, but the situation being what it was, the Master had better beware of behaviour that might cause misunderstanding—

Now I knew what had caused the Mistress to go so pale.

Boys don't cry!

You've been secretly meeting up with Sei, haven't you? I know all about it.

Huh. I can't believe you're crying just because your dog was taken away.

Unable to bear all the nasty snide comments from young Master Kyoichi, Tatsu had punched him. But the young Master was stronger than him. Put on the defensive, Tatsu had said, out of desperation: *I've seen your mother out with a young man, you know.*

***

I placed the letter in the back of the rack the Mistress used for letters addressed to her, where it wouldn't be seen. It was unthinkable that the Master or the young Master would find it there.

If the Mistress was looking for it, that would probably be the first place she would look and might even think she had put it there herself. If I was asked, I intended to be honest - I had put it there. If questioned further, I was prepared to admit to having read it, too, but the Mistress never mentioned the letter again.

What bothered me most was the question of *when* the Mistress had been seen out with the young man.

Mr. Itakura's home wasn't far from the young Master's school, so it was entirely possible for the two of them to be spotted by pupils. But two years had passed since the Mistress had visited him a number of times over the marriage proposal, and I'd thought they hadn't seen each other since then.

The Mistress rarely had the opportunity to go out alone anymore. And if she did, it was only to attend meetings of the Women's League for the Election of Imperial Rule Assistance, or when Miss Mutsuko invited her to lectures by the Japan's Women's Association.

Had Tatsu merely drawn on a memory from two years earlier to lash out at the young Master, like a cornered rat biting a cat?

Thinking about it, however, I couldn't believe the Mistress lost her cool over a love affair that had finished two years previously. I felt utterly unnerved. I had thought I knew everything about the Mistress, having served her since I was fourteen, yet it appeared there was a side to her that I didn't know.

At dinner, when the Master inquired about the young Master's black eye, the boy awkwardly told him and the Master scolded him for form's sake. A distance was beginning to open up between the two of them. I didn't know whether it was because they were not blood relations, or if it was just that the young Master was at a difficult age.

It was a while later, in autumn, that the Mistress had another shock.

That day, unusually, the young Master's elder cousin Masato was over.

Young Master Masato had graduated from high school and was going on to the science faculty at the Imperial University, and Mistress Tokiko's sister, the Mistress Azabu, boasted at every opportunity about how clever he was.

In contrast, the young Master Kyoichi's school grades were extremely poor. He always took the lead in school events and was cheerful and energetic so he was popular with the teachers, but when it came to exams his marks were always low.

Mistress Tokiko was worried and had asked the young Master Masato to home tutor him, in preparation for entrance to middle school the following year.

Mistress Azabu scoffed, 'Lately new schools are sprouting up like mushrooms after rain, aren't they? The Prefectural Twenty-Third opened recently as I recall. As long as he doesn't try for the Prefectural First or Fourth, it shouldn't be so difficult, should it?'

The Prefectural First and Fourth referred to the most prestigious high schools of the time. Up to about the Prefectural Tenth were long-established schools that would only accept children with exceptionally good marks. Of course, even with the new schools it was still difficult to get into the higher grades. The population of the Tokyo suburbs was growing, and however many new schools were built, they were still highly sought after.

I steamed some sweet potato to take to the two boys studying upstairs, but as I approached, it didn't look like they were studying at all. Young Master Kyoichi was good at flattering people, and he'd managed to get young Master Masato all puffed up.

'Once you go to middle school your studies will get a lot harder since you'll also start learning English and classical Japanese. Anyone who can't keep up is left behind. You really have to put your mind to it, you know,' the bespectacled youngster was saying pompously.

'Is English all that difficult?'

'That depends on your attitude.'

'You don't find it particularly hard, do you Masato?'

'If pushed, I'd have to say I'm rather good at it.'

'How do you say, *Uchite shiyaman* in English?'

'*Uchite shiyaman*? I just read that in a magazine. I think it's, *Until the enemy is crushed.*'

'Anchiru ze...?'

'Until the enemy is crushed.'

'Anchiru ze enemee izu crashuto.'

'Buzzzz,' the young master said, circling his hand above his head, 'Whirrrr, thud-thud-thud kaboom,' making noises of a plane being shot down.

'I think "Until the enemy is crushed" is a motto that can be useful for studying. Not long ago, when I was browsing *Student Days* in the bookstore for the first time in ages, I came across a really interesting article.'

'*Student Days* is that magazine for middle school pupils preparing for exams, isn't it? But you're already at university, Masato! And you didn't even take entrance exams for high school, so why were you reading that sort of thing?'

'Because I like studying! And because their story competition is really good. By the way, that article was titled "Please analyse the phrase *Uchite shiyaman*". It's basically *Uchi-te-shi-yama-n*. Of all the parts of the phrase, the most important is that intensifying adverbial particle '*shi*'. If you're interested in that sort of thing, studying becomes a lot more familiar, you know. One bit of knowledge always leads to another, and in this case it's what sparked my interest in classical texts like the *Record of Ancient Matters* and *The Ancient Ballads*.'

Compared to young Master Kyoichi, his cousin simply didn't seem all that much fun. When he saw the tray of snacks I'd prepared for them his eyes lit up, and he quickly sank his teeth into a sweet potato.

That night, young Master Masato joined the family at dinner and it was quite a lively occasion. Suddenly, the Master announced, 'Mr. Itakura's call-up orders have come. Well, given his age, it's rather late.'

'Call-up orders…?' the Mistress repeated quietly.

In those days everyone knew call-up orders could arrive any time, so she didn't look so much surprised as taciturn, as though recalling something. Young Master Masato asked who Mr. Itakura was, and the Master answered that he was one of his employees.

'Masato, you're currently exempted from conscription, aren't you?'

'I'm studying science, so I can't be sent to fight. My cohorts in the humanities will be going to the front in the autumn, though.'

That's how I remember the conversation, but even young Master Masato was called up in the last year of the war. All those who had originally been told they were exempt were all eventually sent off to fight.

'He's due to enlist in seven days, in his home town of Hirosaki. I told him the factory can manage, so he should go right away and spend some time with his family. However, in his case his only remaining relative is his brother who's been adopted into another family as husband, so there would be nothing for him to do. We'll be giving him a rousing send off at the company tomorrow night.'

'Is that so?' the Mistress said in a small voice. Then, as if having made up her mind, she raised her head and smiled brightly. Her expression was the one she had always worn to wheedle the Master. It was the first time I'd seen it in ages.

'Darling, Mr. Itakura always played with Kyo, and he often came to visit too. He won't be at all comfortable in his brother's house. It's not much, but we could offer him some home cooking for a few days. What do you think?'

For a few moments the Master's chopsticks stopped in midair and he appeared to be considering something. Then he turned to look fixedly at the Mistress, and said, 'Yes, you're right, that is a good idea. Let's do it. Tomorrow I'll enquire about his plans.' Then added, 'I heard he'll probably be sent south.'

He sounded terribly cold as he said this, but maybe it was just my imagination.

Two days later, Mr. Itakura came to visit the Hirais.

It was almost two years since I'd last seen him, and it felt a little strange to see him wearing the nationally mandated khaki civilian uniform. I had a mental image of him with his usual white shirt and light grey trousers, no necktie, and sleeves rolled up.

We'd had a big harvest from the chestnut tree in the garden, so I added some to the rice as I steamed it. I made soup with fish dumplings from the sardines we received on rations, and stewed some sweet potatoes from the garden.

We still had quite a lot of sake left from when I'd called in a favour with the liquor merchant to stock up before sales of alcohol were restricted, so I made hot sake to serve with the dinner. Mr. Itakura wasn't such a big drinker, so I decided to serve it undiluted.

It was a gathering of trusted people, and the congenial atmosphere was accentuated in the dimness of blackout. Mr. Itakura discussed art and architecture, and even commented on details of the house's construction as he had in the old days. He praised the quality of the crockery, and commented on a pot with an arrangement of flowers from the garden. He looked as if he was enjoying himself so much he'd forgotten that he was off to war.

'When are you departing for Hirosaki?' the Mistress asked him, offering him tea.

'I plan to get the night train the day after tomorrow.'

'Oh my, you are in a hurry.'

'I've heard there's a week at most to enlist. Today, thanks to you, I have good memories to look back on,' Mr. Itakura said politely, and bid us all goodnight.

The next day, the Master and young Master were out, and I was doing some gardening when the Mistress called me from inside the house.

'Taki, I'm just popping out.'

I went back inside through the kitchen door to find the Mistress dressed up ready to go out. She was wearing plain meisen silk, but her hair was done up and she was carrying a bundle.

'Oh, where are you going?'

'Um, well.'

'Oh. What time will you back.'

'Um, ah.'

She was being so evasive that alarm bells went off in my head.

It's late, so I'll stop writing for today.

Whatever I write now will no longer be secret, since Takeshi is also reading this. In other words, I have a reader. Meanwhile, that young editor may get back in touch. In which case I might let her read it, too.

I think I should consider this carefully.

I knew in that instant exactly what the Mistress was about to do. And I was at my wits' end thinking I really shouldn't let her do it. It was the middle of the day, and she never knew who might see her visiting his apartment. It was soon after the Master's fight with Tatsu, so you never could know what people might say, even if they just happened to see her at the station.

What's more, society was different back then, reflected by popular slogans like: 'All-out war', 'A decisive battle' and 'Fight to the end'. Even just doing something that could blunt the resolve of a soldier going off to war was enough to invite rumours and accusations of being unpatriotic, which wouldn't affect the Mistress alone, but her entire family, too.

Was this something that Master Konaka would say needed to be burned on the fire? In his story, the maid was considered clever for having done something for her Master that he couldn't do himself, but Mistress Tokiko's circumstances were quite unlike those of the English scholar.

Was it my duty to rein in her passion since she was unable to do so herself? Or should I assist her in what she truly wanted to do?

My head was in a spin.

There were two conflicting urges within me. On the one hand I shouldn't let them meet—they absolutely shouldn't be doing that sort of thing in wartime. On the other, I felt I should help them meet this one last time, since they would probably never see each other again.

Even now I am still undecided, I still don't know.

'Ma'am,' I said. 'It would be better not to go.'

'I'm only going to give him a thousand-stitch belt, you know.'

'In that case, I will take it to him for you.'

'What's up Taki? Why are you being so nasty today?'

'I'm not saying it to be nasty.'

'Get out of my way, will you?'

'No, I won't.'

Even now I am still undecided, I still don't know.

***

'Ma'am,' I said. 'This is what we'll do. Write him a note, and I will deliver it to him today. If he wants to meet tomorrow at one o'clock, he should write you to say so.'

'But why?'

'To get him to come here tomorrow.'

'But why?'

'Because if you go there, you might be seen by someone from the young Master's school, and that would cause problems.'

The Mistress opened her eyes wide in surprise, then looked at me sternly.

'If it's here,' I went on, 'Even if somebody does see, I can come up with an excuse.'

'An excuse?'

'You don't need to hide anything from me. I will think of an excuse. I'll be here, so nobody will gossip about it. But if you don't see Mr. Itakura tomorrow...'

'What then?'

'Please give it up.'

The Mistress put her bundle down on the table.

The following day, before returning to Hirosaki, Mr. Itakura came slowly up the hill. He wore a grey suit with pleated grey trousers and a white shirt with thin necktie.

The Mistress wore a long-sleeved dress made from an old striped cotton kimono. The modern pattern, with the vertical stripes cut on the bias and matched with the arrowhead pattern had been designed by the Mistress and stitched by me. She was more beautiful than ever, with light make-up and her loosely braided hair twisted into a chignon.

The orange blossoms of the sweet osmanthus filled the garden with their heady autumnal fragrance.

I don't know what the couple spoke about, or indeed whether there was any need for them to talk. When Mr. Itakura came into the house, I went outside and concentrated on gardening.

That day, in the little house on the top of the hill, the curtain came down on their love affair.

Chapter 7

Back Home

'Taki, don't you think it's about time for you to head home?'

It must have been towards the end of 1943 when the Mistress called me in and said this to me. I felt as though something had shattered deep in my heart.

I left the Hirai household in March 1944. My time with them is forever stopped there, as vivid as ever despite the passing of the years.

After the war, I served in numerous households, but that was different, on a separate thread of time. Indeed, with each passing year memories of the old days come back to me more distinctly than ever. That's what ageing is. Youngsters like Takeshi don't understand at all.

My chest constricts a little when I recall the slight distance that opened up between the Mistress and myself.

After Mr. Itakura was conscripted in the autumn of 1943, the Mistress lost all her vitality and became listless, no longer speaking much. When sometimes our eyes happened to meet, she quickly looked away, and I began to wish I could reverse what I had done. Even now, at my age, I still don't know whether I did the right thing.

Once cracks open up in your feelings for someone, they will never return to the way they were before. I think a number of things started that day when I read the letter from the teacher at the young Master's school. Or maybe even before then. Just as there was a side to the Mistress I didn't know, she must have felt there was side to me that she had never seen before too.

A secret sometimes strengthens the bond between people, but in some cases it can drive them apart. The fact I knew the Mistress's secret became a dead weight in our relationship.

That autumn, the plan to evacuate Tokyo was announced. Air raids on the city could happen any time, and people in dense residential areas were to evacuate by spring 1944. Buildings were to be demolished, since leaving them standing made them a fire hazard in any bombing raid.

The Hirai house was located amidst the woods and farms of the suburbs, outside the evacuation area. Nevertheless, now they were in the 'critical phase of the war' as the Mistress called it, the atmosphere was oppressive, and all people could talk about was how terribly difficult it was to get hold of food.

In the spring of 1944, young Master Kyoichi entered the middle school he'd set his heart on. The entrance exam had lasted three days, the first day being an oral examination, the next day athletics - long jump, pull-ups, and sprinting, and the third day written examinations. Prefectural Twenty-Fifth was a newly established school and easy to enter according to Mistress Azabu, but for the young Master who hated studying he'd had to work hard to get this result. At any rate, everyone was happy his next school had been decided.

Nonetheless, I'd had it in mind for some time that I would stay on with the Hirais only until the young Master went on to middle school. It was partly because the Mistress had suggested this herself, and also because I'd received a number of letters from home, warning me that it was too dangerous to stay in Tokyo with the threat of air raids and urging me to come home.

Whenever such letters had arrived before, the Mistress had always said, 'I don't want to think about what life will be like without you, Taki,' and I hadn't been able to make up my mind to leave. Now, though, it was time. Looking around, there were very few households with maids left. Neither the Master nor Mistress said anything, but I was aware that people generally thought I was an unnecessary expense for the Hirais.

One winter's afternoon shortly before the young Master entered middle school, I was taking in the washing from the line when he came home and hugged me from behind. He caught me off guard and I fell backwards onto my bottom. Fortunately, I was holding the laundry in front of me so it didn't get dirty. The young master apologized and went to help me up, but then his hand slipped under my arm and touched my breast.

'Hey!' I shouted, and ducked down, clamping my arm to my side, but his fingers had already reached round to the front and I simply succeeded in holding them in place as he squeezed my breast.

I hastily ran from him, but the young Master came striding after me trying to grab me again. I threw the washing down on the veranda, and finally managed to shake myself free of his hand.

'Oh, what a shock you gave me! What do you think you're doing, Master Kyoichi?'

I glared at him, but he just laughed foolishly. He had by now grown taller than me, and a dimple formed in one cheek when he smiled. He had inherited the best of the Mistress and her first husband, and was a good-looking boy with well-defined eyebrows, destined to break a lot of hearts.

In spite of myself I sat on the veranda floor and laughed with him. It was a sunny winter's afternoon, and white camellias were blooming in the garden.

'Kyoichi, go upstairs and do your homework,' came a voice in a rather strict tone from inside. The Mistress had recently stopped calling him by the diminutive Kyo and started using his full name, Kyoichi.

After watching him go upstairs, she came out onto the veranda.

'Kyoichi is no longer a child, you know. What are you laughing about? It's imprudent. You must be more careful.'

'I'm sorry,' I answered.

Things were changing before I even realized it.

I had lived with the Hirais for a little more than eleven years. I had been with the Mistress and young Master Kyoichi since before then, so it must have been over twelve years in all. There can't have been many maids able to serve in one place for so long, and really the Hirai household was everything to me.

To celebrate young Master Kyochi's graduation from elementary school and entrance into middle school, the Hirais held a lively party to which even Granny and Grandad Suga were invited. This was to be my last major event in their service.

It was a luncheon early one afternoon at the end of March, just before the school year began. I made a scattered sushi dish with some white rice I had been hoarding. The main ingredients were strips of pickled gourd and shelled clams, with a touch of colour added by some daikon radish leaves pickled in salt, nori, and a little scrambled egg.

I twisted together strips of daikon radish and carrots to make it look like a decorative cord as a garnish for the soup, grated some yam, and made tempura out of butterbur buds from the garden sprinkled with salt. I also made a dessert from dried persimmons soaked in sweet potato liquor and jellied with agar-agar.

'Oh my, you do put on a good spread in your house, Tokiko,' Granny Suga said appreciatively.

Even with such simple ingredients, by putting in time and effort and being inventive, it did look like a feast of sorts.

The Mistress was good at arranging the food on the plates. With grasses from the garden and red-tinged celestial bamboo fronds to add colour, the meagre dishes looked especially appetizing when served. These decorations weren't edible, but they were soothing for the soul.

After the meal, the young Master paraded his new khaki uniform, and played a card game matching lines from famous patriotic poems. The party ended before it got dark and Granny and Grandad Suga went home, but the young Master was running around in his uniform until late. Dinner that night was a simple savoury rice porridge.

I left the Hirai household two days later. In order not to upset the household's daily routine, I decided to leave quietly, without fanfare, while the young Master was out at his Youth Group meeting.

Of course, I wasn't going to leave without saying anything, and had chosen my moment carefully to inform him. 'Japan's going to beat all her enemies, so you'll come back then, won't you, Taki?' he'd said. I think that only a short time ago he would have cried, too, but he was a big boy now, already starting middle school, and contained himself.

During the last few months the relationship between the Mistress and myself had grown awkward, but even so, she packed up some kimonos and clothes for me to take.

'Ma'am, I can't accept these. You'll be able to exchange them for food, so you should keep them.'

'It's okay. It's a token of my sentiments. I had always intended to give you a new kimono and some jewellery when you married.'

There were so many of them I didn't know what to do. I decided to get her to choose one kimono and one dress for me to take. I had lived in this house for over ten years and what little I had in the way of personal belongings would fit into two cloth bundles to take home with me.

'And this,' she said, holding out a gold-edged teacup.

'Oh no, I couldn't possibly accept anything as valuable as that.'

'But look, we've been using this set for so long that we only have two cups left. I can't use them for entertaining guests, and the truth is I had thought of putting them out with the metal collection, but it completely slipped my mind.'

'But Mistress Tokiko, it's a gift from when you were married, isn't it?'

'Taki, your memory is really sharp, isn't it? But you and I are the only ones who know that. This is what I want to do: I want you to take one, and I will keep the other. We'll each keep one cup and one saucer from the set. Don't you think that's fun? It's a memento of our long time together. When the war's over and things have calmed down again, if you still haven't married yet, you can bring it back to me.'

'I'm not going to get married. I don't want to, and there isn't anyone for me to marry anyway.'

'You don't know that. Once we win the war, a lot of soldiers will be returning in triumph, you know. A healthy young woman like you will be in high demand, Taki.'

'I wonder.'

'Of course you will! With your training, you can be a bride in the best of families,' the Mistress said, laughing merrily. I got a little sentimental, but the Mistress didn't cry. That was one of the things I liked about her.

When it was time to leave, I gave her all the details about the tradesmen, including the farmer Mr. Kitamura, and the fishmonger I was friendly with. Mr. Kitamura, who had a farm in Nerima, had contacts in the army and the military police, so they turned a blind eye to his black market goods. He sometimes had not just the vegetables and fruit he'd grown himself, but also rice and beans, or even butter or canned foods. If she gave him money, he'd share some with her. In the case of the fishmonger and rice merchant, these goods were rationed, so they couldn't be so flexible, but given how accommodating I'd been with them they'd still sometimes slip me an extra flounder or reserve the bigger fish for me.

'Oh my, you really did do all sorts of things for us, didn't you? How are we going to manage without you, Taki?' the Mistress said worriedly when I finished explaining.

'Don't worry, it'll be fine. I've asked everyone to give this house special treatment.'

I didn't want to leave, but it was time for me to go and get my train.

The Master came out to say goodbye. 'We're going to miss you,' he said, although he wasn't normally one to let his feelings show.

It was ten years since I'd last been back to Yamagata. I had taken advantage of the one-day holiday servants were given twice yearly, at New Year and in the summer, to go home during my first two years in service. However, I hadn't been back since 1934, when there had been widespread crop failures in the Tohoku region and a letter came telling me they didn't have enough food, so I ought not to come home.

I had occasionally been to visit my relatives in Kasukabe, just north of Tokyo, when I'd had some time off, but I'd stopped doing even that. Before I knew it I felt more at home in Tokyo. Whenever I think of 'home', it's in that red-roofed house on top of the hill with the Mistress and the young Master. I never knew when I might be married off, and at some point I'd started hoping it would be to someone who lived close enough to the Hirais that I could continue working as a maid for them.

This was always something that worried me about going to see my parents. Where I was from, it was the norm to get married before twenty, so I was already long past it. They were bound to marry me off. And once I'd been married off to a not-so-young man left in the village, it was highly unlikely that I would ever be able to return to Tokyo.

I was planning to leave on the night train departing Ueno at seven that evening, but I left the Hirais before noon. I hadn't exactly wanted to take a last look at Tokyo, but the Mistress told me she couldn't make me work right up until the very last minute and sent me on my way early.

I changed onto a train for Ueno at Shinjuku Station, and suddenly found myself reminiscing about my time in the city. Reluctant to go home, I started fantasizing about going to Shinagawa and boarding a train for Kamakura. Of course, I didn't actually do it, though. Kamakura was a distant memory full of nostalgia.

In the end I didn't do much, and spent the time hanging around in Ueno Park. These weren't the times for sightseeing.

The reason I decided to go back home in March had nothing to do with my own circumstances. Rather, it was because tickets for long-distance travel would be restricted from the following month and I ran the risk of not being able to get one at all.

And I wasn't the only one: Ueno Station was jammed with people evacuating the city, so there was a long queue just to buy a ticket. I thought of going into a savoury rice porridge restaurant that everyone was talking about at the time, but there were long queues there, too, and in the end, they sold out just before it was my turn. I hadn't expected much from it, but still it infuriated me to find I couldn't have any.

From what the old lady next to me in the queue said, one serving was not enough to fill your stomach, so lots of people went back for seconds and even thirds. I got indignant all over again thinking that it was their fault there was such a long queue in the first place.

There was a little more time before my train, so I went into a cinema near the station to see *Colonel Kato's Falcon Squadron*.

I got on the train still feeling hungry, changed trains at Fukushima in the middle of the night, and finally reached my family's home the following morning. I had been away for so long that I didn't feel particularly emotional or happy to be back.

I recall being dressed in striped baggy pants with a dark brown overcoat, and my little sister telling me that my coat reeked of Tokyoite.

I hadn't seen my parents for over ten years, so of course they had aged, but still my mother was delighted to see me and welcomed me home with a delicious stew. It had been a long time since I'd tasted the rich local miso broth full of potatoes.

Of my five siblings, my eldest brother had returned injured from the war and been working in a factory in Sendai but had now moved back home together with his wife and two children due to the fear of air raids on major cities.

My next eldest brother was still serving as a soldier overseas, but my two elder sisters had evacuated with their children after their husbands were sent off to war and were living here too. My youngest sister, some years younger than me, had never left home, since she was not yet married. Takeshi is this sister's grandson, incidentally.

The house had never been intended to accommodate so many family members, and I worried whether there was really enough space for me to be here too.

I didn't have to worry for long, however, since I was soon conscripted to work in an aircraft factory in Yamagata city. As it turned out, the time I spent living with my parents and siblings was very brief, and I moved to the worker dormitory in the city a short hop across the mountains.

Communal meals were just rice with daikon radish or rice with sorghum, and we all shared a large room, so it was a huge change from the life I'd led at the Hirais' in Tokyo. The dormitory was infested with fleas and lice, like everywhere in those days, and I was at my wits' end being bitten constantly.

Furthermore, whenever I inadvertently talked longingly about Tokyo, someone would inevitably say spitefully, 'Putting on airs again, are we?'

The others had all been conscripted, too, of course. There were some elderly carpenters and a group of rural women from the red light district's ladies' volunteer corps, which sounded a lot to me like a 'geisha kamikaze squad'. They had thrown themselves into the work after the local paper flattered them for being good at making fiddly aircraft parts, due to their dexterity from playing the shamisen.

In the ten years since I'd last been home, Yamagata had become a major centre for aircraft manufacture. It came as a surprise, since the only industries I associated with it, other than agriculture, were silkworms and textiles. They'd had to do something in order to survive the famine that followed widespread crop failures and the depression, as well as restrictions on textiles exports. I was told so often that I had calluses on my ears that as we hurtled into the final stages of the war, it had become the biggest aircraft producer in all Japan.

And the changes hadn't just occurred in the prefectural capital.

'Luckily our prefecture has mountain forests with lots of beech trees. Given our expertise, we can increase production further with excellent wooden fighter planes!'

The slogan 'Increase Production for the Nation!' written in big letters was stuck up on the factory wall, and the manager would recite it at the top of his lungs every day at the morning assembly.

I was tasked with polishing wooden propellers day in, day out, but they reminded me of the toys the Master used to make, which upset me. Once tinplate ran out, he had ended up making toy aeroplanes from plywood, paper or rayon. The tinplate fighter planes the young Master had been so proud of were fitted with exquisite propellers.

If we ever stopped making wooden propellers Japan would probably lose the war, I thought, but anyway, I focused on the work I had before me. If I thought about anything it was about life in Tokyo, and about the Mistress and the young Master. It wasn't for the likes of me to talk about the state of the war or aircraft manufacture.

When I heard that middle school pupils from all over Yamagata were to be roped into the construction work on a new airstrip at Jinmachi Osanagihara and made to carry construction materials in straw bundles hung from a long pole, the image of the young Master came keenly back to me. It was around April 1944, when I was working in the factory, that work was to start in the desolate, flat-as-a-pancake piece of land in the Murayama Basin.

Rumours started of schoolchildren, only one or two years older than the young Master and not yet fully formed, being woken up at four in the morning and marched over snowy paths in the dark to the construction site, where they were made to work all day long without even being fed.

I couldn't bear the thought of the young Master in his new school being mobilized into hard labour that even robust adult men would find hard to bear. He was stronger physically than he had been as a child and was in good enough shape to do as well as the best of them, but he had been brought up in the city and was delicate, not at all suited to physical work.

Whenever I heard words of sympathy for the boys, I would feel so unspeakably sad that I wanted to cover up my ears.

With the arrival of summer, a new job came my way. It was decided that my village would take in schoolchildren evacuees. A woman was needed to cook for them and take care of their needs, and I was the one singled out for it.

Around forty children were coming from Tokyo, accompanied by one male teacher and a matron. Whoever was going to care for this group of children separated from their parents ideally needed to be able to speak standard Japanese and have knowledge of life in the city, said the chief priest of the temple where they were to stay. Being told that I was the only one capable of providing all-round care as well as managing the kitchen and laundry, I could hardly refuse.

The chief priest negotiated with the village leaders and I was let go from the aircraft factory. The children were due to arrive early in September. I was happy to leave the town, but I was reluctant to go back to my parents' house, already filled to the rafters, and so it was decided I would live at the temple.

I was excited about being able to look after boys and girls from Tokyo. Beaming widely, I went to the unmanned station in our village to greet them with a banner that said, 'Welcome, good children!'

However, looking after schoolchildren evacuees was not as easy as I'd thought. They were all from the fourth to sixth grades of elementary school, but they had an entirely different air to the children at the school the young Master had attended. Plus, they had never been separated from their parents before, so it was hard on them.

They slept six or seven together in rooms with a sixth grader as group leader, but when night fell, oh boy did they start crying for their parents, wetting their beds, secretly taking laxatives to give themselves diarrhoea, and slipping out of the temple to set out for Tokyo along the railroad tracks, so that I couldn't take my eyes off them even for a moment.

To begin with, perhaps helped by their nervousness at coming to a new place, they did at least do as they were told, obediently studying in a classroom borrowed from the local elementary school and helping with farm work, but after a month or so their true characters began to show and they stopped listening to me altogether. It was terrible!

If I didn't do spot checks during the night, the bad ones would be ordering others around and bullying the weak ones, sandwiching them between mattresses and suffocating them almost to death, so I couldn't get a good night's sleep.

It really was no joke. One night when I went to check on them, in one room I found all the mattresses in a big pile, with six or so children jumping up and down on top of them and one big boy bellowing out orders, 'Jump higher!' When I made them stop because it was dangerous, there was a groan from inside the pile of mattresses, and who should crawl out gasping for breath but one of the boys.

'What do you think you're doing?' I shouted, blowing my top. 'What if he died? I'm going to tell your teacher about this right now,' I stormed, and turned on my heel to go tell the supervising teacher without further ado. However, the skinny victim, barely breathing, rushed out into the corridor after me, threw his arms around me, and tearfully begged me not to say anything.

I looked down at the boy with his arms around my waist and noticed a patch of his hair had been ripped out. They must be hurting him regularly. If I said anything, he might be treated even worse behind my back.

I had never seen such a pitiful child before. My heart ached at the thought that back in the city these children would all be cared for by parents who cherished them, even if they weren't spoiled to the extent of the young Master.

I ended up not saying anything, but I couldn't ignore what I'd seen and had to patrol every night to ensure there were no more mattress sandwiches.

When I thought that young Master Kyoichi might have been in one of these evacuee groups had he been born a year later, I couldn't sleep for the horror of it. The young Master was a strong fighter, so he probably wouldn't be killed in a mattress sandwich, but what scared me most was not just the thought of it happening to him, but that he might actually be the one doing it.

On top of that, there wasn't anything to eat. In Tokyo I had connections and insider information, and could use my influence on the various traders that came to the house. Plus, the Hirai household had money and belongings to trade, so I could stock up on items when available. But here there was no way of ensuring a sufficient supply of food for the children beyond the rice rations and living expenses we received from the municipal office.

When the chief priest of the temple had gone to Tokyo to pick up the children, the parents had apparently pressed him on whether there was enough food, since Yamagata was known to be a poor prefecture. He had seen red and retorted caustically, 'As long as their bellies're full, wass' there to complain about?'

When I complained about the lack of food, he fumed at me that even if it was impossible to keep their bellies full, I should somehow contrive to make it go around. But a fighting spirit simply wasn't enough when it came to managing the kitchen.

'Er, but we got over forty mouths to feed, right? There jus' ain't enough to go round.'

'Use yer head woman. Go and beg any farmers yer know. Get 'em all to give a bit.'

'But what if I'm found out and get into trouble?'

'So make sure yer don' get found out!'

'But it's the black market, and I won't get nothin' fer free.'

'Humph,' he gave a disgruntled snort and took off his mantle. I took it from him wordlessly.

'It ain't just breakfast and supper, though. I have to make 'em all a packed lunch too, but there ain't no rice or nothin'.'

'Sort the details fer yerself, woman! It's not fer a chief priest to have to worry about lunch boxes dammit!'

I couldn't argue with that, so I decided to think about what to put in their lunch boxes myself. I often gave them devil's tongue jelly pickled in miso and wild herbs in sweetened soy sauce scattered on top of their ration of brown rice.

The priest was a stickler for table manners and would chant a sutra before meals and say, 'Thank you to all the soldiers,' bowing his head. After the meal, he would have the children put their hands together as in prayer and say in unison, 'Receiving such delicious food gives us a hundred times more courage to work hard for our country. Thank you for our meal.' I felt terrible when they said this. Even though I'd made the food myself, it wasn't in any way tasty and hardly deserved the thanks.

I carried black market rice and vegetables hidden in a big cloak and did everything I could to give them enough to eat, but even so it was never enough. Some of them would steal the raw rice cake offering to the Buddha to crunch on, or someone else's lunch boxes. Sometimes they would steal persimmons hung up to dry in local farmhouses. They really were a bunch of little devils.

Now and then parents would come from Tokyo to visit, and then they would again be angelic little darlings, laughing merrily and enjoying being spoiled. This was a harsh reminder of how terrible it was to separate such small children from their parents. I felt so sorry for those who received no visitors that I resorted to making my little sister bring some stewed pumpkin, so we could spend some time with them eating it.

The boy who had almost died in the mattress sandwich turned out to be from a surprisingly wealthy family. His sweet-looking mother came to see him and gave him food, but by the next day it had all been stolen by the other children. He apparently didn't tell her about being bullied, but I wonder what she thought when she saw his bald patch.

One day, the same boy brought a frog to the kitchen.

'I found it while working in the fields. The teacher told me to give it to you, Ma'am.'

The teacher had probably told him to bring it to me to stop the children from fighting over it. I cut it open there and then and skewered it on a stick, doused it in soy sauce, and grilled it.

'Eat,' I said, holding it out to him, but he just looked at me, confused. 'Eat!'

'What?'

'Look, I'm telling you to eat it up,' I said, speaking in a Tokyo accent. 'Nobody's watching. If anyone asks, tell them I chopped it up and mixed it into the rice for everybody to eat at dinner.'

'But—'

'Finders keepers, right? Eat it up, quick!'

'You sound just like my mother!'

He must have felt a little homesick hearing me speak in a Tokyo accent instead of the local dialect.

He wasn't like young Master Kyoichi at all, but still there was something that reminded me of him.

Since returning to Yamagata, I had often taken my city clothes out to gaze upon them. Not just the ones the Mistress had given me the day I left, but everything she'd handed down to me since

I'd entered her service aged fourteen and I'd re-tailored for myself to wear. They were all such good quality I couldn't possibly wear them here in the countryside, so the only way to enjoy them was to open up the bundle to look at them.

There were times I got up early in the morning when it was still quite dark, checked that nobody else was awake, then stood in front of the full-length mirror trying them on. Taking each piece of clothing in turn, it was fun to recall the Mistress who used to wear them, and how I'd felt when she'd given them to me. I would secretly imitate the Mistress's gestures before the mirror. Since I was told by that poor boy that I spoke like someone from Tokyo, I tried speaking even more like her.

Recalling life in Tokyo was like a dream. It would come back to me when I was relaxing alone at night before going to sleep.

My memories were all of Mistress Tokiko: the young, still girlish Mistress in a polka dot dress flying out of a side street; the Mistress all excited about the newly built house; the Mistress in a light summer kimono listening to jazz on the company president's gramophone, her expression when she'd wanted so much to go the Kabukiza concert that she lost her temper. I would recall the oil she put on her hair, the folded paper cases she wrapped her kimonos in, her perfume bottles, the black tea in a blue tin—all the items the Mistress had liked so much and their fragrances.

During the day, when I was with the children, it was always young Master Kyoichi who came to mind, but before sleep I always had visions of Mistress Tokiko on this or that day. How proud I was to have lived at her side!

For some reason, someone else I often recalled was Miss Mutsuko, and her cool, dry hands as they enveloped mine.

'Tokiko was really gorgeous when we were at school, you know. She was the prettiest girl in the school, and everyone was in love her. That's how it was back then. One girl in particular was really obsessed with her and wrote her a love letter every day and hung around her on the way to and from school. She was so in love that she couldn't concentrate on her studies and even had to change schools the following year so eventually she was able to graduate and go on to women's college. When Tokiko got married, she went out and got stinking drunk and sank into despair, making a huge scene generally. Beautiful women are cruel, they say.'

Then she'd started quoting a rather difficult passage from a story. What had Miss Mutsuko been trying to say? Did she know something?

My Tokyo was forever cheerful and fun. And as the days went by, in my mind it was painted over with the gay atmosphere that the Mistress had loved so much, the dingy atmosphere of places like the savoury rice porridge dining hall completely shoved aside.

While I was up north looking after the children, though, terrible things were happening in the capital. After the fall of Saipan, the Prime Minister changed from Mr. Tojo to Mr. Koiso, who was originally from Yamagata, and suddenly the newspapers and magazines were full of the possibility of a final showdown on the mainland. The B29s they had been warning us about finally attacked the city in the autumn of 1944. We frequently heard rumours of further air raids on Tokyo after that.

The area I now lived in, however, was sparsely populated and there were no military targets in our village, so we were not at risk from air raids. I found it hard to even imagine what it must be like to have to flee amidst falling firebombs.

As long as I was in the countryside daydreaming, I could keep the illusion of life continuing in Tokyo as I had always known it.

There's not much I can say about New Year 1945. I made a clear soup with rice cakes floating in it for the children, and the priest chanted a sutra in gratitude. That was about it.

In February, there was talk of sending the sixth graders back to Tokyo so they could take the entrance examination to go on to middle school.

Of course, rumours of B29s violating the airspace over the imperial capital reached us. Some of the evacuees had even lost family members and relatives. Even so, the sixth graders brightened up upon learning they were being sent back, probably imagining they would find their old lives waiting for them.

To be honest, I was envious of them. I believed I would never be able to go to Tokyo ever again. But life is full of surprises.

It turned out that the male teacher who had come from Tokyo with them had developed a bad cough and was immediately taken into isolation after being diagnosed with tuberculosis. It was a common story in those times when nutrition was so poor.

That meant that somebody else would have to take the children to Tokyo. The matron who had come with them mostly cared for the youngest children, and was needed to continue their care. In any case, losing both of their original supervisors was not exactly advisable. There had been some talk of someone from the prefectural assembly office in charge of arrangements for evacuees going with them, but he'd said he was far too busy to go, the chief priest grumbled.

An electric charge ran through me. This was my chance to go and see the Mistress. If I missed it, I'd never go to Tokyo again. Every time I heard of an air raid on the city, I would fret about the family's safety, even though they lived out in the suburbs. This was my last chance to see that house with the red roof again.

'I'll go.'

'What? You?'

'I lived in Tokyo fer a long time, and know it well. I'll go.'

'But who'll cook if yer not here?'

'I'll get me sister ter stand in fer me. She comes ter help out sometimes anyways.'

For the first time in ages, I forced myself to think hard. Yes, I'd get my little sister to stand in for me so that I could take the sixth graders to Tokyo. We would probably go by night train, arriving in Tokyo in the morning. If I took the night train back again, I would have some time to myself during the day.

I would take all the rice and wild vegetables I could conceal on my person. That way, I would at least be able to leave some food for the Mistress, even if I wasn't able to meet her. I would get to see my beloved house on the hill one more time.

I was sorry for the teacher who had gone down with tuberculosis, but it was a rare stroke of good fortune for me.

There were some who questioned whether the maid who cooked for the children was capable of supervising fifteen or so sixth graders, or whether it would be better to get someone to come from Tokyo to collect them. However, the chief priest vouched for me and insisted that they would be fine in my hands, and so it was decided.

On 6th March1945, I boarded a train along with fifteen sixth grade children.

'So what was going on with the war?' Takeshi demanded, pouting in frustration. 'Nan, you hardly mention the war at all in your stories. It was getting really bad by then, wasn't it? The navy was being annihilated in the Battle of Leyte Gulf, and the kamikaze were being sent out by then too. And what about the Philippines falling to the enemy? You must have known about Iwojima too, right?'

When Takeshi talks about 'the war', what he really means are 'the soldiers' and 'the navy' and 'the fighting' and that sort of thing.

By the time 1945 came around, even I had to accept the war was getting closer and we could expect fighting on the mainland at any time. As for the overseas territories, what was the point of all the information we were fed daily about them?

The only time civilians ever talked about the war was when things were peaceful for us. Master Hirai used to like that sort of talk. Now that air raid sirens were a regular feature of daily life in Tokyo, however, I doubt there was much talk of the South Sea islands.

The night train departed from our local station at eight o'clock in the evening. The children were super excited and couldn't settle down initially, but they'd all fallen asleep by nine o'clock. I suppose they were exhausted, and also relieved to be going home.

I gazed out of the window into the pitch black, recalling the time I had first taken the train away from my home. That had been such a long time ago. Japan had completely changed over the course of those fifteen or so years.

The train arrived at Ueno on the morning of the seventh. The children gave shouts of joy when they saw their parents waiting and rushed over to them. Little did I know that some of those very children would fall victim to the great air raid that happened three days later.

I had half a day before the night train back to Yamagata would be departing from Ueno. I wasted no time in going to the savoury rice porridge dining hall, so I didn't miss out. The rice porridge with green vegetables was indeed tasty, but not in the slightest filling.

I had sent the Mistress a postcard informing her I would be coming to Tokyo, so after eating, I caught the train straight out to the Hirai house. The Tokyo I saw from the train window had been transformed into something utterly unfamiliar, more like a snaggle-toothed mouth than anything else.

Where there should have been houses were now rude, empty lots. Some of them had probably been destroyed in air raids, but many had been demolished as part of the air raid measures. Part of me couldn't help wondering whether it had really been necessary to demolish them before they were hit, though.

As we pulled out of Shinjuku, the scenery changed to that of the outskirts, with fields and trees planted as windbreaks. At last I could relax and breathe freely. I began to feel as though I'd come home.

When I got off the train and looked around, I saw a military base with antiaircraft artillery in the distance, now occupying a large area on the opposite side of the station from the Hirais'.

Starting up the hill, I looked up to see the house I loved so much still standing there as before. Not only was it unchanged, the trees in the garden had grown even taller, and it blended quietly into the surrounding scenery. The white stucco on the entrance, the Western-style red-tiled roof, the stone steps of the porch, and the thick pillars all added to its poise and charm. The pussy willow wore its silken headdresses, yellow flowers in full bloom.

The front door opened. A figure came out into the garden and slowly approached the gate.

'Taki?'

The Mistress had grown thinner in the time since I'd last seen her and, most unusually for her, was dressed in baggy work pants, a cotton hand towel wrapped around her neck. She came out of the gate and started running down the hill towards me.

'Oh, I've been waiting impatiently all morning for you! It's so good to see you. Really, I'm so happy you're here.'

I felt all the strength leave my body. Holding hands, we went into the house.

The smells and colours, and even the rustling of the garden felt like part of my own body. I was surrounded by things that were utterly dear to me. I had returned to the house that I had already known long ago was the one place I felt most at home.

'The Master is out at a meeting of the civil defence unit. Kyoichi is at school. They're made to do drill after drill—it's really tough, apparently. He's often scolded for not being able to put on his gaiters properly, even though he practices at home every night. I somehow feel that I'm the one being scolded. He started second grade in April, so he's been mobilized into the workforce now, you know. Oh, but I'm so glad you're here, Taki! Really, I'm so happy to see you.'

She showed me into the reception room and told me to take a seat. 'I'll go and make some tea,' she said.

'No, I'll do it. But first, I have to give you these,' I said, taking off my air-raid hood, padded jacket, and bellyband. 'I'm sorry I couldn't bring very much, though.'

'Oh, what's this?'

It had been a lot of work to prepare everything. I couldn't let anyone know I was doing it, so I'd had to work at night when everyone was asleep. I had sown rice into the hood and jacket. To stop it all pooling, I'd made lots of little cloth packages which I'd then stitched into the garments. The rice was fresh from the autumn harvest, and I'd polished it to make proper white rice. I'd got it on the black market from farmers who supplied the military, in exchange for the kimonos the Mistress had given me. In my money belt, I had packed some whole dried fish from a big catch of large pilchards off the coast of Yamagata, wrapped in bamboo sheaths. Normally it wouldn't be anything special, but all fish was precious these days.

'Taki, what the…' the Mistress started, then put both hands to her mouth, speechless.

'You didn't think I'd come to visit you empty handed, did you, Ma'am?'

I headed out to the kitchen to pour the tea.

'Wait. Wait!' the mistress called, running after me. 'Use the roasted green tea. It's on the top shelf of the mouse-proof cupboard.'

Yes, Ma'am, I answered, meeting her eye, and we both laughed.

How can I explain? It was the Hirais' kitchen. In other words, the one and only place in the world that was mine.

The Mistress and I spent the next two hours together, just the two of us.

As I took the tea into the reception room, I felt as though I had never been away.

Mistress Tokiko filled me in on what everyone had been doing, how the Master and young Master spent each day, how bespectacled young Master Masato had been conscripted, and her parents had evacuated to Fukui.

And then a gleeful look crossed her face, as though she had thought up some kind of mischief. 'Hey, Taki, what would you like to eat now?' she asked.

'What? Now? But I had lunch at Ueno.'

'No, no! What I mean is, if you could have anything you liked to eat, anything at all, what would it be? Whenever Kyochi and I start in on this, the Master gets really annoyed and tells us not to be greedy. But where's the harm in it? All we're doing is remembering and having fun. For example, right now I want to eat some Columbin shortcake.'

I looked at her in surprise, and she burst out laughing.

'What's wrong, Taki? I said it was just for fun, didn't I? It's not like I said let's actually eat it.'

In my mind's eye, I could see the building in Ginza 6-chome with a small Eiffel Tower on it that housed the stylish coffee shop called Columbin. And then, somehow, I was inundated with the memories, smells and sounds of the bustling city centre before the war.

'Ma'am,' I said, as a thought occurred to me. 'If that's the case, then I'd like some curry rice from Shiseido.'

'That's the ticket. You always did love curry, Taki, didn't you?' the Mistress said clapping her hands in delight, suddenly quite animated. 'Since we're at Shiseido, I'll have some meat croquettes.'

'And what will young Master Kyoichi have?'

'He's at school, so we'd better take him something for later. I know, let's get him some ice cream.' Shiseido would put vanilla ice cream into a blue thermos pot with a handle for you to take home.

'Restaurant Alaska was always the Master's favourite.'

'And the Tokyo Kaikan.'

'How about the Senbikiya?'

'Fuji Ice!'

'Nagafuji Bakery!'

'If you've had your fill of Western food, then let's ask my sister to bring us some roasted bean snacks from Mamegen in Azabu.'

'Salty and sweet ones?'

'Of course! You can mix salty and sweet ones. But if we're going to get something from Azabu, then rather than beans I'd go for sushi pockets myself.'

'Oh yes, from the Otsuna sushi shop.'

'Oh, what I would give to eat some yuzu flavoured ones now!'

It was hardly surprising that the Master would tell her to stop. This game was fun the first time, but I could imagine it'd be really painful after a while.

After sitting quietly without speaking for a while, the Mistress held her teacup in both hands and gazed into what was left of her tea. 'You know, there's one particular food I sometimes get a craving for. Not in Tokyo, though—I mean the dumplings from the Niraso. Taki, do you remember Mr. Itakura?'

The question was so abrupt I wasn't sure how to answer, so I said nothing. Only a year and a half had passed since then, so of course I wouldn't have forgotten, but it wasn't surprising that the Mistress would ask something so strange. The Tokyo in which Mr. Itakura had existed was long gone.

'I'd thought he'd at least send me a postcard from the front, but not a squeak. I don't suppose he ever gets the chance, but still, I hope he's safe.'

So, she still hasn't forgotten him, I thought bitterly. I sneaked a look at her and was surprised to see her smiling brightly.

'You were so scary that time, Taki.'

'That time?'

'Yes, the day before Mr. Itakura went back to his hometown,' she went on, still smiling. 'You were really anxious for me, I know, but I got a bit short with you after that, didn't I? It's been really bothering me all this time, you know. I'm so glad I could tell you that now,' she said smoothly, then stood up and went over to the veranda.

***

What on earth did I mean to write about?

Even now, at my age, I'm still stung with regrets. By writing all this down I've really opened up a Pandora's box of things I'd firmly locked away.

I wish I hadn't let Takeshi see this. I won't show it to him anymore. I must find a good hiding place for it again.

There hasn't been any sight or sound of that woman from the publishers, but in any case, if I ever do show her anything, it certainly won't be this.

Happy times pass quickly.

I'd finally managed to meet the Mistress again after so long, but now it was time to leave I began to regret having come, only to have to go through the pain of separation again.

Once again she brought out some kimonos from her chest of drawers, and told me to take the ones I liked back with me.

'No, I can't accept those.'

'That's not fair. You brought me those lovely gifts, yet I'm not allowed to return the favour. That's not right, you know.'

'In that case, maybe I could take a jacket, since I'm leaving mine with you.'

Recalling my jacket with the rice bags sewn inside it, the Mistress exclaimed, 'Yes, yes of course!' and smiled. She went to her room and came back with a dark grey woollen coat.

'I can't accept that. It's far too good quality.'

'It's all I have. There's still snow where you are, isn't there?' she said, and wound a woollen scarf around my neck too.

When she urged me to take something else, I asked if young Master Kyoichi might have any books he no longer needed. If so,

I could take them back for the evacuees to read. I still have that copy of Noboru Oshiro's *Expedition to Mars* even now.

The young Master had apparently lost interest in children's manga once he went up to middle school. Now he was set on the naval pilot training course with its seven-button uniform, and had no intention of going on to senior high school, the Mistress said hopelessly, curling up one side of her mouth.

'Do come back once the war is over, won't you?' she said, seeing me off as far as the gate.

'Will this war ever be over?' I asked, unable to imagine it ending.

'Oh, it will. What starts will one day end. I don't know when, though.'

'Well then, I will come back.'

'I'll be waiting for you.'

The Mistress didn't cry this time either. She stood with her hand on the gate, her back straight and a bright smile on her face, waving goodbye.

I don't know how to write about what happened after that.

I went back to Yamagata on the night train as planned, and resumed the daily routine of caring for the children.

Two days later, the eastern part of Tokyo was destroyed in a massive air raid.

Even the local newspaper ran a report with the headline 'Imperial City Carpet Bombed by 300 B29s', but with fifteen enemy planes shot down and fires that had been brought under control, I couldn't even begin to imagine the extent of the damage.

The next day or the day after that, the municipal office informed the chief priest that some of the children who had gone back to Tokyo to prepare for entrance into middle school had died in the air raid.

Hot on the heels of this news, a postcard arrived from Mistress Tokiko.

The factory burned down and the company president and his family are left with nowhere to live, so have returned to their hometown. The fires didn't reach as far as us, and we are safe. My sister in Azabu is talking about going to stay with relatives of her brother-in-law in Yamanashi. The Master is talking about moving further out and starting farming or something. I don't want to leave this house. Take care of yourself. Yours.

I still treasure this postcard today, too.

And my days continued with me cooking rice with sweet potatoes or daikon radish and airing the lice-ridden bedding. The local paper ran an editorial exhorting everyone to 'Win the war in Yamagata—hold out like our brave soldiers in Rabaul!' The chief priest was so impressed he stuck it up on the temple walls.

By then I didn't even have the energy to think how unsuited that sort of thing was to a temple, but having seen it every day, I can remember it pretty much word for word.

Tenacity. Tenacity is what determines whether you win or lose. If we do whatever we can to drag the war out as long as we can, which is what the enemy wants least, there will be nothing to fear from them reaching the mainland. If each

of our prefecture's one million residents swears to kill one
person, then in that way alone a million enemy soldiers will
be exterminated. Even if the fires of war reach all corners of
the mainland, if our people are determined to fight to the
last, the final victory will be ours. We share Prime Minister
Koiso's belief that all we have to do is be prepared to give
our lives in service at all times. Everybody in the nation is
willing to fight like crazy without the need for thinking or
speaking. This will gain us time. Women too must kill the
enemy, taking up bamboo spears against the invaders and
stabbing them through. Let's look to our brave soldiers in
Rabaul, building an impregnable fortress determined to win
even now when our planes and ships cannot reach them.
Let's make our Yamagata like Rabaul!

Yamagata probably wasn't the only prefecture putting out rallying
calls like this. All around Japan, people were saying, 'Be like
Rabaul!' and even Miss Mutsuko's magazine *Housewives Delight*
printed slogans along the lines of: 'Kill as many as you can!' on
every page.

I don't know how to write about what happened after that. I
really don't.

My days continued unchanged. I cooked rice with
sweet potato or daikon radish and aired the lice-infested
bedding.

'It's the very tenacity of Yamagata natives, stolid and bovine,
that will lead our nation to victory,' the chief priest would say. I
couldn't tell whether he was being pompous or servile, but either

way I was fed up with his sermons. Meanwhile, I continued to care for the children day in day out.

The days passed without me knowing anything about the things that really mattered. And before I knew it, something important had happened.

The great air raid on eastern Tokyo on 10th March had coincided with Army Commemoration Day, and some people were saying something similar might happen on 27th May, Navy Commemoration Day. There were so many rumours flying around in those days, though.

But then, two days before Navy Commemoration Day, the capital city was attacked again, this time by two hundred and fifty B29s. Even the Imperial Palace had been bombed, the newspaper said, but His Highness had been safe in the palace sanctuary three floors underground. It didn't say anything about which parts of the city had been firebombed, though.

The one time I felt really afraid for myself was in July when I heard Sendai had been bombed. Everyone was saying that Yamagata would be next.

I heard vaguely about a new type of bomb having been dropped on Hiroshima, but more immediately I recall the sky over the Jinmachi airstrip turning red on 9th August. The aircraft factory where I had once worked was also destroyed in that air raid. On the 10th, Sakata, Tsuruoka, Shinjo, and Tateyama were hit, and on the 13th Jinmachi was hit again, and everyone was whispering that all towns in the prefecture were done for.

On 15th August I listened to the imperial broadcast announcing the surrender on the temple radio. I don't really remember what I felt at the time. I think I was relieved. Just as the Mistress had said, what was started sometime had to end. And the war had ended.

Even so, my days continued unchanged.

The quantity of rice with sweet potato or daikon radish was reduced even further, but still I carried on making it and hung the bedding out to air. The children had pitifully distended bellies from a lack of nutrition.

The war ended, and the jeeps of the occupation forces came to the countryside too.

But how should I write about that?

Each and every day that went by was leaving behind something really important.

My daily life continued unchanged, the war ended and I saw the occupation force's jeeps, all without having any inkling that the Mistress's life was now forever in the past.

I don't know how to write about those two strange threads of time that never intersected.

My mementos gradually increased: mixed in with the many other items, the young Master's manga, the Mistress's wool coat and dresses, the photograph taken to commemorate the construction of the house, and the gold-rimmed teacup, there was a small tinplate jeep of the occupation forces.

I put it on the palm of my hand and gazed at it.

Yes, let's talk about that small tinplate jeep.

One Final Chapter

The Little House

Virginia Lee Burton published her picture book *The Little House* in 1942, just one year after the start of the Pacific War. Momoko Ishii's translation into Japanese was published only twelve years later, in 1954. The copy that Shoji Itakura had kept in his study was the English original, and not only was it clearly well-read but the binding had been restored, probably by the artist himself. It remains unclear where or how he got his hands on a copy.

However, according to the curator's explanation, Itakura's own mysterious work titled 'The Little House' was thought to date from the early 1950s, judging from the unique touches in his style. This work was clearly modelled on the composition of Burton's *The Little House*, so he must have come across the original piece early on.

Shoji Itakura was a Showa-period manga artist known for his works run through with dry black humour, but early in his career he also painted kamishibai picture-card stories for children. 'The Little House' is one of these kamishibai, yet it has a sensibility that is entirely unlike that of the works he created for children, and he clearly hadn't intended it for publication.

Many critics have commented on how the increasingly savage content in the latter half of 'The Little House' is not unrelated to the artist's experience on the frontline. In fact, this work was only made public after Itakura's death and was not well known.

The lawyer charged with managing his estate announced that in accordance with his last will and testament, a plot of land in western Tokyo would be bought for the construction of the Shoji Itakura Memorial Museum to house his extant works.

Given Itakura's cult following, the construction of the museum attracted considerable attention. It was widely rumoured that the building was being constructed to closely resemble the Western-style house in his kamishibai 'The Little House', according to instructions in his will. The reason this early, hitherto unknown work was suddenly under the spotlight was because it was now thought to be closely related to his younger years that he rarely talked about.

In Virginia Lee Burton's work, the house is the protagonist and the people living there are not mentioned, but in Itakura's work the house is occupied by three people, two women and a young boy. However, although each picture is numbered, there is no dialogue or written story, and the relationship between the three is unclear. We do not even know which of the two women is the mother of the boy, or whether the two women are friends or sisters. There is no adult man, so it is possible the boy does not have a father.

'Shoji Itakura never commented on "The Little House" during his lifetime. It therefore holds many mysteries,' the museum's curator said. 'Nevertheless, we have come to consider it as one of his most important works, since we can see in it the beginnings of the style he developed in his work throughout his life. Extraordinary innocence enveloped in shocking black humour is a common theme. However, while innocence is mocked in his numerous representative works, in this early piece it feels somehow warmly preserved by the artist. Given his stated desire to reconstruct the red-roofed house in this piece, we have to consider that it must be deeply linked to his personal memories.'

The conditions he left in his last will and testament included detailed plans of the house. He also left extraordinarily detailed paintings of certain features of the house, including a stained-glass panel featuring a tree and bird, a wickerwork ceiling, and a French window in the upstairs bedroom. In fact, it would have been technically difficult and prohibitively expensive to recreate all the excruciating details of the house, so certain compromises had been made in the construction of the museum.

'It is possible that this is why he never tried to recreate the house during his lifetime,' the curator said, quietly touching her glasses. 'He probably already knew that he could never recreate the house exactly as it was in his memory.'

Itakura remained single throughout his life and had no heirs to leave his considerable fortune to. He donated his estate, which includes original paintings and future royalties, to the small company run by his friend that published his complete works of manga, on the condition that they open the museum.

This year marks three years since the museum opened, and an exhibition will be held of the original paintings in 'The Little House', taken out of storage for the first time in many years.

After checking that all the visitors had left, the curator turned to me. 'So what was it you wanted to see me about?' she asked.

She resembled my girlfriend from when I was in college.

It's four years now since Nan died. She was healthy and her mind still intact, but as death approached she became depressed and kept going on at me for having hidden her 'memory notes' somewhere. I'd never heard this term before and at first didn't know what she meant, but after a while I realized that she must be referring to the notebook full of her memories of the war, crammed in with her tiny handwriting.

At one time she'd pressed me to read it, but a long time had passed since she had suddenly stopped showing it to me, and I had completely forgotten about it. I can't say her writing was easy to read, and at that age I didn't find it all that interesting, so I was quite shaken when she angrily accused me of having taken it. She had apparently hidden it from me, and then forgotten where she had put it.

Nan was rather pitiful towards the end of her life. I was the closest to her in my family, but I only visited her at most once a week, and she was alone the rest of the time. I would take food to her when my mother told me to or go to change a light bulb or whatever when she asked for my help, but otherwise I was more interested in college life than going to spend time with her. When her legs were still good, she would sometimes walk the one kilometre to our house to visit, but by the end she no longer had the strength to do even that. She spent every day waking up and going to sleep alone.

I sometimes found her asleep at the kotatsu and worried whether she had actually stopped breathing, but she had just dozed off. The worst was that time I found her crying alone.

What on earth was torturing an elderly woman like that, her face crumpled as she wept, full of regret for her memories? All I could do was awkwardly rub her skinny rounded back, but then she bawled even louder. You should have just left her, my mother said. If you're kind to her, she'll never stop crying.

My mother isn't particularly mean or anything, but she never warmed to Nan. My father had lost his parents when he was still young, so Nan was like a mother to him, which meant she was like a mother-in-law to my mother. She had fearsomely high standards in housework generally, and annoyed my mother when she was a young bride.

I wonder why the gods didn't give Nan more peaceful twilight years. She could be difficult, and a little nasty at times, but she had the right to be happy at the end of her life, surely. When I found her collapsed on the kitchen floor, the police and doctor said she had died two days earlier. The police always investigate this type of case unless somebody dies in hospital. They questioned us about whether anybody had hated Nan and how her estate was to be divided up, although they did say it was for formality's sake.

At least her face hadn't shown any trace of suffering, which was some small comfort. She hadn't died crying, full of regrets. That's what I told myself, anyway. I was sorry I hadn't gone to see her before, but as my mother said, that's life. Nan herself often said she'd lived too long.

After Nan died, her belongings were mostly disposed of. The notebook in question was found in the rice chest. Written on it in Nan's writing was, 'Please give this to Takeshi', so I decided to take it.

Yet now that the one person I could give my impressions to was no longer with us, I felt like I'd taken on something rather tedious and a year passed without me even looking at it.

I'd already split up with that girlfriend who'd been intent on becoming a picture book illustrator, had left university and gone alone to Tokyo to take up a job there. It was only when I was clearing out my apartment I finally got around to reading it. Packing was a chore, and I thought it might be interesting to read what she'd written about Tokyo now that I'd moved there.

So, it turns out I do regret not having asked Nan to let me read more before she died. But when had she started hiding the notebook from me? And why? To tell the truth, I have no idea. I'm forever regretting things only after losing them. I have so many regrets. Maybe I've somehow inherited that nature from Nan.

Nan's 'memory notes' came to an abrupt end: *Yes, let's talk about that small tinplate jeep.*

It was left unfinished with that last line. Had she lost the urge to write? Could she no longer manage to write? Or had death robbed her of time? What did she mean, a 'small tinplate jeep'?

When I asked my father whether he knew anything about it, he'd looked up from his newspaper with a puzzled expression, and suggested I get in touch with Uncle Gunji. Uncle Gunji was his cousin, the son of Nan's elder sister, and had likely lived with her at some point during or after the war, so might know something.

'People who lived together during the war share a special bond, one that people like us, born after the war, have never experienced,' Dad said.

Uncle Gunji was already over seventy, and lived together with his wife in an apartment in Kuramae in Tokyo. I felt a little awkward about visiting, but if I didn't ask now, I would probably regret it forever.

'So you're cousin Satoshi's second son, are you?' he greeted me, very much like someone from up north. 'I thought Aunt Taki would never die!' I couldn't help laughing.

'Right?' I said automatically, although having been with her in her final years I'd been well aware that her time was approaching. When had Nan stopped seeing people altogether? She had probably wanted people to remember her as the Taki who was always so healthy and energetic. Maybe having shrunk and become unsteady on her feet had wounded her own self-image. She never looked at herself in the mirror towards the end.

'The last line in her notes was, "Let's talk about the small tinplate jeep". I'm really curious to know what it was she was going to say about it. When I asked Dad he said you might know something, Uncle Gunji.'

'A small jeep? Hmm, it sounds vaguely familiar. What was it, now?'

He stuck his finger in his ear and wiggled it around, cleaning it. Maybe that was his habit when trying to remember something.

'Oh, I know. What about that Kosuke jeep?' came Aunt Keiko's voice behind him.

'Ah, that must be it! The Kosuke jeep. You've got a good memory, haven't you?'

'Well, I've heard it so many times, after all. It was around the time we got married.'

Uncle Gunji told me the story, with Aunt Keiko correcting him here and there. It really did sound like the episode that Nan had wanted to write about. Maybe she'd simply no longer had the energy to write about it, however much she wanted to.

The first time that Nan—that is, my great aunt Taki Nunomiya—went to Tokyo after the war was in New Year 1946.

The schoolchildren evacuation had ended in November 1945, and Taki had seen them off at the rural station, then gone back to her parents' home. At that time, the Yamagata home was packed with Taki's siblings and their families all living there. Uncle Gunji was still in elementary school, and things got even tougher since many of the siblings had more children after demobilization.

Taki probably wanted to go back to Tokyo anyway, and eventually left the deep snow of Yamagata for the capital on a train stuffed with people seeking to buy goods on the black market. Being the person she was, she was probably carrying sweet potatoes and rice with her.

Tokyo had been completely razed to the ground. It was even worse than she had seen in March the year before. The north-western suburb where Taki had lived had also been burned out in a huge air raid on 25th May.

When I hear 'northwestern suburb of Tokyo' I automatically think of the Tamagawa area, but back then the suburbs were much closer to what is now central Tokyo. The red-roofed house had been on one of the railways leading westwards from Shinjuku. It wasn't that far from Shinjuku and even now is counted as one of the high-class residential areas. I don't know why, but Taki never named the area or the station, and Uncle Gunji didn't know either, so I wasn't able to visit it.

Even so, I went to the area where it was likely to have been located, to find a wide highway and new developments underway. According to information I found in a local library, after the air raids had destroyed all the buildings they had undertaken a large scale replanning and road improvement, and no records were left of the how the area had once looked.

At any rate, Taki Nunomiya had gone there in 1946. She knew very well where it was, so she must have found the location despite the devastation.

How had she felt walking around the area where everything she had known had been totally wiped out? There were so many things I wanted to ask her, but now I'd never have the chance.

Aunt Taki had been so disheartened that her legs had given way and she had sat down on the spot, Uncle Gunji said.

Apparently it was some time before she could move again. There was probably nothing left of the house at all. When she spoke about it she couldn't stop crying, so it wasn't something he'd wanted to hear about much.

Nan had sat down in the charred remains of the stone porch of what had once been the red-roofed house. Time passed as she sat there vacantly. There was no one she could give the sweet potatoes and rice to that she had brought with her.

And then, somebody—a man—came and spoke to her.

A man. Middle-aged. Wait, the young Master's... yes, the father of one of the young Master's friends. He had just been released from prison.

No, not just released. He had come out, then gone to Kyoto, and bought that toy jeep there.

So went the conversation between Uncle Gunji and Aunt Keiko.

In other words, Taki had gone to Tokyo, visited the Hirais', been shocked to find the area completely flattened, sat in the stone porch, and a man had come to talk to her. That man, as far as I could make out, had been Seita Ishikawa's father. He had been arrested in 1941 on suspicion of spying and remained in custody until the end of the war.

Catching sight of Taki, he had spoken to her for old times' sake. 'I don't suppose you're the maid who worked for the Hirais, are you?'

Taki recalled having seen the man before. He was Sei's father. The boy the young Master had been close friends with before his father was arrested.

Sei's father had lost his house too, and not having anywhere to go he had gone to stay with a relative in Kyoto, where he didn't know anyone. He had found the small toy jeep in a department store there.

It was a superb tinplate miniature of the khaki-coloured jeeps with stars on them that the occupation forces were using all over Japan at the time. The Kosuke Factory had started selling them immediately after the war ended, and they were made from things like the coke cans discarded by the American soldiers.

'I thought my son would like it,' the man had told her. 'I remember how he used to tell me that Kyo had lots of tinplate toys and would beg me to buy some for him too.'

The man had bought one of the Kosuke Factory jeeps that were flying off the shelves at the time and, like Taki, went back to Tokyo in the new year to search for his wife and son.

It hadn't occurred to him that his son was no longer nine years old, but fourteen, long past the age of playing with tinplate toys. In his mind, his son was still nine. He hadn't seen him in all those years.

The reality waiting for him was even more cruel. When he got to the city and contacted everyone he knew, he learned that his wife and son had died in the big air raid in May.

He was wandering aimlessly around the burned-out ruins when he recognised the remains of the red-roofed home where his son used to play. And that's when he saw Taki sitting on the porch looking tired.

'Are you the maid who used work for the Hirais, by any chance?' he'd asked her.

And after telling her his own story in brief, he pressed the tinplate jeep into Taki's hand.

'If you do find Kyo, please give him this. He's too old to be playing with this sort of thing, but give it to him as a keepsake of Sei. He used to write to me and tell me how well he got along with Kyo, and Tatsu too.' He wrapped his big hands around Nan's, making her grip the tinplate jeep.

Apparently Seita Ishikawa's father had not been a spy at all. He was suddenly arrested one day at the printers where he worked on suspicion of illegal activities. Evidence had been found inside a package a good-natured colleague was supposed to have given him, but he didn't recall ever accepting it. Neither had he known that the colleague was involved in underground activities. But as so often happens in history, the truth didn't matter. In exchange for the bone in his left finger, shattered during torture, he signed the confession with his right hand.

At Mr. Ishikawa's urging, Taki visited an acquaintance who had miraculously survived and was living in the burned-out ruins on the other side of the station. This person had walked all around the devastated area after the raid, and was able to inform Taki that both Master and Mistress Hirai had died in their air raid shelter.

The Hirais' shelter had been under the camellia tree in the garden. The Master, who was fond of novelty, had built it at a time when air raids on the mainland were still just a remote possibility, and it had been quite large and completely impractical for the purpose. He probably hadn't realized how dangerous air raid shelters could be, that acquaintance had said. Many people got trapped inside them with no means of escape.

And so Nan learned about the fate of the Master and Mistress. All she was left with was the Kosuke jeep.

'So Mr. and Mrs. Hirai died, but what about the boy Kyoichi? Did he survive?' I asked Uncle Gunji.

'I don't rightly know,' Uncle Gunji said. 'But apparently there wasn't any body of a child with them when they were found. Aunt Taki did everything she possibly could to find him. She was more fond of him than she was of her own nephews and nieces, you know. She found out where the boy's grandparents lived— where was it now? Out west somewhere, although I'm not sure whether she actually went there.'

'We didn't hear anything about her having met him,' put in Aunt Keiko. 'She just cried over the Kosuke jeep. She bawled her eyes out, you know. And the story more or less ends there.'

'She wrote in her notes that his grandparents had evacuated to Fukui, so maybe that's where he went?'

'I really couldn't say.'

I found it really odd that Nan hadn't gone there to look for the boy she was so fond of, but Uncle Gunji said simply, 'She probably thought it would be considered odd for a servant to go to those lengths.'

'And look,' Aunt Keiko, at his side, put in wryly. 'At the time Japan was in a complete mess, and people didn't even know where they were going to get food to eat that day. Aunt Taki came back to Yamagata and worked in the vegetable fields with the rest of us. Eventually she somehow managed to head to Kasukabe and start work as a domestic helper, then took in your father and his siblings and raised them. It was really tough, you know. I wish she'd written more about that side of things, to be honest.'

Come to think of it, it had been Kasukabe that Nan went to after leaving Yamagata again. She was quite familiar with it, since she had often visited her relatives there in the past. She apparently hadn't wanted to go to Tokyo, for reasons that I think are quite obvious, and until she retired and moved to Ibaraki, she worked for families who lived along the Tobu train line.

And that was the story of the tinplate jeep I heard from Uncle Gunji.

I found the small tinplate jeep inside the sweet tin in which Nan kept her memory notes.

And that wasn't all I found inside it: there were also two black-and-white photos. One was of the Hirai family together with

Nan in front of the newly built house, and the other was of the Hirai family alone, probably the photo taken in the Ginza studio on the occasion of the Empire's 2600th Anniversary celebrations.

Nan was a plump, healthy young girl built like a small tank, and Tokiko Hirai was as beautiful as a movie star. Kyoichi was an adorable little boy with big eyes, and Mr. Hirai, the executive director, had a surprised expression, perhaps due to his bottle bottom glasses.

There were also postcards from exchanges during the war, which Nan, always a stickler for neatness, had kept in order by person, in bundles secured with a rubber band, each one ordered by date. One letter was simply marked 'Tokiko Hirai' on the back, but there was no addressee, and that one alone had been left unopened. The envelope was of quality traditional paper, but one edge had yellowed over time.

I should perhaps have been satisfied with that. Now that I'd heard the story of the tinplate toy jeep, Nan's story had come to an end. I don't think she wanted to write any more after that. It had always been the story of the red-roofed house, and once the house had been lost that was the end of that.

Still, I just couldn't shake it from my mind. Whatever had become of young Master Kyoichi? Was Miss Mutsuko still alive? And most importantly, had Mr. Itakura come back from the front?

The easiest one to find was Miss Mutsuko. Nan had never mentioned her surname, so in order to find out I went to the National Diet Library to check old copies of *Housewives Delight* for articles on Helen Keller's visit to Japan. I recalled Nan, who had a prodigious memory had quoted one she'd written:

'In these times of crisis, Japanese women have much to learn from the many great achievements of Madame Keller, whose extreme benevolence was gained from the extraordinary effort of overcoming her triple handicap of not being able to see, hear, or speak, to eventually become an accomplished public speaker.'

I found an article with a similarly bold tone that had been written by someone called Mutsuko Matsuoka. Her articles were still appearing in the much reduced *Housewives Delight* the year the war ended, saying things like: 'You're not telling me that the true beauty and strength of Japanese women's spirit has been beaten by those beastly American women!' Being a propaganda magazine, *Housewives Delights* continued publishing without a break, including a combined issue published in the autumn after the war ended, and had a bilingual Japanese-English cover for the duration of the GHQ censorship, after which it revived itself as a popular magazine with women's faces on the cover.

Mutsuko Matsuoka was apparently reformed of her previous support of militarism and became a champion of democracy, a journalist espousing a bold new ideology. She remained active until the 1970s as a freelance commentator on housekeeping matters. Despite everything, she apparently didn't espouse the sudden rise in women's lib. Instead she lamented the steady loss of the fine customs of traditional Japanese women, so seemingly, the traditional Japanese woman as personified by Tokiko Hirai remained her ideal until the end. A Wikipedia page on her says she died in 1976.

Having managed to find out about Miss Mutsuko, I hit a dead-end. Around then I started my first proper job in the accounts department of an electronic parts company. It wasn't particularly big, but there was a lot to learn and I had my hands full. Since I wasn't all that interested in art, I hadn't heard about the opening of the Shoji Itakura Memorial Museum. Three years passed without me knowing anything about it.

I eventually learned about its existence purely by accident, when I chanced upon an acquaintance's name in a bookshop one day. Actually, it was the name of my former girlfriend.

She had been connected to Nan by a quirk of fate years ago. That might be something of an exaggeration, but it was thanks to the old copy of *Mizue* that I borrowed from Nan that we got together. It was the 1940 edition devoted to the Empire's 2600th Anniversary celebrations. She had looked at all the paintings by famous artists and commented that none of them depicted war.

She'd always worn beige and lime-green clothes, with her light brown hair loosely tied back in a ponytail. And she often talked about picture books. I learned about illustrators like Maurice Sendak, Marie Hall Ets and Robert McCloskey from her.

'My dream is to be an illustrator,' she would tell me daily, yet that didn't stop me from being seriously shocked when she was actually hired by a publisher while still a student. 'I don't know why you're so surprised,' she'd said, and set about preparing to move to Tokyo without further ado.

I tried to persuade her to at least stay until after graduation a few months away, but her brown eyes glittered with disappointment and anger. Of course, I had every intention of following her after graduation. I had already found a job in Tokyo. But things didn't go well. It probably often happens that way.

And after three years had passed with me still hung up on her, just when I finally thought I was over thinking about her every single day, I came across her name on the shelves of a large bookshop that opened near my office.

It was on an edition of the quarterly illustrated books magazine *PUCK* devoted to the works of Virginia Lee Burton. Virginia Lee Burton had been one of her favourite picture book authors. She'd given me the amazing science book *Life Story* for my birthday. Her gifts always included a picture book, and if she ever gave a sweater it was always wrapped around a book.

The magazine included a number of interviews with picture book authors, including one with her. 'On Growing Up with Virginia Lee Burton' was the title of the piece. I hesitated a moment, then bought a copy of the magazine. She was pictured wearing bright green clothes just as she had done long ago. She hadn't changed at all, but I couldn't help thinking she looked like an illustrator, not like my girlfriend. It was kind of amazing to think we'd been together for two years.

And that's how, by some crazy coincidence, I came across an essay in the same magazine entitled 'Enchanted by Shoji Itakura's "The Little House"' and happened to see a photograph of the Shoji Itakura Memorial Museum.

But everything is connected, and now I've even come to think that Nan knew it would happen like this. The essay was by the curator of the Shoji Itakura Memorial Museum. The colour plate at the start of the essay was a three-quarter page photograph, with an outline of the essay in the bottom quarter. The essay took up eight pages, including a number of large photographs.

Seeing that house, I felt quite nostalgic. I felt like I knew it well. And after gazing at it for a while, I realized that I had actually seen it before.

My parents' place in Ibaraki was about two hours by train from Tokyo, so that weekend I went home and took Nan's sweet tin from the cupboard. The photo that Nan had treasured of the newly built house: the width of the porch, the front door, the shape of the roof tiles, the windows—it was the twin of the one in the magazine photo, the only difference being the design on the stained glass. If pushed, I would say that the design itself wasn't different, but that the museum's version had been made by a different artist and didn't resemble the original that closely.

It was like reading a mystery, beginning to connect up all the dots in my head.

Shoji Itakura was obviously the same Mr. Itakura as in Nan's story.

Enchanted by Shoji Itakura's 'The Little House'

Shoji Itakura was a manga artist active in the late 1950s and early 1960s, known for works like *Aubergines and Brown Crabmeat*, the *Gumbo Mix* series, and *Waking Up From the Darkness*.

He has a core fan following for his distinctive style, but his best-known work is probably *Gumbo Mix*, which is less harsh than the rest of his oeuvre and was adapted for TV anime in the 1960s and 1970s.

Itakura started out as a kamishibai artist around 1947. However, hardly any of his works from that time are left. Many were lost in a fire at his Komazawa home in the Setagaya ward in the mid-1950s, which is thought to have been started by him smoking in bed. Not only were his early kamishibai works limited in number, but many were either scattered and lost, or became worn out through repeated use and were discarded.

I was therefore extremely surprised to find 'The Little House' in perfect condition in the north-facing semi-subterranean studio at his home in Higashi Jujo, Kita ward, where he lived at the end of his life. This was at a time when construction of the museum was about to start, following plans drawn up in line with his own very detailed sketches. It was wrapped in newspaper dated 2nd August 1952, so must have been painted before then.

'The Little House' is a kamishibai made up of sixteen original pictures painted by Itakura. Other than the original owned by the Museum, it is thought no other copies exist. It appears that he painted it as a personal memento rather than with any commercial aim in mind. It does not have any story attached to it, although the pictures tell a story much in the same way as a silent movie. The reason it is thought to be a personal memento is that the sketches for the Shoji Itakura Memorial Museum closely resemble the house portrayed in the kamishibai.

As a kamishibai too, 'The Little House' is rather special, in that the house is contained within a circle at the centre of the rectangular painting. Seen from a distance, it resembles the design of the Japanese flag. Inside the circle are scenes from the house, snippets of daily life in the entrance hall, the garden, the living room, the reception room, the veranda, the porch, and so forth, all in surprising detail. Each part of the house is identical to the sketches he drew for the museum, the only difference being that the sketches are realistic and lacking individuality, whereas the kamishibai clearly reflects Itakura's early style.

There are actually two concurrent stories in 'The Little House', as the world enclosed within the circle and the world outside the circle progress at the same time without interacting.

This unusual form is both distinctive and actually innovative, not dissimilar to one of his representative works from the late 1950s, *Awaken from the Darkness*, with its so-called manga within a manga nesting-box structure. It is an extremely interesting discovery as we can see Itakura adopted this format in his work very early on.

There are three characters in the world inside the circle: two young women, apparently sisters, and a small boy who is either a younger brother or the child of one of them. The two women mostly do housework, and the boy plays with paper aeroplanes.

The sixteen pictures do not tell a particularly dramatic story, but can rather be thought of as sketches of daily life. In one of the pictures, a typhoon rages outside the circle, while inside the three are soaked to the skin and shivering in a rather comical scene. This is the only picture in which outside and inside are clearly connected. No such connection can be detected in the other pictures, although we can understand from this one picture that inside the circle represents being under the protection of the house, while outside the circle represents the circumstances happening around it.

What isn't clear is the relationship between the two women. They could be friends, sisters, or even lovers. In the last picture, the boy is playing outside, while the two women watch him from a window, their heads close together and holding hands. In this picture, the outside world is painted completely black, creating an effect rather like the shrinking circle on screen at the end of an old black and white movie.

Also, scribbled in English on the back of this last picture is 'sacred/secure', which can be considered a theme of the whole series.

Inside the circle represents tranquil daily life with little action, while dramatic changes can be seen taking place outside the circle. Let's give the background to each of the sixteen pictures.

1. A tranquil spring day.
2. The seaside in summer.
3. A typhoon.
4. People walking on the street in Ginza preparing for winter.
5. Fruit and vegetables.
6. Various animals, mostly dogs.
7. Grummans and B29s.
8. The jungle.
9. The jungle.

10. Yet more jungle.
11. Poisonous mushrooms and bits of human bodies scattered around.
12. The remains of fires in the jungle and burned human arms.
13. Skulls, and other bones.
14. Faceless soldiers marching.
15. Birds of prey flocking.
16. Blackout.

Itakura was conscripted in 1943 and sent straight to the frontline in a dispatch of troops to New Guinea. He was demobilized in the autumn of 1945. His depictions of the jungle here and in later works can clearly be considered to be based on his military experience.

However, Itakura rarely spoke of his own life in the military. In this sense, too, 'The Little House' is a valuable work.

So, just who were those people living in 'The Little House,' the model for the Shoji Itakura Memorial Museum?

There is one mysterious piece in the remarkable, short manga collection from Shoji Itakura's late period, *Aubergines and Brown Crabmeat*, 'The Fragrance of Osmanthus from the Garden of the House on Top of the Hill', which is notable for showing the characters poking their heads out of the many 'o's in the title.

At the top of the hill lives a widow, who has an osmanthus tree in her garden. Characters come out of the 'o's of the title as if drawn by the fragrance of the osmanthus, go into the house, and leave by the back door transformed into animals. The conversations the animals have with the widow are quite uniquely surreal.

This widow's house is, in fact, extremely similar to both 'The Little House', and the sketches for the Shoji Itakura Memorial Museum. It is now thought to be modelled on the same house.

One of the characters is a male manga artist, who is clearly in love with the widow. It is not actually confirmed whether or not this piece is linked with Itakura's own past. However, Keizo Fujisaki of Kairindo Comics, who is director of the museum and Itakura's friend, accepts that Itakura had special feelings for the red-roofed house and the woman who lived in it.

'There are two reasons he remained single throughout his life,' Fujisaki responded in an interview in the art magazine *Moon and Light*. 'He once said that the widow in the house on top of the hill was modelled on a real person, and I commented, half teasingly, that she can't be the reason he'd never married, but in his response he implied that she was. When I tried to question him further on this, though, he became evasive and I don't know the details.

'I think a much bigger reason why he stayed single is because of his experience in the army. He did at one point say that he wasn't the sort of person suited to having a family. That was when he was talking about the weird craziness that slips into his works, and the stench of death that is always present in his black humour.

'Now that the "The Little House" has been discovered, I am practically convinced that he had a powerful experience at the front that I daresay was so appalling that it jeopardized his humanity. This has been continually reflected in his work throughout his life. And it probably is not unrelated to the fact he lived his life without having a family.'

The quotation is long, but it reveals why although Itakura has outstanding artistry and storytelling skills, his piercing black humour and the intense darkness oozing from his works has attracted a cult following, while repelling mainstream readers. It has been pointed out before that his unique insanity stems from his experience of war, and no other work demonstrates this more directly than 'The Little House'.

While Itakura's experience is reflected clearly in this work, the one thing that distinguishes it from his other works is that he never hurts the three mysterious people inside the circle.

He frequently pillories innocence in his works, thoroughly making fun of it, turning it into a laughing stock, leaving it wounded. Take, for example, the story 'Directionless' in his collection *Aubergines and Dark Crab Meat*. This is an archetypal so-called roleplaying story in which an innocent boy called Takeru goes on an adventure, opening doors with the keys he finds. Takeru is utterly hopeless with directions and always picks the wrong keys, encountering something frightful whichever door he opens.

Even readers who feel Takeru's pain find their sympathy completely numbed by the abnormally stupid choices that send him full tilt into hell every single time, and they end up laughing despite themselves. Eventually Takeru loses his arms and legs and, converted into a human ball, continues to roll resolutely along in precisely the wrong direction. By the time readers reach the last scene, they are splitting their sides with nervous laughter.

This characteristic display by cult author Itakura is frequently cited as his best work by manga artists, movie writers, and novelists from later generations.

The only people in his work who are portrayed as sacrosanct and their innocence left intact are the women and boy inside the circle in 'The Little House'.

The building in 'The Little House' not only closely resembles the house in 'The Fragrance of Osmanthus in the Garden of the House on Top of the Hill', but it is probably safe to assume that the widow in the latter and one of the two women in the former (or both of them) are likely modelled on the same person.

Perhaps it is a little too sentimental to think that the pictures inside the circles in 'The Little House' depict those he wanted to protect his whole life.

'So, what was it you wanted to see me about?' the curator of the Shoji Itakura Memorial Museum asked me. Her long, soft hair was tied back in a ponytail, and she wore rather unconventional green-brown clothes. She reminded me of my ex-girlfriend.

As soon as I saw the special edition of *PUCK* devoted to Virginia Lee Burton, I'd immediately headed for the museum. It was in the Tama area near the end of the Seibu line, some distance west from where the original house had probably been.

I told the receptionist that I wanted to talk to the woman who had written that article. She gave me a somewhat suspicious look, but seemed to pass my message on and came back to inform me that although she was showing a group around at present, she would see me once she'd finished. I decided to unobtrusively tag along with the group.

As I listened to her explanations, though, I had a change of heart. I no longer wanted to show her the photo or Nan's memory notes that I'd brought with me.

There was no doubt about the museum having been modelled on the red-roofed house that Nan had loved. But it was being analysed by researchers, and Nan's photo would be put in the museum for all to see, and the love affair between Tokiko Hirai and Shoji Itakura would be exposed. What was the point of groups of tourists all knowing about it?

What was the point of having Tokiko Hirai remembered not as Nan's 'Mistress', but as Shoji Itakura's muse? It would be a ground-breaking discovery in art history and the cult manga world, but I didn't want any part in it.

However, having gone to the museum expressly to talk to the curator, I couldn't just say that I'd changed my mind and leave without saying anything. I wracked my brain trying to dredge up some kind of question I could possibly put to her.

'How did you know that "The Little House" was influenced by the original book of the same name? It's true they have the same title, but the Japanese translation came out after Shoji Itakura had already painted his work. They might both be focused on a house surrounded by changing circumstances, but even so they do look very different. Virginia Lee Burton's house always looks the same, while Shoji Itakura's shows different parts of the house and has people in it. Also, the portrayal of the surroundings is much more abstract. How can you be so sure it is based on the structure of the original *The Little House*?'

The curator was rather taken aback and was silent for a moment. Then she said, 'Of course, you weren't there at the start of my explanation, were you?' and suddenly put her hand over her mouth and giggled. 'I'm sorry. I just remembered seeing you in that party of the Seniors Association from Chitose Funabashi taking lots of notes,' she said, chuckling. I didn't think it was all that funny, but still it broke the ice and I felt myself relax.

She turned over the first page of the kamishibai and showed it to me. There, in the same handwriting as the 'sacred/secure' on the last page, was written 'The little house/Memories of the little house.'

She asked me if I had any other questions, and when I said no, said, 'Please take your time in looking around,' and went into the staff room.

I was left alone in the reception room. The museum was very quiet in the absence of any study groups. I followed the white arrows indicating the route through the museum and looked around the house.

It had been built three years ago, but still felt brand new. In each of the rooms stood a wooden plate indicating its function:

reception room, living room, veranda sunroom, bedroom, and so forth.

The objective of the museum had been to reconstruct the rooms according to the documentation they had, and to store and display the belongings left by Shoji Itakura. This meant that what would originally have been tatami floors had been replaced with wooden floors, and bookshelves and glass display cases had been installed where none had been originally. The maid's room that Nan had loved so much had a wooden plate that read: 'Maid's room/Staff room', but I couldn't go inside.

I went into the upstairs 'Children's room/Reading room', a small space about 4.5 tatami mats in size, and picked up one of Shoji Itakura's manga. The drawings were exquisitely beautiful, but also somehow scarily dark, not at all for children. Even so, I found them extremely appealing.

I left the children's room and went next door into the library that housed the collection of foreign picture books and comics that Shoji Itakura had collected during his life.

I wandered over to the French window and gazed down on the garden. It was May, and new buds were sprouting, covering the garden in fresh green.

Beside the window there was a small bookshelf with several visitors' books, the oldest with the year the museum had opened on the front cover. It was a beautiful notebook bound in the Japanese style. I casually picked it up and flicked through it.

And then I saw it.

The name Kyoichi Hirai, together with his address in Ishikawa prefecture.

I couldn't believe my eyes! I hurriedly looked for something to write it down with.

I am not one to believe in psychics or spirits or messages from the gods. However, I couldn't help feeling that Nan, as energetic and businesslike as ever, was sending me instructions from the other side.

I decided to send a letter to Kyoichi Hirai. Indeed, I felt bound to do so. I wrote about Nan, and her memory notes. I said I had found his address at the Shoji Itakura Memorial Museum.

A while later, I received a reply from Mr. Hirai's wife in his stead, which concluded, 'My husband's eyes and legs are bad, and he is disabled. At his age, getting out and about is difficult. If you have time, though, he would be very pleased if you could pay him a visit.'

It was two months later, in summer, that I was finally able to visit.

Kyoichi Hirai lived near the sea in a small town in Hokuriku. He had been employed for many years in the town hall, and had built a house there upon retirement. His children were grown, and the house he and his wife had moved to was small, yet nicely furnished. It was not in the slightest reminiscent of the red-roofed house, but it did show good taste.

Mrs. Hirai showed me through to the living room. A white-haired old man was sitting in an armchair. He was wearing lightly tinted glasses.

'Welcome. Pleased to meet you,' he said, then went on, 'So Taki passed away, did she?'

'Yes, four years ago. She left some notes she'd written about the red-roofed house. I brought it with me today.'

'Oh, really? Thank you. But you know, I can't read any more.'

'That's right,' his wife put in quietly.

'I was in fairly good health until a few years ago, and even visited the museum, but I've gone down quickly since moving here. I'll be eighty next year. I've lived quite a long time,' Mr. Hirai said, although his chiselled, clean cut features belied his years.

He gave me a brief account of what had happened. By chance he had gone to stay at a friend's that night so escaped the air raid, but lost his parents and so went to his grandparents in Fukui. After the war he transferred to a middle school in Fukui, and ended up going to Kanazawa University and getting a job in the council of a small local town. He married, had children, they flew the nest, and now he had a twenty-year-old grandchild.

'How did you find out about the Shoji Itakura Memorial Museum?'

The corner of his mouth twitched into a smile. This almost eighty-year-old man had a dimple in his cheek! 'Because I'm a fan of his work.'

'Since when?'

'Oh, a long time. Maybe around the early sixties? I was still young then. A new colleague brought in a manga of his, and I made a sarcastic comment about newbies reading manga at work these days. But still I borrowed it, and I enjoyed it.'

'When did you find out that it was the same Shoji Itakura?'

'Oh, I always knew. I could tell right away it was him. The name was his, and I'd grown up seeing his drawings. And they were things I knew. Not just the house, but the streets of Tokyo, the things people were carrying, stuff like that. It's hard to explain, but only someone who had lived in Tokyo before the war could have drawn those sorts of things. And he did it well, too.' He removed his glasses and wiped the rim. I don't think he was crying. He looked amused, showing his dimple.

'Didn't you ever get in touch with him?'

'With who? Mr. Itakura? No, never. It never even occurred to me. What would have been the point?' This time he laughed quietly.

When he put it like that, I couldn't think of any good reason.

Mrs. Hirai came in carrying a tray with a bottle of beer and two glasses on it, along with a couple of plates heaped with salt-pickled yellowtail and a bright green, leafy vegetable with dressing.

'Local dishes,' Mr. Hirai said. 'They go well with beer, so please help yourself.'

It was my first time to try the rolled yellowtail Hokuriku was famous for. It had apparently been soaked in sake to remove the saltiness.

After that we talked for quite a long time. We talked about Nan, about Taki. Mr. Hirai recalled a lot of things about her, how she went about her work, the jokes she told, the mistakes she made, the games she played with him, the sort of food she cooked. He told me everything he could remember.

After two hours, Mrs. Hirai told us we should have dinner. 'Oh yes, please do stay to eat,' Mr. Hirai told me, 'And you're welcome to stay over too.' I'd already booked a hotel room, so I refused his offer to stay, but accepted with pleasure the invitation to dinner.

Mr. Hirai said he would show me around while his wife prepared dinner.

'But dear, what do you mean?' she said, looking somewhat put out, but he gave her a charming smile and said, 'Don't worry, young Takeshi here will push me.' 'Of course I will,' I said. 'Assuming you mean in a wheelchair.'

Mr. Hirai put on a sun hat, and with his wife's help transferred himself into his wheelchair. Mrs. Hirai showed me how to operate the chair, and the two of us went outside together.

The sun was stronger than I expected, and I commented with amusement how it was hotter here than in Tokyo. It took some effort to manoeuvre Mr. Hirai's wheelchair down the country lane overgrown with weeds, and I could feel my back grow damp with sweat.

We crossed over a single-track level crossing. Weeds grew thickly along the side of the tracks, which described a slow curve before disappearing into a tunnel in the distance. Mr. Hirai might not be able to see, but he confidently told me to turn left and continue straight on, then turn right when I saw a road going down a slope.

There was nobody on the country road other than an occasional bicycle going past, and the only sound was the gentle rustle of the breeze in the trees and grasses. Zigzagging down the slope, we saw a beach down below. Beyond the beautiful white sand was the Sea of Japan.

'I really wanted to live by the sea,' Mr. Hirai said, his cheeks relaxing as though he had noticed the scent of the sea air. 'When I was a child, we would go to Kamakura for the summer. There weren't many people on the beach back then, so we could enjoy swimming in the sea at our leisure. Taki didn't come though, and I don't recall having ever seen her in a bathing suit. My father was too busy with work to come to the beach either. My mother was proud of her white skin and scared of getting sunburned, so she would immediately put up a parasol and retreat into the shade. She was proud of her beauty. Clothes, makeup, and accessories were the only things that interested her.'

'My eyes always start watering when I come out in the sun,' he said. That must have been why he kept wiping away tears with his handkerchief.

Even in the calm of summer the waves on the Sea of Japan were big, and the sea breeze relentlessly fluttered Mr. Hirai's short-sleeved shirt cuffs. The white surf matched the white sand.

It had been a long time since I'd seen the sea. Its surface reflected the sunlight as though alive.

'What do you see?' Mr. Hirai asked me, pursing his lips in amusement.

'I see the sea glittering as it reflects the sunlight, and then I see the horizon and the summer clouds,' I answered him.

'Ah, you see the summer clouds? How lovely,' Mr. Hirai said, nodding with satisfaction.

Before I forgot, I took out the tinplate jeep from my canvas shoulder bag. 'Here,' I said, handing it to him. 'Nan was given it the year after the war ended by Seita Ishikawa's father. Seita died in the air raid, so he asked Nan to give it to you instead, as a memento of his son.'

'Sei's dad...' Mr. Hirai murmured in surprise, holding out both hands.

I gently placed the jeep on his dry palm. 'A toy manufacturer called Kosuke Factory put it on sale right after the—'

'It's tinplate, right?' he interrupted, and then roared with laughter. 'A Kosuke jeep, I suppose?'

'Yes, a Kosuke jeep. Do you know it?'

'I was a presumptuous middle school pupil in my day, and I thought they were terribly unprincipled for putting out this sort of thing the moment the war ended. You are a strange one, though. I never thought that at nearly eighty years of age I'd be given something like this by anyone. Still, you've made me happy. Happy, but surprised.'

Mr. Hirai took of his glasses and wiped his eyes with his handkerchief again.

'There's something else, too,' I said, reaching into my canvas bag and taking out the sealed letter.

'What's that?'

'A letter. From Tokiko Hirai.'

'From my mother?'

'It's in its original envelope, unopened, and it's not addressed to anyone. Nan had it in her belongings, but if it were addressed to her, she would have opened it, I'd have thought. Since it isn't addressed to anyone, the correct thing to do would be to return it to the sender, or since in this case she is deceased, to her next of kin.'

'How old are you?'

'Me? I'm twenty-six.'

'You're terribly honest, aren't you? You take after Taki, I suppose.'

'Oh, I don't know about that. But it doesn't feel right to just throw it away.'

'You could have opened it. It's from decades ago.'

'But it's somebody's letter.'

'You're a funny kid, you are.' He laughed teasingly, his cheek dimpling, and patted me on the arm.

'I am?'

'Well, all right then. I'll put all my trust in you. Open it now, and read it to me, will you?'

'Right now, this minute?'

'You said it's alright for her next of kin. You don't mind, do you? Let's read it. In any case, I have a good idea what it says.' He stopped talking, held his chin in his hand, and closed his eyes.

I clumsily opened the letter. Inside were a few lines in beautiful, feminine penmanship.

To: Shoji Itakura
Please come tomorrow at one o'clock. I do so want to see you.
Be sure to come.
Tokiko Hirai

As I read, I was more embarrassed than I'd ever felt in my life. Next to me, Mr. Hirai slowly moved the muscles in his cheeks and opened his mouth as to say something, but no words came out.

I dropped my canvas bag. The unbleached cloth handle burrowed into the sand, and the edge of Nan's notebook peeped out. Mr. Hirai cocked his ear in the direction of the sound, as if wondering what had happened.

I picked up the notebook and flicked through the pages. If memory served, Nan had written about this letter, and about the afternoon Shoji Itakura visited Tokiko Hirai for the last time before taking the night train back to his hometown to enlist in the army.

'What are you doing?' Mr. Hirai asked. His white freckled hand with raised veins trembled as he reached out and touched my hand.

Was whatever had caused Nan's regrets in her last years contained here in this letter? This was the sole thought that went around and around in my head with nowhere to go, like a cat that had climbed a tree and was unable to get back down again.

I was even less able than before to grasp what exactly she had hoped to achieve from leaving everything written down. She had written in great detail about things in her small, neat handwriting in that dog-eared notebook, expressly labelled 'Please give this to Takeshi', but it didn't reveal anything to me.

What was clear was that she had not delivered the note that she had urged Tokiko Hirai to write when she'd been about to visit Shoji Itakura just before he went off to enlist. It had remained unread for sixty-six years, still in its lovely traditional paper envelope.

Could it be that she hadn't handed it over because, as she wrote in her notes, the sentiment that 'You shouldn't do that sort of thing in wartime' had won out? Or had it been for a completely different reason? Even that was a puzzle.

In those times, everyone was forced to make choices that went against the grain, Mr. Hirai had said. 'Some were forced into it, but others did things willingly, and only realized much later it wasn't what they really wanted. That sort of thing happens. Like me refusing to play with Sei any more, even though I wanted to play with him. I just didn't know it at the time.'

That was probably true. With hindsight, due to the demands of the time Nan may well have made a wrong choice, only to realize so later on.

However, gazing at the picture on page sixteen of the reproduction of 'The Little House' that I had bought at the Shoji Itakura Memorial Museum, a new thought occurred to me.

Had Nan been in love with her beautiful Mistress?

'Fancy seeing evidence of my mother's infidelity now, when I'm nearly eighty!' Mr. Hirai said after a while, pursing his lips in amusement. 'Well, it's long in the past now. I always knew about it anyway.'

After that, Mr. Hirai turned his sightless gaze to the horizon and said, 'My mother always was quite a handful. She was a bit unbalanced, the sort of person who took chances and needed to be protected by someone. I wanted her to be there for me more, and was unhappy that she didn't give me, her only son, her full attention. She really was beautiful, and everyone fell in love with her. And she was good at making them fall in love with her. That's the sort of person she was.'

We didn't say anything, and just listened to the melody of the waves coming in and going out, over and again. As the sun went down, I pushed Mr. Hirai's wheelchair slowly back up the slope.

A delicious aroma came from his house, and I was treated to his wife's home cooking and local fresh fish. I said thank you and goodbye, then took the last local train back to Kanazawa.

In my hotel room, I opened up the reproduction of 'The Little House'. Enclosed in a circle at the centre of every page were three people. There was no adult man, unusually, and the small boy was always playing alone. The two women were always together, doing housework or chatting about something.

On the last page, they were holding hands, their heads close together, gazing out through the window. They appeared a little anxious, as if fearing another storm was brewing.

What were they gazing at?

How had they appeared in Shoji Itakura's eyes?

I would never know.

I would forever be searching for answers to questions I hadn't asked.